KELLY, SUSAN

E

FOR LOVE OR M

COMBERTO

20.

11

20. OCT 00

CW00351002

BARH		MELB	
BASS		SAWST	
COMB	9/00	SWAN	
COTT		WATB	
FULB		WILL	
GAMI		LIPT	10 10
GSHI		CSMOB	
HIST		CTMOB	
LINT		SMOBC	

FOR LOVE OR MONEY

Susan Kelly

This first world edition published in Great Britain 2000 by
SEVERN HOUSE PUBLISHERS LTD of
9–15 High Street, Sutton, Surrey SM1 1DF.
First published in the USA 2001 by
SEVERN HOUSE PUBLISHERS INC of
595 Madison Avenue, New York, N.Y. 10022.

British Library Cataloguing in Publication Data

Kelly, Susan, 1955-
   For love or money
   1.   Escort services - Great Britain - Fiction
   2.   Love stories
   I.   Title
   823.9'14 [F]

   ISBN 0-7278-5617-0

Typeset by Palimpsest Book Production Ltd.,
Polmont, Stirlingshire, Scotland.
Printed and bound in Great Britain by
MPG Books Ltd., Bodmin, Cornwall.

Spring

Time remembered is grief forgotten,
And frosts are slain and flowers begotten
And in green underwood and cover
Blossom by blossom the spring begins.

"Atlanta in Calyzon" – Swinburne

It takes all sorts

"I need a man," Zoe said. "It's for a special occasion."

The woman's voice at the other end of the telephone answered this request without surprise, although it sounded bizarre to her own ears. "That's what we're here for, madam. We have gentlemen in all sizes, colours, ages and shapes . . ." She paused as if expecting some response here, perhaps a laugh, then prompted. "What do you have in mind?"

Zoe hooked the receiver under her pointy chin and looked out through the study window at the rain-soaked front garden. It was the first of April and there'd been scarcely a glimmer of sun for weeks.

"Hello?" the woman said in her ear. "Are you there?"

"Sorry. It's for a literary dinner for the Robert Drewe Memorial Prize – so someone who knows one end of a book from the other would be nice."

"Most of our male escorts are resting actors," the woman said, "so they're quite . . . artistic."

Zoe wondered if that was a euphemism for gay. She wished she'd thought this out properly before picking up the phone and dialling, trying to think what ingredients she wanted as if ordering a pizza, but if she'd thought about it too much she wouldn't have done it.

"A man in his thirties," she said finally, "not *too* tall – say, five ten, five eleven – good-looking, I suppose." Might as well raise a few curious eyebrows. Was she fussy about colour? She thought not.

"All our escorts are good-looking." Zoe could hear fingers tapping at a keyboard on the other end of the line and the woman asked, "When's it for?"

"The twenty-ninth of April. Evening. Oh, and it's black tie."

"No problem. And where is the function?" Zoe named an expensive new hotel off the Strand. "I think I have the very thing. Let me check availability and I'll get back to you, hopefully within the hour. What was the name?"

Zoe hesitated. She'd used her pseudonym for so long and it was the name the public knew her by. Her real one gave her anonymity and peace.

"Rosalind Tate," she said finally.

"*The* Rosalind Tate?" The other woman's voice took on a new respect and she said she knew someone who'd read one of her books. Zoe made the expected noises of gratitude and appreciation, divulged her telephone number and hung up.

"The very *thing*." Was that an odd way of putting it? As if he, the man, were an object to be purchased.

She hated waiting for people to call her back. She couldn't settle to anything. She was in her study, a cool room at the front of the house, quiet since her road dead-ended at the river. It was square except for the bay window, with shelves of books taking up two walls. Framed dust jackets for her novels hung on either side of the door, in more than one language.

Si Monumentum Requiris Circumspice.

She sat down at her desk and picked up the photograph of her husband Oliver, which she kept next to the word processor like a talisman. It was a four-by-three-inch colour snapshot in a plain silver frame. He looked pleased with himself, standing in his climbing gear, a coiled rope jaunty on his narrow shoulder, crampons in one hand.

He couldn't in all justice be described as handsome but it was a nice face, a kind face. His sandy hair with speckles of white was dishevelled behind its widow's peak where he'd removed his balaclava for the camera, knowing that she wasn't fond of the terrorist look. His grey eyes were smiling, narrowed, because he gazed into the low sun, sending horizontal wrinkles back towards his ears.

She could see his shadow behind him, very tall and distorted against a rock, telling her that it was evening and the end of a long day's climbing and that he was looking forward to a pint of real ale in the pub.

He'd died in a climbing accident eighteen months earlier, a

mountain in Scotland that no one had heard of, an unforecast mist, a fatal slip. She thought of it now as Widow's Peak.

September 28th.

He'd been with John Morrow, his oldest friend, his former roommate at Cambridge; a single man who never talked about anything but climbing and the merits of different brands of beer. He'd died too, which meant that she would never know what had happened, why those two experienced and careful men had fallen to their deaths on the rocks on that day and no other, on that peak and no other. Which of them had been leading? Who had first lost footing? How much terror had there been in Oliver's heart when he knew that it was all over, and how long had it lasted?

Please God, let it not have lasted long.

Oddly, one thing that had survived the fall was John's camera, and his sister had had this photograph developed for her from the half-used roll inside it. This was Oliver, had he known it, on the last evening of his life.

"You stupid sod," she told the picture, but without heat; it was an old argument, rehearsed without passion. "What was the point of it all? Because it was there?" Tears formed in the corners of her eyes and now there was heat. "You selfish bastard."

The phone rang and she blinked back the tears and took a single deep breath before she picked up the receiver. "That was quick," she said, when the now-familiar voice identified itself as Jean from Allsorts of Escorts.

"The first one I tried is free that evening and seems ideal. Matthew Groves. He's thirty-two, five foot eleven, blond, handsome—"

Zoe cut in. "He sounds fine." She'd never fancied blonds, but it didn't matter. He was for show: an accessory like her good pearl necklace, so the world could see that she was successful and prosperous and happy.

The woman was still talking. "It's four hundred pounds for the evening. You pay two hundred and fifty now and the balance to Matthew on the night, in cash if possible. You pay his expenses, naturally."

"I haven't done this before. I'd be glad if you could . . ."

5

"No problem. If it's a social gathering requiring, say, trips to the bar, it makes sense to give him a few pounds beforehand so he can seem to be paying. It goes without saying that Matthew will not mention the nature of the monetary relationship between you unless you wish him to do so."

"Do I – I dunno – tip him?"

"That's not necessary." Jean coughed, her voice taking on a delicate tone as one speaking to an invalid who hasn't long to live. "Any personal services . . . any *extras* must be negotiated directly with the escort."

Zoe didn't pretend not to know what she meant. She didn't bother to take offence or to say, her voice a little shrill, that there was no question of *that*, even though there wasn't. Jean wouldn't believe her, would think she was protesting too much. Anyway, she'd already passed on to taking details of Zoe's address and arrangements for the meeting and the moment when she might have said "Not guilty" had passed.

"He lives in Hammersmith," Jean concluded. "Not far from you. You'll like Matthew, he's very popular. Clients often ask for him by name. I could book him out twice every night of the week. Lucky you rang well in advance."

The Matthew is one of our most popular lines.

Zoe entered into a verbal contract, promised her a cheque by the next post, and hung up.

She wished Jean hadn't put such a stupid idea in her head, but then it was All Fools' Day.

A moral, somewhere

S he recognised him easily, as the hotel bar where they'd
arranged to meet wasn't busy at ten to eight on a drizzly
Tuesday evening in late April. Recognised implied that she'd
seen him before; more accurate, perhaps, to say that she knew
at once who he was. She saw a young man sitting alone with
his back to the wall so that he had a good view of the door,
nursing what looked like mineral water, barely touched, its
bubbles breaking haphazardly for the surface.

As she came in he was glancing at his watch. Ten to eight.
Almost five to eight. It should have been a quarter to.

He was certainly handsome, with regular features and thick
corn-coloured hair, well cut, reaching to his collar. He had
a brilliance in his cheeks, evidence of fresh air and regular
exercise: he looked healthy and wholesome. She was forty-one
and he seemed very young to her, but she reminded herself
that if he was thirty-two then he'd been grown up already for
fifteen years, was probably a husband and father of three.

He stood up as she made her way across to him, knowing
her in the same way she knew him, relieved that she was here at
last. He was a little clumsy, faintly nervous, scraping his chair
back with a hard noise on the polished floor. She saw that he
was slim and elegant in the evening dress she'd specified –
not a rented one, if she was any judge. Start-up costs must
be high in this business, she thought, what with having to kit
yourself out. He even had the spotless white silk scarf.

"Matthew?"

"Ms Tate?"

"Rosalind."

"Rosalind." He smiled for the first time, showing the white
and even teeth of his generation, fluoride in the water from

birth, no fillings. "Jean makes us address clients formally until they say otherwise. She's very strict."

"Yes, she sounded it."

They shook hands and looked at each other helplessly for a moment. This, she thought, was worse than a blind date, and she hadn't been on one of those since she was nineteen. Perhaps this was his first time too. But no, the Matthew was a popular line. She could see why. He wasn't what she'd been expecting, however. She'd anticipated something smoother, blander, prettily commonplace: all things to all women. His smile looked real and not part of his kit. There was nothing ingratiating in it, nothing of the whore.

Zoe had developed a way to cope with awkward social situations: she became someone else. She became Rosalind Tate, who was confident and at ease, fluent, incisive and amusing, even streetwise. It was easy to be all these things when you didn't exist. As she took on the mantle of Rosalind she felt her strained body relax and she touched him lightly on the arm.

"We'd better be going. I'm a bit late. Traffic."

He followed her out to the chauffeured limo she'd hired for the evening – the driver darting to wield the door for them – and they settled into the back seat. She took an envelope stuffed with ten-pound notes out of her evening bag. "Let's get this out of the way."

"Thanks." He put it in his inside pocket without opening it, either not wanting to count it or not liking to in her presence. The car pulled smoothly away from the kerb, the engine inaudible to its cloistered passengers.

"Matty Groves," she said, "like the song."

"Sorry?"

"It's a folk song. Don't you know it?" He shook his head, intrigued. "I won't inflict my singing voice on you." She began to recite a little too quickly. "Hi-ho, hi-ho, holiday, the best day of the year. Little Matty Groves to church did go, some holy words to hear."

"Doesn't sound much like me," he remarked.

"He spied three ladies dressed in black, as they came into view. Lord Arlen's wife was gaily clad, a flower among the few. She trippèd up to Matty Groves, her eyes so low cast down, saying 'Pray, oh pray, come with me stay, when you pass through the town.'" Zoe stopped and shrugged apologetically. "It goes on a long time, at least twenty verses."

He said, "Dare I ask what happened to him?"

"Nothing good, I'm afraid."

"I thought not. Nothing good ever happens to anyone in those old songs. Worse than the blues."

"He took her up on her offer, but her page sneaked to Lord Arlen and he came rushing home, found them in bed together, and ran Matty through with his sword. I can't remember if he killed the wife too. I expect so."

"So there's a moral here somewhere, perhaps?"

"Perhaps."

They looked at each other and began to laugh. She felt more comfortable and the short journey was over. A gloved hand was reaching out from a uniformed body – burgundy with gold frogging – to open her door; an umbrella was being manipulated above her head despite the presence of an awning.

Clearly Rosalind Tate was a person of importance.

She took Matthew's arm as if she had every right to be on it and sailed through the foyer to let herself be announced to the crowded hall.

"You did well," she said as they settled back into the car afterwards. She felt as if she'd been on show for hours. She wanted to kick her shoes off and soak her feet in Radox and she wished she had the car to herself, but credit where it was due. "With the sponsors especially," she went on.

The patrons of this award were a national supermarket chain and their senior managers filled up the tables with their excited wives or, occasionally, husbands.

"My father was a supermarket manager all his working life," Matthew said, "so I was able to talk shop quite knowledgeably."

"Has he retired now?"

"Yes, home to New Zealand."

"You don't sound like a Kiwi."

"That's because I'm not. I've never been there. All I know about it is that there are more sheep than people. Oh, and that it's God's Own Kingdom, of course." She laughed. "I was born after my parents came over in the sixties," he continued. "They'd heard the streets of London were paved with gold. They hated it, but they stayed anyway – didn't want to go home to 'I told you so', I guess. They went back three years ago when Dad reached sixty-five. I was a late-born child."

"Me too."

The car drove along the Strand, sticking in a short tailback on the threshold of Trafalgar Square. Only one or two of the theatres were coming out as yet and the pavements were quiet except for bundles in shop doorways where youngsters slept rough. Zoe sensed their hostile eyes on her long, shiny car and felt guilt. They burst through at last, past Nelson's Column with its attendant lions and into Pall Mall.

He put his hand over hers as they swung into Piccadilly, not threatening, not amorous, only friendly. "I'm sorry you didn't win tonight, Rosalind."

"I didn't expect to."

"We all say that but we hope. I say I don't mind when I do a blinding audition and still don't get the part, but I mind like hell."

"Being shortlisted is almost as good."

They were soon in Knightsbridge, heading past Harvey Nicks at speed. She removed her hand from under his and looked at her watch. She no longer wished him gone. "It's not late. Do you fancy another drink, Matty? Is it all right if I call you Matty?"

"Whatever you like. And I'm at your disposal till midnight," he added with mock primness, "after which I turn into a big fat pumpkin and you can kick me home like a football."

He drank orange juice in the wine bar, while the limo waited on a double yellow line outside. She ordered red wine but mostly for something to twist in her fingers. It wasn't as good as the claret at dinner, which had been supplied by their hosts from their Superior Dining range, and she'd had enough to drink. She left most of it.

"Have you been doing this long?" she asked.

"Almost a year. It was when I moved into my present flat. My flatmate is also an unemployed actor and he does it four or five nights a week."

Not married then, she thought, or not at the moment.

"It sounded preferable to bar work or waiting at tables," he went on, "more fun and better paid, so he introduced me to Jean and she looked me up and down like a prize cow." He pursed his lips and she heard Jean's fluting voice with its slippery estuary vowels coming miraculously out of his mouth, so that she might almost have turned to see if the woman had crept up on them. "Oh, yes. You're the XR3."

"The what?"

"Ford *Escort* XR3 – top of the range. Apparently."

"Oh, I see. Very good."

"I'm sure it's a line Jean has used on more than one occasion. I suspect she was checking that I would laugh at the clients' jokes. One must laugh at the clients' jokes, you see, however feeble."

"Yes, I can see that. Do you like the work?"

"Depends on the client. I enjoyed tonight." He sounded sincere but she reminded herself he was an actor and, for all she knew, a good one.

"Did your parents encourage your theatrical ambitions?"

"I was an only child, and a late one, as I said. They doted on me and gave me whatever I wanted. So I was a horribly spoilt little brat."

She said rather wistfully, "I don't think anyone goes to the bad through too much love."

He laughed agreement. "I didn't go straight to drama school, in fact. I was at university reading English and history and I did a lot of acting there, but I dropped out halfway through the course – couldn't seem to see the point of it any more, didn't know what I wanted to do . . . Time came when I was finding it increasingly difficult to get out of bed in the mornings."

"I thought that was normal student life," she said drily.

"I messed about for a couple of years, doing odd jobs, then one morning I woke up and thought, 'What I want to be is an actor', so I somehow managed to bluff my way into the London Academy of Music and Dramatic Art and I've been trying my damnedest ever since with very little to show for it."

"These things take time," she said lamely.

She felt comfortable with him. He was friendly, pleasant, easy to talk to, but not in the least flirtatious. She'd been afraid that an escort would think it necessary to flirt, that it was part of what he was being paid for – and that was something she hated, the dishonesty of it, shrinking instinctively from the men who made an art of it. Poor Oliver hadn't had a flirtatious bone in his body, which had been one of his chief attractions.

A moment later he excused himself. When he returned she summoned up whatever there was in her of bravery or foolhardiness and said, "I was wondering if you would like to come home with me. I mean, I can pay . . ."

She felt the blood rush to her face and was glad she'd been careful with her make-up that evening. He'd already picked up his glass of orange juice and she saw his hand shake slightly as if she'd taken him completely by surprise. She gabbled on because it was too late to stop. "Jean said I should talk to you direct about . . . personal services. Extras."

He didn't answer for a moment and she wanted to die of shame. What if he said, "No, sorry, you're too old and ugly"?

Pray, oh pray, come with me, stay.

When he spoke it was without looking up from his drink, apparently finding the depths of the glass fascinating, "It's two hundred for the night. In advance. Your place." He looked up at last and gave her a brilliant smile. "And you make me breakfast."

She heard herself say, "Will you take a cheque?"

"Um, I suppose."

"Or we could stop at a cashpoint."

"A cheque will be fine."

"You have condoms, I assume."

He thought about this. "Actually I've run out. I daresay we'll pass a late-night chemist."

"Or a garage," she said. "They sell them at garages."

12

"Do they? I don't see the connection."

"No, nor do I."

"I don't drive," he said. "Can't afford a car."

"Me neither. I mean I *can* afford one, but it's not worth it where I live. There's plenty of shops and restaurants and cinemas in Richmond, you see." She knew that she was babbling now. "And two excellent theatres. And it's only twenty-five minutes to Waterloo by train."

If she could go on talking randomly forever then they'd never have to leave this place.

He drained his glass and said, "Shall we be off?"

"Too narrow to turn round here." The chauffeur grumbled as he drew up outside her house.

"You can turn round at the bottom, by the river," she said coolly, "as you did when you picked me up." She handed him a ten-pound note through the open glass screen. "This is for you."

He brightened up and touched his cap. "Thank you, madam." He got out of the car and opened the back door for them.

The house was a generously proportioned two-storey building at the end of a row of six. It looked tidy and comfortable with its brickwork mellowed by time to a warm brown, leavened by a creamy clematis. It was well cared for with its fresh clean paintwork in petrol blue, its recent guttering. It was a place prosperous cultured people came to settle in their middle years.

She'd left some lights on and for a moment it was like someone else's house, already inhabited, not for her. But then she unlocked the front door, mortice and latch, and the hall was full of familiar things – the mirror opposite with its pretty painted frame, the umbrella stand, the bowl of early roses on the secretaire. The door to her study stood open to her right and she realised by the humming noise that she'd forgotten to switch her computer off when she went out, which was again alienating as if someone had been working away in her absence.

She must pull herself together and either go through with this or pay Matthew and send him away, preferably the latter.

13

But as she stood there hesitating, he put his arm round her shoulder and she felt its warmth even through her jacket and blouse, and there was a spasm in her pelvis such as she hadn't felt since September of two years ago and which she recognised with surprised welcome as lust.

He said, "Are you OK, Rosalind?

He must be used to this, to clients who got cold feet, to reassuring them.

"Yes. Absolutely. I'm fine."

He wasn't a machine, she thought: he'd probably like a bit of time before they went to bed, some sort of build up. She certainly would. She led the way into the sitting room. "Would you like another drink. Or maybe I should say *a* drink since I notice you were on fruit juice all evening."

"I'm not a big drinker at the best of times and drunkenness on duty is not encouraged."

"Is Jean strict about that?"

He gave a mock shudder. "Very. A whisky would be nice."

"Sit down. Make yourself at home."

He bounced down on the sofa, his long legs pushing the rug a little away. "What a lovely room to come home to." There was a wistful note in his voice. "Elegant but comfortable at the same time. So . . . welcoming."

"Isn't your place nice?"

She opened a door from a range of cupboards that filled the wall opposite the fireplace, selected the bottle of twenty-three-year-old Clynelish which was her personal treat, and poured the straw-coloured liquid into a crystal glass, holding it up to the wall lamp to admire its deep lights.

He said, "You know what rented flats are like. Or perhaps you don't."

"Oh, I know all right. Here. Would you like water?"

"Is there any ice?"

"You don't put ice in single malt."

"OK. I hope I can do it justice." He sipped it, keeping it in his mouth for a moment to savour it. "Mmm. Lovely. Smoky." He smiled up at her. "Aren't you having one?"

"I think I've drunk enough. Excuse me a moment."

14

She went next door to her study, snapped off the computer and wrote out the cheque, scribbling "sundries" on the counterfoil. She came back and handed it to him. He put it in his inside pocket with the envelope of cash without looking at it, then took his jacket and scarf off and draped them over the end of the sofa. He patted the seat next to him and she sat. He put his arm round her again and looked deep into her eyes. His were very blue with a corona of silvery grey. She noticed that he'd drained his glass already, but he could hardly be as nervous as she was. After all, he was used to this and she most definitely was not.

"It's OK," he said, as if he sensed her misgivings. "It's really OK."

His hand stroked her hair which was glossy, heavy and the colour of chestnuts. Her best feature, as her mother had said when she was in her teens, always succeeding with this qualified compliment in making her feel plain. It was soothing, as if she were a nervous animal being stroked to quietude.

"Such beautiful hair," he said. He put his glass down on the side table, cupped her narrow face in his hands, leaned forward and kissed her. It was gentle but not in the least platonic.

She opened her mouth to his, tasting the mature malt on his tongue. Eighteen months since anyone had kissed her, and never anyone as beautiful as Matty. Hadn't she read somewhere that prostitutes didn't kiss? This one did, and very nicely. Dry. She hated sloppy kisses that left your mouth drooling.

"More whisky?" she asked when they disengaged. He shook his head.

She stood up rather too quickly, as if the fire alarm had sounded. "Are you ready?"

He sat forward, winding his strong arms round her, loosening the silk shirt from her waistband, pushing it up and kissing the softly rounded flesh of her belly. She threw her head back, arching into the pleasure of it, twining her fingers in his clean hair. His hands moved up to unfasten her bra without difficulty, setting her small breasts free.

He said, "I'm ready."

Things Zoe would be too shy to write

She switched on one of the bedside lamps, giving some light and some places of refuge. She pushed back the patchwork quilt to the end of the bed; they would be warm enough.

He undressed her, which didn't take long, his hands warm and dry on her skin. He slid her shirt over her head, causing her unfastened bra to fall away, then undid the waistband of her evening trousers so they dropped to the floor and she could step out of them and kick them aside. She thought that if this had been premeditated she'd have worn some sexier – or at least some *newer* – underwear.

When she was naked and under the sheet, he quickly stripped himself.

She scrutinised her purchase openly and was pleased with what she saw. His cock was of average length and thickness, uncircumcised, snapped up at attention against his belly in a way that Ollie's had been when they first met, declining with imperceptible slowness over the years to the right-angled – the tea-pot-spout – position until she'd forgotten that it had ever been any different.

Thank God he was aroused. It would be have been so humiliating if he hadn't been, if he'd had to use his hand to ready himself.

"Tell me what you like," he said.

"Everything. I like everything. All of it."

She'd never understood women – and she'd met plenty – who said they loved the foreplay and the afterglow but would be happy to forego the penetration altogether. That for her was the real pleasure, a quite separate one from orgasm which she had at her fingertips at any time. There was no substitute for a cock – the hardness yet flexibility of it. It was eighteen months since she'd had a man inside her and that was starting to look like a serious oversight.

She said again, "I want all of it," and he smiled at her fervour and got into bed beside her, tearing open the packet of condoms they'd bought on the way and extracting one but not yet putting it on.

He began to kiss her again but then stopped, brushing the hair back from her face, and said, "You're very tense. Turn over."

"Huh?"

"I'm going to massage you, loosen you up. You'll see."

She turned obediently on her stomach, her head sideways on the pillow so she was gazing at the bedside lamp in its primrose shade. She couldn't see him, was aware only of a presence – a shadow, strong and male, a masculine smell not masked by shop-bought scent – but she felt his hands moving firmly over the knotted muscles at the nape of her neck, then outwards across her bony shoulders. They were sore at first and she let out a little grunt with each circular motion of his thumbs, but then the knots began to relax and unravel and soon she was barely blinking at the light like a subject in a trance.

She felt his lips in the small of her back, on her buttocks, butterfly kisses. Or did she imagine them, so delicate were they? She could hear her own breath, each one longer and deeper than the last. After a few minutes she said, "Enough," and rolled over beneath him, feeling his erection bumping round her thigh, the silkiness of the taut skin of its head. "I shall go to sleep if you're not careful."

He broke off to put the condom on, deft, not fumbling, before resuming his caresses. The butterfly kisses had been no imagination, they were settling now on her belly and breasts before flying away.

It was gloriously liberating to realise that she didn't have to please him, that it was his job to ensure her pleasure. As he touched her he was paying attention, watching and listening, gauging her responses. He licked her skin – arms, legs, stomach – then blew softly on the damp patch till the hairs stood erect with a tingling sensation that was almost unbearable.

She told him: "This" and "Here" and "Yes, like that" and "No, not yet" and "Yes, definitely, now". As he moved easily into her when she told him she was ready for him, he whispered, "Rosalind!"

Yes, she thought, it was Rosalind Tate who was doing this outrageous thing, Rosalind Tate who didn't exist, not Zoe Kean, respectable widow.

It was her last coherent thought for some time.

She hadn't supposed that she'd be able to sleep with this big, alien body in her bed. Indeed, she'd intended to leave him afterwards and go and spend the night in the spare room – the thought of lying unconscious in his presence more worryingly intimate to her than the merging of their sweating bodies – but she fell deeply asleep before her sedated muscles would respond to her commands to move.

When she woke up hours later she thought she must be in the middle of an erotic dream. Matthew was making love to her again as she hovered in the no-man's-land between dozing and waking. It was something she'd fantasised about, being woken in this way, but on the one occasion when she'd ventured to mention it to Ollie, he'd expressed doubts at managing it successfully, at not waking her until the right moment, totally relaxed and halfway to heaven.

Matthew must be a mind reader. Unless that was what all his clients dreamed of in their hidden worlds. She sighed with the pleasure that suffused her body and opened her eyes, seeing his intent face close to hers in the twilight.

He whispered, "Good morning," and kissed her.

With one quick movement she turned him onto his back and straddled him, taking him deeper into her. He laughed in delight as their limbs tangled in the sheets and she kicked herself free with a savagery she had not suspected herself capable of. His torso came up to meet hers, his mouth sucking at her breasts like a greedy baby, his thighs strong under her.

She came almost at once, collapsing forward on him,

pushing him down again as an irresistible force against the pillow, and felt him stroke her hair as it tickled his face and neck.

"Your turn now," she said as he stayed still inside her. She was sure he hadn't come yet, although she'd noticed last night that he was quiet at climax, with none of the noise – let alone the running commentary – which some men seemed to think obligatory.

He said, "No hurry."

One thin gleam of daylight, where she hadn't pulled the curtains properly in her haste the night before, fell across them, drawing a line to link their hot bodies. His hands fondled her buttocks, his neat nails rippling across the pearly skin, making her shiver.

He said, "We can give you another turn first," and began to move again with long, slow thrusts.

She said, "Please, no more," and he said, "You don't mean that," and, as it turned out, he was right.

He looked incongruous sitting at her breakfast bar in evening dress, the shiny stripe down the outside of each leg, the white shirt, a little limp now, the black bow tie – not ready made, as she had discovered – streaming loose from the collar. Unshaven, but well showered.

As if reading her thoughts, he said, "I shall feel silly going home on the tube like this."

"Pretend it's a new fashion." She opened the fridge. "Bacon and eggs?"

"My God! A woman who has real food in her fridge instead of some lettuce leaves and half a low-fat yoghurt with mould on the top."

"Was that a yes?"

"Yes, please."

She was in her Chinese silk dressing gown, blue and white like willow pattern, feeling pleasantly slatternly since she always dressed for breakfast. Next thing you knew she'd be wandering about with rollers in her hair and a fag hanging out of the corner of her mouth calling people "luv".

She fried while he drank coffee. She cooked for two

19

since she had a ferocious appetite this morning, crisping the bacon the way she liked it and flipping the eggs over without breaking them. She'd never had a one-night stand before, hadn't realised how liberating it could be. What did it matter if her body wasn't perfect, or if she made strange and embarrassing noises as she came? In a few minutes he would leave and she need never see him again. Who was he going to tell?

"You're divorced I take it," he said after a while.

"Widowed."

"Oh, I'm so sorry. It didn't occur to me. You seem too young."

"He died in a climbing accident eighteen months ago. He was forty."

"That's too young to die."

"You're never too young to die."

"Children?"

"We never felt the need. We had each other."

"And now?" Matthew asked.

Oliver had volunteered to have a vasectomy four years after their marriage and she'd been able to come off the pill and hadn't had to worry about contraception for more than ten years. Last night had been her first encounter with a condom. This morning her second. And suddenly she was embarrassed, feeling the flustered red stain start at her breasts and spread up her neck, sprinting for her cheeks.

"I'm sorry," she said quickly, scrabbling for plates and knives and forks. "Did you ask me something?"

"I was wondering if you wished, with hindsight, that you'd had them."

She wanted to tell him that this was too impertinent a question, too private, but that was an absurd thing to say to a man with whom you'd had vigorous intercourse twice in the last twelve hours, a man who had acquainted himself with the most private recesses of your body with his lips, his fingers, his tongue and his cock.

Rather stiffly, she said, "I don't see children as an emotional crutch."

A child to mourn his father's loss. Or her own loss. Or

would Ollie have given up climbing if he'd had a child to consider? She would never know. She put his breakfast in front of him and sat, concentrating on her own food as they ate in silence.

He cleared his plate, then there seemed nothing else to be done or said. She glanced at the clock on the wall. They'd fallen asleep again after their dawn exertions and the weak spring sun was now high in the sky, although she could see the tops of the trees along the railway line shaking in the wind, strong enough to send leaves cascading on to the track as if it was autumn and they were providing an excuse for late running.

He took the hint, if that was what it was. "I'd better be going, let you get on." He wandered into the sitting room in search of his jacket, not putting it on but draping it round his shoulders, stuffing the silk scarf into his pocket. "I expect you'll be working today."

"I usually go for a walk in the mornings. It clears my head and lets me plan my afternoon's work."

He hesitated, unsure how to take his leave. "It was nice meeting you." He held out his hand for her to shake and she looked at it, perplexed for a moment, and then they both began to laugh. He pulled her to him and kissed her lightly on the mouth. "Bye, Rosalind."

She said, "Thank you," then cursed herself for a fool. She turned from him, flustered, and tugged the front door open.

He said, "Yes, thanks," hesitated again, then stepped over the threshold.

She gave him directions to the station and shut the door behind him, not watching him go up the road. She went back upstairs to shower and dress, to brush her hair and find some earrings. She cleaned and flossed her teeth with extra care. She tried to straighten the king-sized bed but they'd made too much of a jumble, as if at least six people had been holding an orgy in it, and in the end she stripped it and started from scratch with fresh sheets.

She noticed the unused condom from the packet of three lying on the bedside table like an accusation. She wrapped it in a tissue to camouflage it and threw it in the bathroom bin.

21

She went down to her study and booted up her computer but then stared at the screen without opening any files, not even to write her diary. Where to begin? No one else read her journal and yet she was ashamed to write in it the plain facts of what she'd done, let alone how it had felt. Suppose she fell under a bus today and somebody read that file? Her solicitor and executor, a bland man who gave an impression of being easily shocked which sat ill with his calling? The next owner of the machine, more excited than he'd anticipated by his second-hand bargain?

She'd always considered men who went to prostitutes as beneath contempt, but this was different, wasn't it? But how? Because she liked Matty and really fancied him. Because he must at least fancy her. Mustn't he? Or he wouldn't have been able to . . . But she'd read somewhere that many male prostitutes were gay and got it up for a female by closing their eyes and thinking of a pert male bum and a wad of money.

Wasn't there still a gender difference, a feeling that died hard even in the final years of the twentieth century, that men were always up for it, that no woman could exploit them sexually? She despised herself at that moment, but physically she didn't remember when she'd last felt so good. It was as if her whole body had been expertly stimulated, then expertly relaxed. And wasn't that the point of sex, after all – not the excitement of the moment but the purity of the rest that followed?

She looked at the picture of Ollie in his climbing gear, at his open, honest face, then turned it down on the mouse mat. She laid her head on the desk and closed her eyes. A dry sob shook her body.

She was still lying like that ten minutes later when she heard a key turn in the front door.

"Ollie?" she croaked, panic stricken. Caught almost *in flagrante.*

"Zoe? You in?"

Sarah. It was Wednesday, of course, and her cleaner came on Wednesdays and Fridays. She wiped her eyes on her cuff, switched off the computer, lumbered to her feet and went out into the hall. A woman, thirtyish, in a tracksuit, was removing her fleecy zipped top and hanging it on the newel post at the foot of the stairs, revealing a purple T-shirt with a heart appliquéd on it.

She'd dumped a three-month-old baby in its carrycot on the wide bottom step where it slumbered deeply with its mouth open. Zoe found this minuscule human alarming. Its reaction both to her smiles and grimaces was identical: total indifference.

Sarah said, "Oh, you are in. I wasn't sure, you were so quiet."

She fiddled with the waistband of her tracksuit trousers, hoiking it up over the bulge where she had still to regain her figure. Her reddish hair, caught back in a towelling headband, looked greasy as if she never had the leisure or the inclination to wash it any more, having fulfilled the reproductive function allotted her by nature.

Zoe said, "Is it that time already?"

Sarah consulted her Teletubby watch. "Yep. Half ten. How are you this morning?"

"I'm fine. How's . . ." She gestured at the cot.

"Myrtle? She's grand."

Myrtle. Zoe knew the baby's name, she just couldn't bring herself to say it. She bent dutifully over the cot. The baby opened its eyes, looked at her and began to grizzle. At least that made a change from indifference. Zoe mumbled apologies and plucked her jacket from the coat cupboard as Sarah began to soothe the baby with clucking noises, her blotchy face filled with an inner light as she pacified her child.

"Just going out. Get from under your feet for a bit."

Sarah called after her. "Do you want me to change your sheets today?"

"No! I changed them myself. Spilt coffee."

Zoe shrugged on her jacket and left the house.

Through fat and thin

"Well, Zoe!"
"Well, well, Zoe Kean. Who's been a naughty girl, eh?"

She drew herself up to her full height of five feet six and glared over the fence at her neighbours, the Jims: Fat Jim and Thin Jim. Thin Jim was thin only in comparison to Fat Jim, who'd achieved a sphericity that barrage balloons envied. They were such a cosy and long-established couple that she half expected to find them dressed in identical jumpers, like twins, although she never had yet. Her glare had no effect except to make them giggle.

"You're scaring us," Thin Jim lied.

"We saw him leaving," Fat Jim said. "Very tasty."

"And young," Thin Jim added.

She said without acrimony, "Sod you both."

"Seriously, darling." Fat Jim leaned his belly against the boundary fence, which groaned complaint, and hugged her. "It was high time."

Fat Jim McLaverty was a Glaswegian of red-Irish descent and gave the impression of being a real hard man, almost a gangster, the last man in the world you would suspect of being gay. He looked as if he'd beat you up at the merest suggestion of it and bite your nose off for good measure. He looked as if someone had bitten *his* nose off more than once and sewn it back on slightly more askew each time. He owned three nightclubs in darkest Surrey which enabled him, as he put it, to live somewhere civilised. The most successful of the clubs was called the Screwdriver: not because that particular cocktail was fashionable at the moment, but because most of its clientele drove there to pick up someone to screw.

Thin Jim Cooke – a blond and cheerful Geordie, who'd
left Newcastle because random bursts of cheerfulness were
frowned on there – had come to work at one of the clubs
as a temporary bartender ten years earlier and had quickly
progressed into his boss's bed and then into his house. It was,
as Fat Jim said, as clear a case of sexual harassment at work
as you could hope to find.

Fat Jim was pushing fifty, Thin Jim was thirty-five. They
were devoted to each other and to a series of Welsh terriers
called, for no discernible reason, Trefor. Trefor mark three
was a puppy, Trefor two having met a premature end after an
unequal fight with a removal van on the Green the previous
winter. He was currently sitting on the doorstep, one drop
ear cocked, as if he was certain he could understand what
his lovely humans were saying if he only concentrated hard
enough.

"So what's his name?" Thin Jim said. "Where did you meet
him? What does he do? When are you seeing him again?"

"Nosy!" Fat Jim said, then, as Zoe didn't immediately
answer, added impatiently, "Well?"

"Marmaduke, in a Turkish bath, he's a taxidermist and . . ."
Inspiration failed her. "I must get to the shops." She left.

She liked the walk across the Green into town. Rounding
the corner at the top of the road and seeing the space opening
out before her – a tamed acreage of lawns and trees, paths and
benches, with graceful houses on every side and the distant
prospect of the baroque Victorian theatre – could banish all
but the most stubborn blues.

Zoe returned an hour later with a bag of groceries and
another full of books. She could hear Sarah vacuuming
upstairs, halfway through her two and a half hours. She
padded across the kitchen floor and flicked on the coffee
filter. She threw open the French windows in the sitting room
and went out on to the terrace. She lugged the terracotta pots
full of spring flowers into position to hold the doors open and
walked down the two shallow steps on to the lawn, breathing
in the clear, cool air.

"By the way" – Fat Jim's head and shoulders reared up over
the fence, causing a partial eclipse, and she stifled a sigh. She

loved the Jims dearly but they never knew when they weren't wanted. They'd appointed themselves her guardian angels after Ollie died, although she'd never envisaged a pair of gay guardian angels with prominent love handles. "Dr Lincoln was looking for you last night," Jim continued, oblivious.

"Sam? Was he?"

"I told him you were at that . . . what was it?"

"The Robert Drewe Memorial Dinner."

He laughed. "I wonder if he was that pompous when he was alive. Yes, the dinner you didn't invite us to and now we know why."

"I explained that I had only one spare ticket," she said patiently. She could have asked one of the Jims to escort her – both had evening dress for work in the clubs – but they couldn't be relied upon to behave.

"I believe you," Fat Jim said. "Thousands wouldn't. Anyway, young Sam said he'd forgotten about that and he'd look round today after he'd done his house calls. Thought you'd like to know."

"Lucky he didn't come too early this morning." Thin Jim's voice came floating invisibly over the fence, making her jump. "While your little friend was still here. The green-eyed monster. Ooh!"

"Oh, shut up. Both of you."

Fat Jim grinned and his head and halo vanished below the parapet.

She could have asked Sam to escort her but she hadn't.

She poured herself a mug of coffee and fetched a deckchair from the shed. She sat on the terrace, sheltered from the wind by the side wall, pretending to read a novel. A few minutes later the doorbell rang.

Through the glass panes that flanked the entrance she could see the familiar shape of her friend Sam Lincoln, distorted though it was by the mottled effect of the panels that rendered them opaque and therefore useless as windows. She flung the door wide.

"The Jims said you were looking for me last night."

"Hi, Zo." Sam came into the hall and went instantly through the sitting room, making for the French windows in the manner

26

of someone who knew the house intimately and was sure of his welcome there. He sank down in her deckchair with a sigh of relief, wiping his heavy dark hair which badly needed cutting back from his forehead, revealing an endearing streak of grey on the underside. Zoe smiled at him with real warmth and perched on the low parapet that separated the terrace from the lawn.

Sam had almost bullied her after Ollie's death, respecting her grief but refusing to allow her to shut herself away from the world, to retreat into an eremitic existence from which she might never have emerged. There had been times when she'd screamed abuse at him, even struck him, her fists banging uselessly against his chest in inarticulate frustration because he wouldn't let her give up on life now that the main point of it was gone. She'd thrown him out of the house on more than one occasion, telling him not to come back, but he always had come back, and the worst had passed, as he had promised, just at the moment when she believed it never would.

Their common struggle had fostered a true intimacy between them.

"Coffee?" she asked.

"I just had one, thanks. I can't stay long. Annie's with Diana next door but she's got a hairdresser's appointment in half an hour."

He always explained too much, she thought, with a surge of affection, had to account for himself, as if people might not otherwise make allowances. He was a little taller than she, perhaps five foot eight, and strongly built: not in the least fat but looking as if there was something to get hold of, and not only physically. He was a GP at the health centre where she was registered, but not her GP. He was popular with his patients, especially the women, who brought him home-made cakes and chutney and called him familiarly Dr Sam.

He was thirty-eight but came on like he was middle-aged and had been born that way, although she remembered a more light-hearted Sam from her early days in Richmond, the counterpart of a more light-hearted Zoe. There were worry lines on his forehead which he accentuated by active furrowing. He wore a dark-blue suit that had grown baggy from years of overstuffed pockets, along with a cream shirt, ironed only at the front, and a blue and red striped tie which he now unknotted and shoved into one of them. He didn't have to undo his top button: there wasn't one.

"I came to see if you could man the phones Friday," he explained, "or whatever more politically correct verb I ought to use. Kate's grandmother died suddenly yesterday afternoon and she's got the funeral to see to."

"Oh, I'm sorry."

"Well, she was in the right place when she heard."

She and Sam were colleagues at the local Friends in Loss – FILO – office, counselling the bereaved. Sam had brought her into it a year ago, stressing her qualification for the task: that she had experienced the unique pain herself. Zoe had only recently finished her training and Sam was her supervisor but he never acted as if he knew better than she did, not about anything. He had none of the arrogance she'd come to expect from young male doctors.

She had a couple of clients but mostly she did administrative work in the office, dealing with letters and answering the phones. She thought she was better with that than at handling raw grief face to face, although one elderly man, robbed of his wife after forty-five happy years, had told her what a comfort she'd been and had hugged her as he sobbed on her shoulder.

It was vital that someone answer the phone during the day: when you were wondering how you were going to go on, you didn't want to discuss it with an answering machine. Outside office hours people did have to leave messages but someone – usually Sam – rang in to collect them and return the calls the same evening. It was not uncommon for him to be on the phone half the night, listening to a familiar yet unique tale of grief.

"Of course I can do Friday," she said.

"Thanks." Sam leaned back in the deckchair and closed his eyes. "God, your garden smells good."

"Hard day?" she asked.

"Heavy morning surgery. I overran by more than an hour."

"Any special reason, or shouldn't I ask?"

"Nothing confidential, an outbreak of unseasonal flu among

the local children which their mothers are convinced is meningitis. I have to examine each one carefully, in case it *is* meningitis."

"You work too hard."

"I know." He sounded proud of the fact, boastful, like most people who acknowledged they worked too hard. Zoe had never bought into the Protestant work ethic: she put in a few hours a day at her desk at times that suited herself; otherwise it was coffee and a good book on the terrace, walks by the river and in the park, visits to the cinema and her friends. Why did you have to justify time spent on yourself? Why could you not stand and watch sunlight sparkle on water and not feel guilty about it?

Thinking of guilt she blurted out, "What do you think about casual sex, Sam?"

"Not right now, thanks, Zo. I'm knackered." He opened one spaniel eye and looked at her from under long lashes. "Seriously, for obvious reasons, I'm against it."

"Even safe sex?"

"There's no such thing, not a hundred per cent." He closed the inquisitive, beautiful eye. "No, I'm not going to ask why you're asking."

"But what if you have a one-night stand and it's fan-fucking-tastic – miles better than anything you've ever had with . . . a regular partner?"

"I don't believe that stuff, about how sex with a stranger is better than with someone you love and trust. It's crap. It has to be."

Something in his voice told her that he very much wanted it to be crap and she didn't pursue the subject. They sat in comfortable silence for a minute then she said, "What about Annie?"

"Shit! I forgot." He jumped to his feet and headed back into the house through the French windows. "Your garden is so peaceful I could sit here all day."

In the sitting room he paused at an ornate chess set placed out on its board on a japanned table by the fireplace. He picked up a piece, flourished it dramatically, put it down in a different place and announced, "Bishop to queen six."

"No, Sam."

"No?"

"Bishops can only move diagonally, as you very well know."

He grumbled and made a different move. "Did you ever meet a bishop who could only move diagonally?" He zig-zagged down the hall, his hands folded over his head to simulate a mitre. "Like this? Bloody stupid game." She saw him out, kissing him on both cheeks at the door. He turned halfway down the path and said, "You seen that new Spanish movie at the Filmhouse yet?"

"I thought I'd go Saturday afternoon."

"Mind if I tag along? I should be able to get a sitter."

"No. Great. I like to have someone to discuss it with after."

"And maybe it'll keep you out of mischief. Bye." And he was gone.

She thought that his lot had been harder than hers. His partner had died of Aids six years earlier, the infection undiagnosed until the last possible moment when a bad cold turned rapidly into pneumonia and even more rapidly into death, unverified till the post mortem. Sam could only conclude that she'd contracted it during the two years she'd spent doing VSO in Africa in the late seventies when she was eighteen and nineteen.

She must have been infected before anyone, but a few worried doctors, had even heard of it. The mercy – the miracle – was that Sam and their then infant daughter, Annie, tested negative. Annie was now a happy, lively eight-year-old who had no memory of her mother.

Family secrets

Joanna Aimery was a woman of Zoe's own age, give or take a year or two, a plump, dishevelled blonde who arrived for her first counselling session that Thursday evening with a hurt look in her striking grey eyes.

The initial hour was the most difficult in Zoe's experience. It was often the first time the clients had seen any sort of counsellor and they were wary of opening their suffering hearts to a stranger, groping for the words to express their loss, their despair and – worst of all – the feeling that it would never end, that this blank misery was now part of them.

They didn't usually come to FILO until some time after the death, believing, in the early days, that the numbness would pass once the funeral was out of the way and life returned to some semblance of routine, finding to their dismay that the grieving got worse before it got better. The counselling rooms were designed to put them at their ease: cheerful pastel-coloured walls with undemanding landscape prints and neutral carpets, comfort foremost with Zoe and Joanna head to head in cushioned armchairs, a low pine table between them scarred with the rings of a thousand hot coffee mugs.

The single mother of two boys, Joanna worked part time teaching music at local schools to make ends meet, giving private piano lessons so that the ends might overlap. She was intelligent and lucid and Zoe liked her at once: she had to be kind and gentle to her clients, but she was only human and the fact was that some of them were irritating, whiny and self-pitying.

The most difficult to deal with were the ones who demanded assurance that there was something beyond the grave, that they would be reunited with their loved ones in heaven, an assurance which Zoe couldn't possibly give. She would have referred them to their priest but they were seldom churchgoers, wanting the comforts and ritual of religion at the crucial landmarks of life without the daily grind of adherence.

At first she'd feared she wasn't cut out to be a counsellor, that she hadn't the necessary empathy and kindness, but Sam had laughed at her misgivings and explained, "We all feel like that in the beginning. If you thought you were ideal for the job, *then* there would be a problem."

Joanna's mother had recently died in her mid-eighties, but that wasn't why she'd come to FILO, or not the only reason. Clearing out her mother's house, sorting through her papers, she'd come across the great family secret: her mother was not her mother but her grandmother – her real mother her "big sister" Valerie, fifteen at the time of her birth.

"I feel doubly bereaved," she explained on this first visit, articulate, eloquent and dry-eyed, "doubly and trebly bereaved. I've lost a mother, a grandmother and a second mother. I feel betrayed, and as if I can never trust anyone again."

"Is Valerie dead?" Zoe asked.

"No. At least, she might be. I don't know. She married a Canadian airman when I was five and went back to Canada with him. At first she used to write to Mum – or whatever I should call her now." A look of distress flickered across her pretty face. "What should I call her?"

"What's wrong with Mum if that's what you've always called her?"

"All right. I'll pretend it was a pet name and not an age-old appellation reserved for mothers by their offspring. Anyway, after a couple of years it was a cheap card at Christmas – love Valerie and Dwight, no message – and, for the past fifteen years, nothing. Why couldn't they tell me? Why did we have to live this *lie*?"

"Such lies are born of fear rather than deceit," Zoe offered.

"I also feel incredibly stupid that it never occurred to me: after all, my 'mother' was forty-five when I was born which was pushing it a bit. How deeply in denial can a person be?"

"Do you remember her?" Zoe asked. "Valerie?"

"Dimly. A pretty teenager, allowing for the hideous fashions of the day – the beehive hairdos and false eyelashes like a spider had crept there and died, the panstick make-up. I remember her always getting ready to go on a date with yet another new boyfriend, always being yelled at to turn her music down."

"And how was she with you?"

Joanna considered this for a long time and Zoe might have thought that she didn't want to answer, but she knew that childhood memories could be – not buried for the sheer misery of them – filed away, perhaps under an unexpected heading, and difficult of retrieval.

"She ignored me," Joanna said at last. "I was the nuisance kid sister. I remember once how her current bloke stepped on one of my dolls and broke its plastic head and I burst into tears and she told me not to be such a cry baby. Even the man was kinder. He promised to bring me a new dolly next time he came, but he never did come to the house again. She'd dumped him like the rest. Until the Canadian. Dwight."

"Perhaps she'd been badly hurt by your father," Zoe suggested, "and you were a constant memory of that pain."

Joanna said, "You read about adopted children seeking out their birth mothers and about the mothers weeping on their shoulders and telling them how they hated to give them up, how it broke their heart and how they've thought about them every day since. There's no danger of that with Valerie, even if I knew where to find her. I'm a mother myself. I know how it feels to give birth and to hold a baby in your arms for the first time. How can any woman do that and then . . . put it aside, forget about it?"

Joanna remained on cordial terms with her ex-husband but had been unable to express her feelings to him, or not in a way that he could understand. "He's not comfortable with emotion, never was, like so many middle-aged men. He can't see why it matters to me that all the woven fabric of my life has been torn to shreds."

"So he's not supportive."

"Oh, yes. He pays his maintenance every month on the dot."

"No, I meant—"

"Yes, I knew what you meant. But paying alimony and so on is Henry's way of proving he still cares, you see. Working hard and supporting his family financially is the way a man shows his feelings, to his way of thinking. It's what his father did and *his* father before him. Like when you ask a man if he loves you and he says gruffly 'I wouldn't be here otherwise, would I?' You know?"

Zoe nodded as was required, although Oliver had never been slow to tell her that he loved her.

"As to the rest," Joanna concluded, "he thinks I should forget about it and get on with my life."

Unresolved anger about the break-up of her marriage, Zoe thought, but she wasn't a relationship counsellor and could deal with only one source of misery at a time. "Did you love your mother?" she asked. "I mean the woman you thought was your mother. Tell me about her."

"Yes, very much. She was a tough old bird, the sort that worked her socks off all her life, keeping to a tight budget, making sure the house was spotless, always putting herself last in the queue for attention. Nurturing."

"I know the sort." Zoe's mother had not been like that and she'd envied friends whose mothers wore pinnies and smelled of baking.

Joanna smiled to herself. "She got eccentric after Dad died. I liked that. She took up ballroom dancing when she was seventy. Some children might have been embarrassed but I was proud."

"And is she a different person now you know she wasn't your biological mother?" Zoe asked. "Did she love you less, or you her? Has her personality changed posthumously? Is she any less admirable?"

As their session came to an end Joanna agreed to return the following week. "All my life I've felt like I was in the wrong place at the wrong time," she said, "even living the wrong life, and now I begin to understand why."

"I want you to think between then and now how your life might have been different if you'd known the truth," Zoe said as she saw her out. Because there was a danger that Joanna would blame everything that hadn't worked out in her life on this one primal deception.

She resumed her seat, closing her eyes, taking a few minutes to herself before Sam came in search of her. At the end of fifty minutes counselling she always felt as if she'd spent that time running uphill.

The course of life changed on the most minuscule of decisions, she thought, or not even decisions, things that happened to you. She almost hadn't gone to the theatre that night when she'd met Oliver. She'd been starting a cold and kept sniffing into her handkerchief all morning at work until her fatherly boss had sent her home. She'd taken some patent cold cure which had dried her nose up but made her feel most peculiarly light-headed. So she'd rung Polly and told her she was going to have to cancel but Polly had sounded so disappointed that she'd been persuaded to change her mind.

Then Polly had rushed off to the loo before the performance so that she, Zoe, had taken the innermost of their two seats, the one next to Oliver. The play had been awful and she'd felt him laughing next to her for all the wrong reasons, the same reasons she was laughing, his shoulders shaking silently. And perhaps it was the alienating effect of the cold cure that had allowed her to turn to him as the lights came up for the interval, to raise her eyebrows in shared derision, reducing them both to more helpless laughter, to spend those fifteen precious minutes talking to him and to accept his invitation to go for a drink after the performance.

So if such an important thing in her life had hung on the invisible threads of a cold virus, a weak bladder and a playwright who didn't know his craft, how much more dramatic might the changes in Joanna's life have been had Valerie been a different sort of person, or England before the 1960s less judgmental?

"I'm beginning to understand," she told Sam half an hour later, "that someone doesn't have to be dead to be mourned. Joanna is mourning a relationship that might have existed between her and Valerie."

Sam grunted and drank his beer. He didn't feel it necessary

to reply unless he had something specific to say, not with Zoe.
They were in a quiet corner of the Prince's Head on the edge
of Richmond Green. A regular meeting place situated halfway
between their respective houses.

"In some ways I'm already in mourning for my mother,"
she went on.

Sam spoke then, his voice sounding detached. "When
the personality disintegrates through senility then the relationship dies with it. Death, when it comes, is almost
embraced."

Zoe went to the bar and fetched another round. Sam drained
his half pint of bitter in one gulp and said that he must be
going without moving any of the muscles that would have
accomplished this end.

"It's odd," she said, "but when I was a teenager, and even
into my early twenties, I thought I'd never marry, never meet
anyone I could achieve that level of intimacy with."

"What's odd is not that so many relationships break down
but that so many make it to the finishing line," Sam replied.
"It's absurd, when you think about it, to pile all your eggs into
the basket of that one person who must be lover, parent, child
and friend."

"And nursemaid and counsellor."

"Cook and bottle washer."

"Undress you and put you to bed when you're rat-arsed."

"And hold the bowl for you when you throw up."

"I was nervous of talking to men because I assumed they
wouldn't find me attractive and I was afraid if I tried to be
friendly I'd be suspected of chatting them up in some desperate
way, of running after them. Then Oliver appeared and it was all
so natural and right and I wasn't nervous at all. I think I was
lucky to have had one such relationship. To hope for another
would be over-optimistic."

Sam didn't challenge this. He said, "There's been no woman
in my life since Christine died."

"In six years?"

"It seems like yesterday. You see," he said simply, "I'm
afraid. Don't know if I can take that risk again."

"Of infection? Of Aids?"

He shook his head. "Of losing someone who was my whole life to me."

Zoe had noticed that men took widowhood harder than women. The man was usually the older partner and women lived longer so that, on her wedding day, a woman understood, deep in her subconscious, that one day she would likely be a widow.

For a man it was a lightning bolt from a summer sky.

After a moment he added, "She was the only woman I ever . . ."

"The only woman you've ever slept with?" Zoe queried, thinking she must have misunderstood.

"I was nineteen when I met her. She was twenty-one. She was the first and, as it turned out, I had no need to look further."

"Haven't you ever wondered what it would be like with another woman?"

He shrugged.

Everything had changed in human relationships during her lifetime, she thought, beginning in the late sixties: divorce reform, the pill, the legalisation of homosexuality and abortion, the destigmatisation of cohabitation – "living in sin" as it had been quaintly called when she was a child – and illegitimacy.

All the old rules had been swept away but nobody had come up with any new ones to put in their place and the result was chaos.

So a woman went out looking for love and ended up with a one-night stand; looking for a quick, meaningless fuck she got lumbered with an obsessive stalker; she married in her thirties, believing herself and her partner now mature enough to make that commitment, only to have him pack his bags three years later because he was bored.

Sam said again that he really must go and this time his legs moved as well as his mouth. They went their separate ways. The next morning she rang Jean at the agency.

There were no rules.

Trick questions

She'd arranged to meet Matthew outside Turnham Green tube station at twenty-five past eight. She was a few minutes early and stood with her back to the dingy foyer, looking down the terrace at the brightly lit cafés as young people came and went, talking, laughing, kissing, groping.

To her right the sun was setting somewhere over Gunnersbury Park, turning the few clouds orange as it went.

She was wearing a new silk dress with a cowl neckline that hung in graceful folds about her firm bosom and merged greens and blues and mauves into something that looked like running water when she moved. Her hair was freshly cut, shining with health, the ends curling above the collar bone. A middle-aged man hurrying into the tube station clutching his jacket closed with one hand and holding a *Standard* with the other, took time to look her up and down and wink at her, making her feel stupid.

She felt rather than saw Matthew come up behind her. "Rosalind, hello." He kissed her cheek. "You look terrific. I hope I'm not late."

"Not at all. I was early." She'd forgotten how handsome he was, how incongruous she felt on his arm. Surely she'd been dreaming when she imagined bedding this Adonis in his elegant blue lounge suit.

She led the way down the Terrace to the Chiswick High Road and they crossed to the restaurant opposite. She murmured her name to the hovering manager and they were shown to a table at the front. It was a warm night for early May and the folding doors that made up the front of the building were set right back, giving them the benefit of the slight breeze.

She did what she always ritualistically did in restaurants:

moved things aside to create a clear line between herself and her guest. An ashtray, a book of matches, salt and pepper pots, two carnations in a narrow vase – all made the journey to the edge of the bare table. Matthew watched this housekeeping without apparent surprise, certainly without comment, then reached through the resulting canyon and took her hand, squeezing it once, then holding it loosely in his own as he talked easily about the weather, the view, the day's lighter news.

They separated as a waitress handed them menus, glancing up to smile their thanks. She was a tall girl of about twenty, slender enough to move with ease through the close-set tables and holding herself very erect. She had copper-coloured hair tied back in a loose knot, wispy pieces framing her clear, pale face, her huge grey eyes. She was all in black, harem pants with a drawstring waist and a cropped top, revealing a taut and freckled midriff. Zoe looked at her with admiration.

She said, "Can I get you a drink from the bar, at all?" and her voice was deep with the faintest accent that Zoe thought was Northern Irish.

"Matty?"

"Orange juice please."

"I'll have a kir."

"I thought it was a dinner party," he said, when the girl had gone.

"I think I told Jean dinner. I suppose she assumed—"

"Only I feel a little overdressed."

Glancing round she saw that the other male diners were casually if smartly dressed. "Well, why don't you take your tie off?"

"Good idea." He loosened the knot and removed it over his head, folding it carefully before stowing it in his pocket and unfastening the top button of his shirt. His neck had caught the sun and was lightly gilded, his body hair showing almost white against it. She remembered that the dozen tangled strands of hair in the opening V of his shirt were all there was, like window dressing for an empty shop, apart from a single, darker, line running down to his navel then resuming on the far side into his pubic hair.

So she hadn't imagined it after all.

"It's nice to see you again," he said rather formally.

"I enjoyed our last . . . outing."

"Yes, me too."

"And I don't normally have occasion to employ the services of an escort. I don't get invited to 'functions' much, but then I thought there was no reason we shouldn't simply go out to dinner, or to the theatre."

"No, that's quite common."

She didn't want reminding that she was one of a gang, so she began to study her menu. "The food's good here."

"So I've heard."

They ordered. She was feeling adventurous and chose things she hadn't tried before. She asked if he would choose the wine, because that was what men did, but he said he knew nothing about it and would far rather she chose, so she ordered a Burgundy. She went through the ritual of pretending to taste it and nodding acceptance. The girl poured for them.

Talk began to flow with the wine. The restaurant was full and noisy but their position in the window gave them privacy, intimacy. No waiters pushed past them to serve other tables, no diners making for the lavatories. She asked him about the jobs he'd done over the years while waiting for stardom to knock on his door.

"You name it. I've lugged bricks around for builders. I've sat beaming behind a reception desk until I thought I'd never be able to frown again. Oh, and there was a term's modelling in a life class."

"Life, as in you naked?"

"Me, naked on a dais in front of a dozen elderly women, who stared at me with frowns of what I now see was concentration, although at the time, in my paranoia, it looked like criticism."

"How was it?"

"Cold, mostly. Every so often someone would open the door of the classroom, look me up and down, say, 'Sorry, wrong room' – yeah, right! – and go away again. By the end of term I felt this big." He held his thumb and finger an inch apart. "Then they sacked me in favour of a bloke of seventy-two with a belly like Buddha and more wrinkles than a bloodhound. They said he was more interesting artistically."

"I can see the logic of that. Perfection isn't a challenge to an artist."

"Nice of you to look at it that way, but *I* think there was a casting couch. I think 'Sidney' flourished his wrinkles at Mrs Delaney, the tutor. Still, the worst thing was a month in telephone sales."

He put on an earnest, caressing tone. "Mrs Tate? It's Matthew here from Bathrooms Direct. We're going to be in your area in the next couple of weeks and I was wondering if one of our representatives could – I'm sorry? You're in the middle of cooking supper? And it's burning? – I can go and do *what* to myself? I don't think that's anatomically possible, Mrs Tate. Thank you for your time, Mrs Tate. Have a nice evening, Mrs Tate."

She was giggling by now and he said, "But why are we talking about me? Let's talk about you."

"I'm quite happy talking about you."

He shrugged. "You're the boss."

The copper-headed girl brought plates, dishes and glasses, then whisked them away again when they were empty pausing each time to give Matthew a big smile which he seemed not to notice. "Our waitress is beautiful, don't you think?" Zoe said after one such interlude.

He looked at her quizzically. "Is that a trick question?"

"Sorry?"

"Only usually when women comment on another woman's good looks they want you to say, 'I hadn't noticed her. I have eyes for no one but you, darling.' Or possibly, 'What, that old dog?'"

She laughed, then said more seriously, "I don't like playing games."

"Nor do I."

"Well, then. It was a simple question."

"In that case I think she's very pretty. She's too young to be beautiful. A woman needs a certain maturity to achieve that level of tribute."

She thought for a moment he was going to say that *she* was

beautiful, but he didn't and she was glad. She knew she wasn't beautiful, except to Oliver who had loved her, and she'd have thought less of Matthew if he'd paid her the easy and obvious, the shallow compliment, reminding her that she was hiring him to be nice to her.

Over coffee, she asked if he was coming home with her and he said, "Gladly." She paid the bill and asked the waitress to call them a taxi. She tipped the girl scrupulously, adding a bit extra because she wasn't old enough to be beautiful. As they left the restaurant she held tightly to Matthew's arm and looked up intimately into his face in case the girl had any doubts about what this middle-aged woman was going to do with the beautiful young man when she got him home.

As they walked across to the waiting cab, he said, "That cheque you gave me . . . before."

"I've got cash tonight," she said quickly.

"No, it was just that it had a different name on it. Not Rosalind Tate."

"Zoe Kean. That's my real name. Zoe Rosalind Kean, née Tate."

"I see. So should I call you Zoe, or is that for your special friends?"

There was an edge in his voice and she sensed that he was hurt that she hadn't trusted him before with her real name.

"Zoe, of course. I've been meaning to say. Call me Zoe."

Now she'd done it. She could no longer pretend that it was free-spirited Rosalind Tate who gave this young man money to sleep with her. She'd have to take responsibility for her own actions from now on.

Once they were in the dark recesses of the minicab heading along the Kew Road at speed, he took her in his arms and kissed her with a delicate thoroughness, his long thin hands kindly careful on her breasts. She was constrained by the seatbelt which she'd dutifully fastened but slid her right hand inside his shirt, feeling the fast beating of his heart beneath the wiry hairs around his left nipple.

He was licking the fingers of her free hand, sucking them in turn, his tongue playing across the creases of her knuckles. It was perhaps the most erotic thing that she'd ever experienced.

She felt him hesitate as he encountered the sudden hard bitterness of her wedding ring, before continuing. He made no comment.

"You taste of something," he said instead. "Something like a salad."

"Fresh basil? It grows in the garden. I was picking it this afternoon."

"That's it."

As a street lamp flashed past she saw the Asian driver's eyes on them in his mirror, sardonic. She didn't care, except to think that he should watch where he was bloody well going. She paid him off outside her door and he drove away with a valedictory toot on his horn.

They didn't waste time with small talk downstairs but went straight up to her bedroom.

As Matthew was leaving the next morning, she said, "Would you be interested in making this a regular arrangement? Not via the agency, I mean. You and me . . . Private. Just the 'extras'."

He finally got a word in edgeways. "Yes, sure. Definitely."

"Say, every four or five days."

"What days?"

"What about this Saturday? Sunday?"

"I'm booked up for an escort do on Saturday night but I'm free in the evening on Sunday, although I've promised to play cricket in the afternoon. Pre-season warm-up friendly."

She could see him in white flannels, the V-necked sweater with its colourful stripes knotted casually round his neck, his athlete's body running up to the crease, releasing the leather ball with confident aim. It made her feel hot with desire and she wrapped her arms around her torso and said briskly, "Then come by about ten. Is that all right?"

"See you then."

"I'd better take your phone number." He recited it and she wrote it down and gave him one of her cards. "In case you can't make it."

"Oh, I'll be here."

She tugged at the front door which was inclined to stick, only to be confronted with Sarah, her latch key poised in her right hand, the carrycot in her left. All three adults said, "Oh!" simultaneously.

"This is Matthew Groves," Zoe mumbled rather reluctantly. "Matty, this is Sarah Boxer, who cleans for me."

"And who is this?" Matthew crouched down to peer into the carrycot.

"Myrtle," Sarah said.

"Hello, Myrtle." He touched the corner of her mouth gently with his finger and the sulky child opened her eyes wide at him, as if she liked what she saw, and gave a great gurgle of delight. "She's beautiful." He straightened up and said, "See you later, Zoe. Bye, Sarah. Bye, Myrtle."

"He seems nice," Sarah said neutrally as she pushed the door shut with her ample bottom.

"Yes, he is." *Well, you would think that with him making such a fuss of your stupid baby.* Presumably babies were beautiful before they got old enough to be too young to be beautiful.

She said, "I'll be in the study," and went in, shutting the door hard behind her.

Queen's mate

She thought Matthew would ring and cancel before Sunday, or that she would, but by Saturday night neither had. Their relationship had moved on to another level now, a regular thing. She could no longer tell herself that the night of the Robert Drewe Memorial Dinner had been but a moment's aberration.

She imagined him out at an "escort do" that night; one of our most popular lines. She envisaged another woman like herself, in her forties, not bad looking, if past her peak, shyly offering money, cooking bacon tomorrow morning, frying eggs.

Perhaps it had been mean to tell him to come only at ten on Sunday night. She could have invited him to come earlier, to have a meal. But she wasn't his mother, she reminded herself sternly, or his girlfriend; it was best to keep this on a business footing.

When she was passing the chemist, she stocked up on condoms. She bought two dozen. When they were finished she would put an end to this madness.

He was punctual, ringing her doorbell two minutes after the clock struck ten. She was playing a game on the computer, a complicated adventure game which passed the time, making the hands of the clock go round more quickly than they otherwise would. She was making good progress tonight, her imagination running free over the possibilities, and she was wielding the magic sword of Heronin to destroy the evil dwarf Kantrip and gain the silver cup of invisibility when he arrived.

She would have to remain visible for one more day at least.

Matthew was casually dressed this time: fawn corduroy trousers and a denim shirt topped with a cotton sweater the same blue as his eyes. She liked men better in casual clothes, as if that was the real them, the besuited man a facsimile, a clone he sent to work in his place. He had a small leather bag with him. He kissed her cheek and followed her into the sitting room.

"Did you win?" she asked.

"Yes, by three wickets. I made thirty not out."

"That's jolly good." She picked up an envelope full of twenty pound notes from the coffee table and handed it to him. "Let's get this over with."

"Thanks." He put the envelope in the bag. "Brought a few things," he said following her eyes. "Toothbrush, shaving stuff."

"Good idea. Sit down. Drink?"

"That whisky was nice."

She poured a generous measure of Clynelish for both of them. He didn't sit down but went to look at the chess board. "Please don't touch the pieces," she said in alarm, "I'm in the middle of a game."

"Okay." He put his hands in his pockets to avoid temptation. "What a lovely set. I've never seen anything like it."

"I bought them in Venice a few years ago. They're Murano glass, decorated with black and white gold. I hope they fall this side of vulgarity."

"Well this side. They're beautiful."

"*We* bought them. Me and my husband, Oliver. A present to ourselves for our tenth wedding anniversary."

"I've never been to Venice."

"I love it, or I did. I don't suppose I'll ever go again."

He glanced up. "Why not?"

"Because it's a place for lovers. Here." She handed him his glass.

"Thanks." He went back to examining the board. "Are you black or white?"

"Black."

"You can mate in five. Look." He picked up her queen in his free hand, responding to her cries of alarm with, "It's all right. I can remember exactly where all the pieces are. If you sacrifice your queen like so by taking white's king's bishop then . . ." She listened and watched. "White can't avoid mate," he concluded, "whatever he does."

"Let me write that down."

He repeated it patiently while she scribbled on the back of an old envelope, offering alternative moves that her opponent might make but which would not enable him to avoid his fate. "Of course you might consider this cheating," he concluded.

"So?"

He laughed and put the pieces back where he'd found them. "Is it a correspondence game?"

"No, my friend Sam. The only person I know who's even more useless at chess than I am, but then he tries to make up his own rules as he goes along. That's why I let him be white."

Matthew said, "Want to find a better opponent?"

"No, I like to win." He laughed again and she remembered that you had to laugh at clients' jokes. He flopped down on the sofa. "How did you get to be so proficient?" she asked.

"My dad was dead keen. Taught me to play almost before I could read. We'd play without a board on long car journeys. We'd occasionally differ over where a piece was. Dad was always proved right."

She sat beside him. He put his arm round her and she settled comfortably into the crook of it as if she belonged there. "How did last night's job go?" she asked.

"Oh!" He shuddered. "The escort job from hell. Turned out the client's old man had left her for a girl half their age. She was going to some posh dinner-dance at the golf club and knew he'd be there with the bimbo so my role – as I belatedly discovered – was to make him jealous."

"Do you dance?"

"Not too badly. It's a useful skill for an actor."

"I was packed off to dancing classes at the age of fourteen. My mother said it might make me a bit less clumsy."

"You're not clumsy."

"Must have worked then. So how was the big band sound?"

He rolled his eyes. "Well, the plan worked as far as it went. She, Mrs Hunt, was all over me and hubby came rampaging across to sort me out. It got to the point where I thought I was going to have to yelp, 'Please don't damage any of my favourite organs.'" Zoe laughed. "Seriously," he went on, "he was a pretty rough type, builder, self-made, lots of money but morals out of the barnyard. Said he'd send some of his men round to teach me a lesson I'd never forget if I didn't keep my hands off his missus. If *I* didn't keep my hands off *her*. Mrs Hunt was smirking her head off and the bimbo was sobbing into her Asti Spumante."

"Perhaps they'll get back together and live happily ever after."

"I hope so. They deserve each other. Anyway, I made an excuse and left early. I've had Jean on the phone half the morning chewing my ear off because Mrs Hunt complained, but I'm not a piece of meat."

So he hadn't gone home with Mrs Hunt last night. Good.

He put his hands over his face. "Two of these escort things a week is all I can stand." She didn't know how to reply to that and he slowly took his hands away and gave her a horrified look. "I didn't mean you, Zoe. When I said that I took it for granted you'd realise I didn't mean you."

"Okay," she said a little stiffly and buried her face in her glass.

He got up and she thought he was going to lead the way upstairs to bed and knew that she no longer wanted that, not now, not tonight. She felt cheap. Instead, he bowed, held out a hand, and said, "Would you care to dance, madam?"

She hadn't danced for years: Ollie was your original two-left-feet man. She looked round as if the room was unfamiliar to her. "Is there space?"

"Oh, we needn't do anything elaborate." He took her hand and raised her smoothly to her feet. He crossed to her random collection of records, tapes and CDs, flicked through them and exclaimed in delight at an old LP.

"Hey, Juliette Greco singing in French. Brilliant. Where did you get this?" Without waiting for an answer he took the record from its sleeve, breathed gently across it to dislodge some dust and put it on the turntable. A moment later Greco's smoky brown voice began, a little crackly after all these years.

He put his right hand firmly in the small of her back, pulling her close into him, his left hand seeking her right as her remaining arm circled his shoulder. They began to move slowly in time with the music. Not Fred and Ginger, perhaps, but she wasn't clumsy and neither was he and they soon began to feel the rhythm of the music in their bodies.

"Parlez-moi d'amour," Juliette sang, *"dîtes-moi des choses tendres. Votre beau discours, mon coeur n'est pas las de l'entendre."*

His breath was breezy across the back of her neck the way it had been over the ridges of the record, blowing the hairs erect till they tingled.

He began to kiss her, little sipping kisses at first, then deeper, stronger ones. By the time the side ended twenty minutes later, the needle lay clacking unregarded against the plastic centre as they had danced their way upstairs to bed.

Next morning, after he'd gone, she stood looking at her chess pieces, examining them as she hadn't since the day she'd unpacked them. She picked up the white queen and held her to the light, letting it pass through the glass, the metallic overlay deflecting it into needles of sunshine.

She could see herself and Oliver choosing it, hesitating over the expense for a mere toy, since neither of them played, but she'd known that their vacillation was bogus, that she'd made up her mind, that she had to have it, have *them*.

She pictured herself and Oliver standing in St Mark's Square gazing, not at the golden splendour of the basilica but at each other. It had been a blazingly sunny day but cold, the sky an unmitigated blue but with a bitter wind coming in off the Adriatic. She'd shivered in her too-thin jacket and Oliver had clasped both arms round her and jiggled her warm and passers-by had smiled at them.

They'd walked the streets of Venice for days, hand-in-hand, finding unknown churches in every alley, hopping on and off crowded waterbuses, standing on bridges of wood and stone and brick, eating ice cream and watching the world go by.

It had seemed like a gilded life then, gilded like the chess pieces.

Susan Kelly

Happiness recollected in misery. Was Dante right that there was no greater sorrow? Or did the memories warm and soothe?

Wasn't it better to remember that she'd once been happy? That she must therefore have the capacity for happiness, however deeply it might be buried just now?

50

World's end

Zoe rented a hatchback for the day, a scarlet Peugeot 205, and threaded her way through the streets to the M4, making a brief detour to Mortlake Cemetery to say hello to Oliver whose ashes lay there under a patch of bare earth some eighteen inches square. She'd not got round to ordering a stone for it, putting it off for no clear reason, but feeling it would be a capitulation, an acceptance that he wasn't coming back.

She brushed away the accumulated debris from his grave with her hands and stood quietly over it for a few minutes, empty of that belief in a reunion to come which so many adjacent gravestones proclaimed.

"Wait for me," one mourning husband had had inscribed, "I am coming as fast as I can."

Once she joined the motorway west of the Chiswick Roundabout she put her foot down and was pulling off at junction thirteen less than an hour later. She'd driven for ten years before moving to Richmond and giving up her car and she went confidently along on automatic pilot, except when the vision of Windsor Castle in a sudden blaze of sunshine appeared on the horizon and made her smile at its epitome of Old England.

April showers were lasting well into May this year and she alternated her sunglasses with bursts of the windscreen wipers as she kept pace with the heavy traffic as far as Heathrow airport and the lighter volume beyond.

She turned off the motorway, not south towards Newbury, but north. The Beeches nursing home was a former country house set in twenty acres of parkland near a hamlet appositely called World's End. She went sedately up the tree-lined drive, though taking less care over the sleeping policemen than she might have done had the car been her own, and parked alongside a dozen others.

She sat for a moment in the driving seat as she always did, building up the courage to go in, pretending to admire the architecture. The house was red-brick Georgian, extended at both ends some time during the reign of Victoria, although not without sympathy. The paintwork was a refreshing white and green; the double front doors stood open. Finally she got out of the car and slowly locked it.

She went in, turned left and made her way along the corridor to the day room that ran from the front to the back of the house, overlooking the gardens on three sides. Men and women in simple, hygienic uniforms – white trousers, green and white striped tunics, white nurse's shoes – greeted her as she went along, some by name.

The day room was full of old people, more accurately, of old women, one lone man uncomfortable in his wheelchair, a look of mild alarm in his blue, long-sighted eyes, unsure if he was decent in his dressing gown and pyjamas in mixed company.

She hesitated on the threshold of this waiting room to death, examining it anew, never growing accustomed to it, reluctant to enter.

French windows stood open at the far end and there was honeysuckle on the wall beyond, that most perfect of spring and summer scents, a few fragrant fronds wisping, inquisitive, into the room. Despite the warmth of the day the women wore heavy woollen cardigans and thick stockings on varicose legs. A television was chattering at one end of the room with three old ladies grouped round, not watching it.

On the other side of the French windows a young man in a green and purple tracksuit, his baseball cap worn backwards, was weeding with a good will. He looked about twenty and Zoe wondered if this was a Youth Training Scheme or Community Service: perhaps he was a mugger of old ladies come to make compulsory amends.

She took a deep breath and crossed the Styx, which was also, for most of the residents, the Lethe, and which brought benign forgetfulness.

"Well, hello there, Mrs Kean." A red-headed woman of her own age looked up from her desk with a smile. "I thought you'd be in today."

"Hello, Maggie. How is she?"

"Much the same."

They glanced across the room to where Zoe's mother was sitting with another old lady in a group of three armchairs. The time had come when change could no longer be hoped for, only the final transformation.

Zoe braced herself and walked across. "Hello, Mum."

She placed a hand on her mother's shoulder and a face looked up at her that was both familiar and strange. In some lights, from some angles, it was *her* face although framed by a halo of white and not chestnut hair, but it was not the face Zoe remembered from her childhood. Uncertainty flickered across the wrinkled features for a second, chasing memory, but then her mother caught it firmly and said, "Zoe. Darling. It's been ages."

"A week, Mum. I come every week. On Tuesday morning."

The old woman frowned down at her daughter's hand on the royal-blue wool of her cardigan. "Your nails are filthy, as if you've been scrabbling in dirt. Have you?"

"Something like that."

"So unladylike."

Her mother knew who she was; she had that blessing. She'd seen women led out sobbing as their mothers said with bemused smiles, "Hello, dear. Who are you? Have you brought my tea?" Mrs Tate suffered from something called Multi Infarct Dementia, caused by a series of tiny strokes that had randomly severed the infinitely intricate links in her brain. She knew who she was; she remembered mostly where she was and who Zoe was, but she couldn't recall what she'd had for lunch or what anyone had said to her two minutes earlier.

She reached up and tweaked at Zoe's cotton jersey, not satisfied with the way it hung. It was a habit which had driven her daughter mad in her youth and she gritted her teeth now as she submitted, since resistance was futile. She said, "How are you, Mum?"

She sank down on the spare armchair, clutching her shoulder bag to her as her mother didn't answer the rhetorical question. She smiled at the other woman sitting opposite, older than her mother, almost ninety, and tried not to stare at her obvious red wig, as at any disaster.

She said, "Hello, are you new here?"

The woman said, "I want to go home."

There seemed little prospect of sensible conversation here so Zoe turned back to her mother, social duty done. "I brought you some strawberries." She pulled a brown paper bag from her carrier, the rigid plastic boxes squeaking against each other. "They've got a bit squashed, but they're good. Sweet. English. The first of the year. You can have some with your tea."

"Thank you, dear." Mrs Tate put them down on the table beside her. In a minute she would ask, "Where did these raspberries come from?"

"Have I had my lunch?" her mother demanded, looking round restlessly.

"Not yet, Mum. It's barely eleven. Are you hungry?"

"No." She reached out and picked up a punnet. There was gravy on her sleeve. "Where did these come from? Are they left over from lunch?"

It had become clear by the time of Zoe's father's death three years ago that her mother was no longer able to care for herself at home. There had been much anguished debate between Zoe and Oliver about whether they could cope with her in Richmond. Oliver had been more in favour of the idea than she, but then he was out at work all day.

In the end the family house had been sold and the proceeds used to buy her mother an annuity which, along with her pension, covered eighty per cent of the fees in this comfortable private home amid the same tranquil landscapes that Mrs Tate had known all her life. Zoe made up the rest easily from her own income.

Oliver's death might have been the ideal occasion to rethink, to bring her mother home to Richmond, as company, as someone to look after, as a reason for going on. But Zoe had needed to be alone then and had justified her choice to herself by saying that her mother was settled and would hate another move. She still thought she'd made the right decision.

"No Oliver?" her mother asked suddenly.

Zoe took a deep breath. After all this time it still had the power to pain her. "Not today, Mum. He had to work."

"Is it a weekday then?"

"Tuesday. I come on Tuesdays."

"He's so hard-working, Oliver. My favourite son-in-law." Mrs Tate nudged the other old lady with her foot; the uncharitable might have termed it a kick. "He's my *only* son-in-law. See?" The other woman made no response. "Bonkers," Mrs Tate said loudly. "Can't even keep herself clean." Reverting to the previous subject she added, "It's a pity he never gets over to see me."

Zoe said truthfully, "It would be difficult for him."

She couldn't tell her mother again that Oliver was dead. She'd tried the first few times but it came on each occasion as a new and unbearable shock to her. Zoe imagined how she would feel if she had to keep reliving the moment when she'd opened her front door to the pair of uniformed constables who'd come to break the news, endure again the ensuing hours and days and weeks of anguish, denial and fury.

"So why aren't *you* at work?" her mother asked. "My daughter's a PA," she told the inert woman opposite, "that's a personal assistant, to the managing director of a big company." Which was what she'd done in her early twenties, a safe and undemanding job. She'd decided against university, although she'd acquired the necessary A levels, and taken a secretarial course instead. She'd liked the work well enough but had no regrets about giving it up at thirty-four to write full time.

She'd proudly given her mother a copy of her first book ten years earlier. She'd read it and asked only if it was really necessary to use "that sort of language – the sign of a poverty of vocabulary, darling, and what will people think?" Zoe had continued to give her copies of each book as it came out in hardback but had found them unread, their spines uncracked, when she cleared out her mother's house for the final move to the nursing home.

There was a discreet cough somewhere over her head. She

glanced up and saw the look of pity in the attendant's eye. "Morning coffee, Mrs Tate? Miss Young? Can I get you some, Mrs Kean?"

"Yes, please." The strange comfort of a hot drink.

The coffee seemed to get the ironically named Miss Young started, as if it was the fuel she ran on, and she began to speak in a pre-war, upper-class accent, like Celia Johnson in *Brief Encounter*.

"Do you remember our first ball, dear?" she said addressing Zoe's mother. "How lovely you were in lavender with yellow flowers in your hair. What could they have been?"

"Freesias, I suppose," Mrs Tate replied, to Zoe's surprise.

"And your card was full in no time. You danced six dances with lovely Dickie. What year was it? 1928? Before the stockmarket crash, certainly. That was a good year. We were nineteen and just out and there were boys enough to go round again after the war – the Great War, of course; *our* war." Her face was animated, demanding.

"Dickie," Zoe's mother said, with a sigh of nostalgia. She'd been in her playpen in 1928.

The other woman sighed too, sitting upright as a duchess in her plush armchair, her knees modestly together as her mother had taught her, her feet, neat and small in laceless plimsolls, tucked in beneath.

"Champagne." She giggled. "Lots of it, and boys who were 'Not Safe in Taxis'. NSIT."

"They were the best sort," Zoe's mother said gamely.

"Dickie," the old maid went on, "always so tall and handsome with hair like flax and eyes like cornflowers. He married that brainless little pretty, Dorothy Moore, but I knew secretly that it was me he loved. You always said so, didn't you, dear?

"Did I?"

"If only Daddy hadn't lost everything in twenty-nine, because Dickie hadn't a penny of his own and Dorothy was loaded, for all the good it did her. You should have seen him in uniform, years later. He joined up at once, in his old regiment, to fight Jerry."

"What happened to him?" Mrs Tate asked, sipping cooling

coffee. "Dickie?" She left a smear of pink lipstick on the cup and regarded it critically. She put powder on every day, and rouge, filling in the gaps. It was part of what she remembered of life on the other side of the Lethe, part of her self-respect.

"He didn't make it back from Dunkirk," her companion answered inevitably. "Left Dolly with two little boys to bring up on her own. Hard times we've lived through, Sadie."

"Yes," said Mrs Tate, whose name was Daphne. "Yes."

Zoe looked at Miss Young, wondering. Was there any reality in her memories? Was it legend or only myth? Dickie, with his flaxen hair and impossibly blue eyes, his sad fate, sounded as if he'd crept out of a bad movie, although this house was the sort of place where such parties might have happened seventy years ago, this room the perfect setting for declarations of undying love, by the French windows in the shadow of the honeysuckle. There was no way to tell: nothing in Miss Young's clothes or features, which seemed identical to her mother's. The old moved inexorably into homogeneity, losing distinctions of class, of hair colour, even of gender, as breasts shrivelled and testosterone failed.

Eyes like cornflowers. Hair like flax. That could describe Matty. Matty, who was coming to her tonight for the fifth time. She was suddenly wet, and she blushed as if people could tell from looking at her, as if these dried-up hermaphrodites remembered the sweet spasms of sexual desire, any more than one can remember the taste of apricots.

Miss Young removed a full set of false teeth from her mouth and sighed. "That's better." She put them loose in her handbag.

Maggie, the care assistant, had once told Zoe that if an inmate died in the night the first thing they did, even before calling the doctor or the undertaker, was to put their false teeth back in, otherwise, as rigor set in, it was impossible to replace them without breaking the jaw.

Which had been more detail than Zoe needed to know.

57

Playing the trump

"It was like being lost in some bizarre parallel universe," she said as she recounted the scene to Sam the following afternoon.

He had no afternoon surgery on Wednesdays and they'd picked Annie up straight from school and were picnicking in Richmond Park, sitting on a tartan rug a few yards above Pen Ponds watching the waterfowl fight over breadcrumbs. There had been a burst of summer weather such as often happens in May and the sky was blue with a few puffy clouds, while the sun was beaming down on them like a proud parent.

"Miss Young sounds good value," Sam said. "When life is too much one should always have a spare handy."

Zoe unpacked her knapsack, starting with sandwiches. An ambitious coot began to walk towards them on its overlarge feet, turning its white-topped head to one side, eyeing the wholemeal bread. It stopped hopefully a few feet away and cawed at them until Zoe shooed it.

"And my mother succeeded in making me feel fat and ugly and stupid, just the way she always did," she said.

"But that's not who you are, Zo." Sam shuffled over to her and ponderously hugged her. Physical demonstration didn't come naturally to him and he felt that as a failure. "You're not a miserable adolescent with no self-esteem any more. You're a mature woman, successful, clever and amusing, and you look great."

"Tell her that."

"And she's not herself any more, not the mother who belittled you and undermined your confidence all your life. She's an old woman who's completely lost in the world and you are all she has. You can afford to be kind to her, to repay her coldness with true affection."

"I don't know if I'm that big a person, Sam."

"This is scrumptious." Annie found this adult soul-searching boring and incomprehensible and wanted to divert the attention of two people she loved from subjects that obviously depressed them. She took a cheese and apple sandwich and bit into it. "Isn't this scrumptious, Zoe?"

"Wizard."

Annie was a willowy child, tall for her age, with her father's dark hair, which, like his, seemed unfamiliar with the concept of hairdressing, and with his beseeching brown eyes. Her skin was already tanned.

"You wouldn't be sitting here like this if you were at boarding school," Sam pointed out slyly.

Annie had developed a passion for Enid Blyton's school stories, to her father's dismay, and kept demanding to be sent away to Saint Claire's or Mallory Towers where it would be all midnight feasts and sneaking out to the cove for a moonlit swim. It also explained the archaic vocabulary: scrumptious, wizard, spiffing or, if things were not so much to her liking, beastly.

"That would be like getting a pet cat and keeping it in kennels for nine months of the year," Zoe pointed out. "Bonkers."

"And you'd have to wear a uniform, all starch and big knickers." Sam looked with affection at his daughter who wore jeans torn at the knee, a T-shirt emblazoned with the name of the latest teenage girl group and a baseball cap to keep her hair off her face, although at least it wasn't back to front. She'd taken off her lemon-yellow trainers and sat flexing her long narrow feet against the grass.

Zoe was wearing new navy tailored shorts, a fuchsia T-shirt and white leather walking shoes. Her mother had always told her she hadn't the legs for shorts but she'd noticed Sam glance at them as she'd called for him and Annie in the minicab, and it hadn't been a look that said, "I wouldn't wear shorts with those legs, if I were you".

They would walk back down the hill to Richmond in the

cool of the early evening with Annie holding both their hands,
and passers-by would mistake them for a family.

"Can I have a cat then?" the child asked.

Sam sighed. It was an old war. "It wouldn't be fair, darling,
not where we live, near the traffic and without a garden."

"Zoe's got a big house and a garden," Annie said. "We
could go and live with her and get a kitten."

"But I back on to the railway line," Zoe said quickly. "Think
how dangerous that would be for the poor little thing."

Annie ate quickly and neatly like a starving marmoset and
soon the sandwiches were gone, along with three pieces of
chocolate fudge cake and peaches imported from California,
more appearance than taste, virtual reality fruit. Annie drank
something out of a can that had a name like Woosh! and which
tasted to Zoe like water and saccharine. She and Sam had apple
juice. Zoe produced wet wipes to clean their hands but Annie
did handstands to scrub hers on the grass.

"Can we go and look for deer?" the child asked.

Zoe gestured eastwards, beyond the ponds. "I think I can
see some over there. It's not easy to make them out as the
antlers disappear in the bracken if they're sitting down."

"I'll go and look." Annie skipped off barefoot.

"Don't go too close," Sam called after her.

"I don't suppose they'll let her get close."

"She should put her shoes on. There may be tetanus."

"Surely she's been inoculated. You fuss too much." Zoe
looked after the child with a certain reverence. "She's beautiful, Sam."

"Yes, she is."

"I hope you tell her so."

"Of course I do. Every day." They watched her bounding
across the grass, as if she was a deer herself. "Honestly, the
energy of children." Sam propped himself up on one arm
and looked at her. "Great picnic, Zoe. Thanks for getting
the stuff."

"No trouble. It's not as if I made the sandwiches myself."
As he continued to watch her, she said, "I wish you wouldn't
stare at me like that."

"I'm worried about you."

"I wish you wouldn't. You have enough to worry about."

"You've had too much piled on you these last two or three years, what with Oliver's accident and your mother having to go into that awful home—"

"It isn't awful," she protested. "It's clean and bright and the staff are kind and caring."

"So when are you moving in?"

"I'd rather die."

"Quite. You had all that to deal with and you did – deal with it. You coped. Everybody said how wonderful you were, how strong, but it can build up inside you like in a pressure cooker until you've got to find a way to let off steam or explode."

"Shows how much of a cook you are. If you let the pressure cooker cool for a few hours, the steam condenses and you can remove the lid without so much as a scald."

"Okay, so similes aren't my forte. But I keep thinking about what you asked me the other day."

"Forget it." She lay back on the grass with her arms folded behind her head and gazed upwards. The sun's rays fell on her body, warm as Matty's mouth in bed this morning, and as gentle. "Sometimes sex is no big deal," she said, wriggling. "Sometimes it's the satisfaction of a physical urge, like draining a glass of water when you're thirsty."

"That's what Christine thought."

After a pause she said, "The thing about playing a trump card, Sam, is you can do it only once. You can't play it, then put it back in your hand, then keep playing it again and a-bloody-gain."

His voice went stiff in a way she knew. "You think I take advantage of what happened to Chris?"

"I sometimes think you use it as a garrotte to strangle reasoned debate."

"There are eight deer." Annie came running back to them before Sam could reply, if he had any reply. "All with coat hooks on their heads."

"Young males," Zoe said, "without the civilising influence of female company, budding football hooligans and lager louts." She swept their debris into her backpack and folded the rug over her arm. "Let's go and see."

Annie picked up her trainers, knotted the laces together and slung them round her neck.

One of the deer lumbered to its feet at their approach and stood looking defiantly at them.

"That's close enough." Sam pulled his daughter to him and stood with her held against him, his hands wrapped across her flat chest. She giggled and placed her feet on his so he couldn't walk without taking her with him and he obligingly tottered a few stiff-legged paces. They were now an impenetrable family unit, excluding Zoe.

"Antlers are dead good," Annie said. "Why do they have them?"

"To fight over the ladies."

"Will they fight now?" she whispered hopefully.

"Not until the autumn."

"Not these ones," Zoe said. "These are young bucks, teenagers with acne and chronic shyness. They're the trainspotters of the cervine world."

"Of the *what*?" Sam said.

"Cervine: appertaining to a deer."

"I bet you're good at scrabble."

"Not specially. Words are interesting only in context. It's the red deer stag that fights for his women, in any case. These are fallow bucks and they know a trick worth two of that. Come the autumn they'll find a quiet spot and spray around it—"

"Spray what?" Annie wanted to know.

"Their own special . . . perfume."

She wrinkled her nose. "Ugh! You mean they're going to pee round it, don't you?"

"Yes. Then the female fallow deer, who's called a doe, smells it on the wind and comes to investigate. No fighting and no broken antlers."

"That sounds a much better system," Sam admitted, "although I expect women quite like men fighting over them, don't they?"

"I wouldn't know."

Middle-age spread

"I'm afraid I won't be able to see you in the evenings for a couple of weeks," Matthew said at the beginning of June, "or not till late. I've got a gig."

"You never said."

"No, well, I stepped in at short notice. Spent every spare second learning my part this past week."

"Matty, that's wonderful."

"It's only fringe theatre, pub theatre, doesn't even pay Equity minimum, but it's doing the thing I love most in the world." He looked deeply contented, sitting at her breakfast bar, an empty plate and a full mug of coffee in front of him. "It's a nice part too, and it's the sort of place agents and casting people might see me and then . . . who knows?"

"Where?"

"The Shrub and Firkin in Kew."

"I've heard of it, although I've never been there. It's got a good reputation. What's the play?"

"One of these tough-talking things. Young woman writer setting out to shock with a lot of strong language and explicit sexual violence, but I think she's got something to say underneath the bravado, a genuine poetry in there somewhere."

"May I come?"

He looked pleased. "I didn't like to ask in case it would bore you. I'll get you some comp tickets."

And two days later an envelope dropped on to her doormat with two tickets for the first night, the following Tuesday, and a note: "See you at the cast party after? Love Matty."

The theatre was full, although that wasn't saying much since the room above the pub held only sixty or seventy people on

63

long benches round the square stage. On the first night, it was probably all friends and family with not a paying customer among them. Seats weren't reserved and there was no hint of the space that Zoe's second ticket holder, had she brought one, might have taken up, although no doubt room would have been grumblingly found if necessary. She wondered what happened if all the audience on a given night were fat.

Her neighbour, trying to read his programme close to his face having, as he explained at unnecessary length, forgotten his glasses, kept jabbing her with his elbow and apologising. She twisted in her hands the single sheet of paper the theatre dignified with the name of programme. She'd read it till she could probably recite it by heart. She rubbed the corner between thumb and forefinger, distressing it into a flimsy concertina.

The lights went down. There was rustling, some prophylactic coughing, then shuffling as the actors took their places. Most of the audience stopped talking. Zoe felt nervous, worried that Matthew's performance might not be a success, that she would be able to find nothing to say about it that was both truthful and good.

She needn't have worried.

She hardly recognised Matthew when the lights came up to reveal him alone in the centre of the stage. It wasn't only the costume – the tracksuit bottoms padded into a convincing beer belly, the sleeveless T-shirt revealing tattoos up his arms, his golden hair lank and dirty and a five-day stubble on his chin – he walked differently: a defeated swagger, she thought, if such a thing were possible. And his voice was different – not his accent, but his voice – conveying inarticulate panic, brutal fear.

He was unwholesome.

Scenery was at a minimum and the actors took props and bits of furniture on and off with them as they made their entrances and exits via the four corners of the stage, but she had no difficulty in suspending disbelief as the material absorbed and entranced her. She saw at once what Matthew meant about the dialogue: it wasn't naturalistic and yet it flowed in the cadences and rhythms of the English language like water. You could close your eyes and let it drift over you.

There was no interval, the play running straight through for an hour and forty minutes. A break would have destroyed the tension. Towards the end the action moved very close to her feet and she had Matthew barely a yard from her, his face contorted with baffled rage as he slowly throttled the life out of the waiflike girl who played his pregnant girlfriend, muttering, "Cunt! You lying cunt!" in a chant suffused with evil.

For a moment she was terrified of him, shivering, feeling her heartbeat quicken as adrenalin surged through her blood.

"You made me do it," he whispered to the girl's dead face, and now his voice was full of sorrow and there were real tears in his eyes.

The applause at the end went on and on as the three main actors, and a fourth man who'd played a dozen tiny parts, bowed to each direction in turn. She didn't imagine the extra-hard applause that greeted Matthew when his colleagues made him take a solo bow. There was the usual faint sense of anticlimax as the actors trooped off and people began to glance at their watches and gather their coats and bags. The short-sighted man muttered, "Too depressing."

"Sorry?" Zoe said, since he had to be talking to her.

"Too depressing, and I don't see the need for all that bad language."

She'd never understood the mentality of people who went to see a play about a sexually dysfunctional family and then complained because somebody said "Fuck". She got up without replying, made straight for the ladies then left the pub. It was barely dark – the summer solstice a fortnight away – and she needed a little air and exercise.

She walked as far as the Victoria Gate at Kew Gardens and pressed her face against the bars, looking into the shadows beyond. The day's cloud had cleared during the evening; the stars were out and it had turned colder. An owl hooted somewhere near the Palm House. She wished she could go in and walk about alone in the dark.

A 65 bus came winging along from Kew Bridge, its headlights playing on the dark surface of the road. It pulled up at the stop opposite and she was tempted to hop aboard and go home. Matthew had invited her to the party but he would be surrounded by his real friends and might do little more than acknowledge her presence, leaving her alone and humiliated on the edge of the merriment. She hesitated too long and the bus had closed its doors with a pneumatic "schtum" and moved away towards Richmond.

She decided to make the best of it. She walked briskly back to the pub and returned to the upstairs room. Its stage area was now clear except for a trestle table on which stood bottles of cheap wine and paper cups, some crisps and cheese biscuits.

"Zoe, I was afraid you couldn't make it." Matthew came straight over to her despite the attempts of numerous wellwishers to abduct him on his way. His hair was damp where he'd washed the grease out of it, his face pink where he'd scrubbed his make-up clean. He was himself again, cheerful, clean and reassuring. "I'm so glad you could come." He kissed her, taking care not to sandpaper her with his bristles. "You look beautiful tonight."

She was wearing black trousers in a thin cotton, little more than muslin, tapered into the ankle above black suede pumps. A white V-necked T-shirt clung close to her body and was topped by an embroidered waistcoat. Silver and jet earrings dangled almost to her shoulder and jingled as she moved her head. She'd looked in the mirror before she left the house and, for once, liked what it reflected back. She looked, had she known it, happier and prettier than she had in the spring, perhaps younger.

"You were wonderful," she said.

"Thanks." He made no modest disclaimers. "Did the beer belly suit me?"

"Not hardly."

"No, I think I'll save that till middle age." She put her hand on his arm, pushing up the sleeve of his sweater to reveal the tattoos, fascinated. "I'll leave those," he said. "Takes too long to redo them every day. Anyway." He flexed his muscles. "They make me feel . . . dangerous. Wot d'you fink, Zo?" He was using his voice from the play. "Ow d'I rate as a bi' o' ruff?" She didn't reply. She found it exciting. He looked at her in surprise for a moment then grinned. "Pretty well, apparently."

She blushed and took her hand away.

He glanced round. "Are you on your own?" She nodded. "Can I get you a drink? I can't recommend it."

"I'll risk a glass of warm white wine."

He was gone just a moment, returning not only with her wine but with a very handsome black man, a little taller and more solidly built than himself, whom she'd noticed lounging on his own in the opposite corner, talking to no one. He wore expensive but casual clothes, his well-toned muscles visible under his designer T-shirt. His hair was cropped close, making a feature of his well-shaped head. A black cashmere jacket hung nonchalantly over his shoulder held by one finger.

"This is my flatmate," Matty explained, "Paul McIver. Paul, this is Zoe Kean, a friend of mine. Zoe's a novelist."

They shook hands and Paul said, "The boy was good, wasn't he? I'm sick to my stomach with jealousy." He was older than Matthew, she thought, perhaps thirty-five or-six.

"Oh, yes. You're an actor too."

"Don't listen to him," Matthew said. "He's much better than I am and he's got an audition for TV next week."

"Sure," Paul said, and his accent was suddenly pure Jamaican, "I get to be de dread-locked smack dealer, like always."

"Nonsense," Matthew said, "sometimes you get cast as a pimp."

"How do you manage to cry like that on stage?" Zoe asked Matthew.

"I think of something very painful."

"Like a kick in the balls?" Paul said.

"Something like that."

"Mr Groves?" A well-kept hand fell on Matthew's arm. They looked round to see a short, fat man who wore a lightweight summer suit of crushed cream linen but who still contrived to look hot and a little sticky with bubbles of sweat gambolling along the top of his pink and green spotted bow tie. He was holding out a business card in his left hand, his right hand poised to shake Matthew's. "James Hargreaves.

I'm an agent and I wondered if you had representation, or were thinking of making a change."

Zoe felt Matthew stiffen next to her as he took the agent's hand and his card. Paul drew her adroitly away with a firm grip on her arm. "Let the boy do his stuff," he whispered.

"It's what he was hoping for, isn't it?" she whispered back.

Their heads were intimately together so they might hear each other, and she could smell his subtle perfume and knew that it wasn't cheap. He was examining her, she realised, though discreetly, sizing her up. She was aware of his well-made body, regularly pummelled in the gym, closer to hers than was considered normal in social situations. She knew that her appearance gave little away about her. Her clothes were things that suited her shape and colouring rather than what was fashionable that season. There was no designer chic. She didn't look rich. She didn't look especially Bohemian or artistic.

She thought, You don't read me that easily, my friend.

He said, "So you're a novelist." She nodded, sucking the sour wine into her mouth through her teeth since, for some reason, it didn't taste so bad that way. "Zoe Kean?"

"I write as Rosalind Tate."

"Ah." If he'd been a dog, he'd have pricked up his ears. "Right. You known Matt long?" he asked.

"A few weeks."

"Are you two close?" She didn't answer since she didn't know the answer. "Funny he's never mentioned you," Paul continued when he realised that she wasn't going to reply.

"Well, I . . . don't suppose he tells you everything."

"True. He's a big boy now. When I first met him he was as green as grass." He gave her a slow smile and she felt hot, sure that he knew her and Matty's situation. It was he who'd introduced his flatmate to the easy money of escort work, she remembered.

"You two look confidential." Matthew joined them at that moment, his arm falling lightly and naturally round Zoe's waist. They turned to see the oily Mr Hargreaves dissolving out of the door into the night.

"What joy?" Paul asked.

"I'm going to see him tomorrow afternoon with my CV and my glamour photos and we're going to have a nice chat."

"He's not buying you lunch?" Paul queried sharply.

"No such luck."

"Oh, well. Who's he work for?"

"That's just it. He's at Jackson and Pears. Golden Square."

Paul whistled softly. "My man!"

"Is that good?" Zoe asked.

"They're the best there is."

"I'm so pleased for you, Matty."

"Not gonna have to join the Ugly Agency after all." Paul punched Matthew on the arm and his friend mimed severe pain. Paul looked around. "This party's a dud. It's not even half ten. Let's go somewhere else. A club."

"I've got to stay here for a bit," Matthew said, "accept the adulation of my adoring fans." He said it with such a straight face that for a second Zoe thought he was serious.

Paul made a derisory noise. "Zoe?"

"I'm too old for clubbing."

"Who says?"

"I do. I loved the play, Matty, and you were great, but I'll get off home now." She didn't want to interfere in his private life. She didn't have that right. He was young and beautiful and charming, talented and funny. And poor, which was where she came in, and she mustn't kid herself differently.

"If you're sure." He saw her to the door, kissed her briefly on the lips and murmured, "I don't want to go either but I don't suppose Paul'll take no for an answer. See you Saturday afternoon, yeah?"

"About three." She ran her hand up his tattoos and licked her lips with mock lasciviousness, although she was no longer sure how mock it was.

Afternoon had always been her favourite time for lovemaking.

Summer

Summer set lip to earth's bosom bare
and left the flushed print in a poppy there

"The Poppy" – Francis Thompson

Sufficient unto the day . . .

On her third visit to FILO Joanna Aimery told Zoe that she wouldn't be coming any more. This was not, she explained carefully, a failure on Zoe's part, but the opposite.

"You've helped me think through the implications of what happened, and I've realised that I have enough things to worry about. I'm a single mother with two growing sons, managing on a strict budget while juggling my job – or rather jobs – with the other hand. Why do I want to fret about things that happened forty years ago?"

"I'm so glad you've been able to get through this," Zoe said.

"Now I can go back to mourning Mum. Because she *was* my mother."

"So you won't be trying to trace Valerie?"

She shook her head. "A waste of time and money. From what I remember of her I don't suppose her marriage lasted long, so she's probably changed her name again since she left home, perhaps moved on from Canada. Even if she *is* still there, it'd be hard work trying to track her down with thousands of miles of ocean between us. I'd probably have to employ a private detective and God knows what that would cost."

"If you did find her, what would you say to her?"

"I suppose," Joanna said, "I would ask her who my father was. Did he know about me? Did he offer to stand by her or run a mile? What was he like? Was he musical – is that where I get it from? Am I at all like him?"

As Zoe saw her out Joanna said, "I was hoping we could meet, socially."

Zoe didn't make new friends easily but she replied without hesitation, "I'd like that."

*   *   *

73

"Of course it's okay," Sam said, twirling his swivel chair back and forth until she felt seasick and wondered why he didn't.

"I thought, you know, it might not be allowed. Like you sleeping with one of your patients."

"Well, you say she's now ceased to be a client and I assume you don't intend to sleep with her." He looked at her steadily. "Unless lesbianism is the next step on your quest for sexual freedom."

"Somebody been in the knife drawer?"

"Sorry. I think it's great for you to have a new friend. I thought you and Joanna would get on. You're alike in many ways. She's very strong too."

"You know her – outside of FILO?"

"As well as I know any of the mothers of Annie's class-mates. Her Adam's the same age. I see her at parents' evenings, carol concerts, school plays, sports day and all the other torture schools inflict upon long-suffering fathers and mothers."

"Well, you were right. We do get on."

So it was that on the last Saturday in June Zoe paid her first visit to Joanna's. She lived in Kew Foot Road, a quiet alleyway on the far side of the Richmond roundabout, opposite the athletics ground. The Aimerys had a small but pretty house, narrow Victorian with a bay window on the ground floor. There was hardstanding at the front for the middle-aged hatchback that took Joanna to school three days a week and chauffeured her sons to and from the various clubs and leisure activities that filled their young lives.

Zoe had been invited to tea, rather than to a cooked meal. A sensible arrangement, she thought, since the fledgling friendship might prove incapable of flight when turfed out of the nest, in which case a speedy and dignified retreat would be possible. So far there was no sign that this would be necessary.

The sitting room was two rooms knocked into one, a dining table covered with papers taking up most of the far – the narrower – end, beyond it a single glass door open on to the patio garden. It was the sort of room you'd expect in the house of a single mother with two pre-teen boys: generically untidy, chaotic, the furniture a mixture of styles drawn together by colourful cushions and throws. The piano took up more than its fair share of space, but then it earned its keep.

Zoe never knew what to say to children but it seemed they were none the wiser. The boys – Stevie who was ten and eight-year-old Adam – had grunted an uninterested greeting on being introduced, taken a large portion of the food and disappeared upstairs.

The television was on in the corner, the sound turned down. It was the first Saturday of Wimbledon and the women were keeping a desultory eye on the match as they wolfed down sandwiches and cake. Rain earlier in the week meant that the tournament was behind schedule and a note of desperate urgency seemed to be creeping into the game.

"Who in the men's top twenty would you most like to shag?" Joanna asked.

"Got to be Patrick Rafter," Zoe said after giving this important question suitable consideration. "Although he's a bit hairy."

"How about Agassi?"

"Maybe when he had a bit *more* hair."

"There's no pleasing you – too much hair, not enough hair. I dunno. Can we afford to be this fussy at our age?"

"If I was allowed to stray outside the top twenty," Zoe mused, "then I'd have to say Todd Woodbridge. Great legs."

"Oh, yeah. Woodbridge. Yummy."

"Mum!"

They broke off like guilty schoolgirls as they realised that Adam had been standing in the doorway for who knew how long, a look of baffled outrage on his face such as was worn by males of all ages at the sight of women – especially their mothers – behaving badly.

"Yes, darling?" Joanna said demurely.

"Is there any more Pepsi?" he asked, his hands thrust into his jeans pockets as he tried not to be embarrassed by their talk. He was tall for his age, sturdily built, with a tangle of black hair which he constantly brushed back out of dark eyes. He must take after his absent father, Zoe thought.

"I'm sure I bought some yesterday," Joanna said.

"I can't find it in the kitchen."

"Did you look in the boot of the car?"

He groaned. "That'll be well chilled." They heard him take his mother's car keys from the hall table and the sound of the hatchback being opened and then slammed. The front door slammed next. He yelled, "I've got it!" through the doorway without pausing and they heard footsteps thundering upwards.

"Hannibal and his elephants crossing the Alps," Joanna murmured. "I wanted them to go to ballet classes to give them a modicum of grace, but my husband reacted like I'd suggested bringing them up on purpose to be homosexual."

Peanuts, toy soldiers and stuffed animals

The voice on the telephone was thin and shrill, a little girl's voice.

"Zoe, is that you?"

"Annie? What is it?"

"Sam's very upset and I wondered who I should phone for help and I thought of you first."

"What's the matter, dear?"

"One of his patients died today."

"Oh my God!" This was bad news indeed. Sam had never been able to come to terms with the fact that the death rate among his patients was ultimately a hundred per cent.

"A little boy. Ana . . . ana-something shock."

"No, I can never remember what that word is either. I'll come straight round. Thanks for thinking of me, Annie."

It was less than ten minutes' walk to the two-up-two-down terrace in the centre of town where Sam and Annie lived. Zoe knew that the doorbell wasn't working and was sure that Sam wouldn't have got round to fixing it as he'd been putting it off for the past six months. The theme music from *Friends* was coming loudly and inopportunely out of the open upstairs window next door. She rapped with her knuckles and Annie came to the door, a glass of cola in one hand.

"He's playing with his toy soldiers," she whispered, glancing back down the corridor behind her in a furtive manner.

"Oh, that's a bad sign." Zoe came into the narrow hallway which was made even narrower by the piles of paperback books that took up most of the wall on her left-hand side.

Sam appeared from the back sitting room at that moment. He seemed shocked at the intrusion. "Who . . . ? Zoe. What are you doing here?"

He looked tired, she thought, and pale, almost as if he was himself in shock. "Annie rang me. She said you needed a friend tonight."

"That child is too old for her years," he grumbled. "I'm fine."

"I invited her round," Annie said, "and it's my house too."

Which was literally true: Sam and Christine had owned it as tenants in common and, as Christine had died intestate, everything she possessed was held in trust for Annie until she was eighteen, after which Sam might well have to buy her out.

"I thought I might be able to help," Zoe said, "or at least listen, but I'll leave if that's what you want." She understood that there were times when you needed to be alone with your grief.

"No, don't go," Sam said and added quietly, "Thanks."

"Annie said a little boy died."

Sam took a deep breath before answering. "He had an unsuspected peanut allergy. It was awful. His mouth and throat swelled up and he was dead in less than five minutes, his airway blocked, he couldn't breathe. They called an ambulance, but there was no way it was going to get there in time. He'd gone into cardiac arrest. When they arrived they did everything they knew to resuscitate him, of course, but it was too late. He was only four."

"No one knew about the allergy? At four?"

"No, that was one of the odd things. He'd never had peanut butter – hard to believe when kids seem to live on it nowadays – till he saw some advertised on TV and asked for it. His mother bought some next time she was in Waitrose and the next thing she knew the poor little bugger was choking to death in front of her."

"There's nothing you could have done."

"I know." His head was lowered, his voice faint. "That's what I hate about it most, how bloody pointless and help-less I felt. He was four years old, and his parents' only child. There was nothing I could say to them, Zoe. All my years in FILO, all my training in the right words, it

was useless in the face of that appalling, uncomprehending pain."

Since she didn't know what to say either, she put her arms
round him and hugged him. Annie joined them, still clutching
her glass which banged against Zoe's thighs, her head butted
into her father's armpit.

"You shouldn't have disturbed Zoe like that," Sam said,
breaking the circle and ruffling her hair.

"It's fine, Sam. I hear you've got the toy soldiers out."

"They're not toys."

"Can I play?" Zoe asked and felt Annie giggle against
her.

Sam turned away, back where he'd come from. Zoe looked
at Annie with raised eyebrows and she nodded, so Zoe
followed him. Annie came and stood in the doorway, silently
sipping.

The house had two sitting rooms. Most of the neighbours
had knocked the rooms through into one, but Sam liked to keep
the back room for his hobby: the painting of model soldiers
and the enacting of historic battles. It seemed an odd pastime
for this most unmilitaristic of men but it was one of the few
things that seemed to absorb him and give him ease when he
was troubled. It had been a great trial to Christine, who was
a pacifist, but he'd been doing it since childhood and couples
had to tolerate each other's foibles.

A man needed a hobby.

At nineteen Zoe had spent three months in France one
summer in the futile hope that she could improve her school-
girl French enough to call herself a bilingual secretary. The
middle-aged couple she lodged with lived in a large house in
Tours and had fallen on hard times like so many of their sort
in the late seventies. Monsieur de Dessigny painted horrid
daubs, like something out of a painting-by-numbers kit, and
when Madame called upon her to admire them Zoe had said
rather lamely that it was good to have a hobby.

"Yes," Madame had said earnestly, "especially for a man,
otherwise he may fall into vice."

The solemnity of her tone and the biblical nature of the
language had made Zoe want to giggle and the sentiment as

well as the phrase had stuck with her. It was the one bit of French she could get out without stumbling: *autrement il peut tomber dans le vice.*

It was completely useless on holiday.

The principle did not, in any case, work since monsieur had lunged clumsily at her breasts one day while madame was safely ensconced at the hairdresser, and Zoe had discovered a larger French vocabulary for invective and abuse than she'd dreamed of and which was unlikely to be in much demand in an office. The old man had shambled off muttering about the famously passionless English, his dignity in shreds.

Oliver's hobby had been climbing, which had stopped him falling into vice, assuming he had ever been in such peril, but had not stopped him falling. Full stop.

The light was dim as the back room had only a small window which faced north. A trestle table along one wall bore the battlefield, its contours changing as the war changed: brown hills, green valleys, paths of mud, sometimes a shoreline or river. Last time Sam had been this upset he'd fought the battle of Malplaquet for days until the French inexplicably won, thus changing the course of modern European history.

"Borodino," he explained.

"Ah," she said intelligently. "A French victory," she added hopefully.

"A Pyrrhic victory. Staggering losses on both sides. Napoleon took almost half a million men into Russia with him and brought home less than ten per cent of them a few months later." He shook his head. "Madness. Look." He picked up a natty little man in what Zoe assumed was a nineteenth-century Russian army uniform. "General Kutuzov, representing the Emperor of all the Russias, for the home team."

"You need a CD player in here," she said, "belting out the '1812 Overture', complete with cannon."

She watched as he moved pieces round the battlefield – cavalry, cannon, foot soldiers. There was something contagious in his enthusiasm and she was fascinated rather than bored, although it was so very much a boy's game. In re-fighting the catastrophic battle of Borodino Sam could shut out contemporary tragedies and his own troubled thoughts.

She envied him.

More than two hours passed before she glanced at her watch.

"Fuck!"

Sam frowned, standing with Napoleon upside down in his palm. "You know I don't like you using that sort of language in front of Annie."

"People say 'fuck' at school all the time," Annie said, "and that's just the teachers."

Sam groaned. "Maybe I should send her to St Claire's after all."

"Look, Sam, I've just realised I was expecting someone tonight at eight and it's gone half past. He . . . they're probably waiting on my doorstep."

"Then don't keep them waiting any longer."

"I'll tell them there's been a change of plan and come back."

"No, we're okay. You run along. And thanks."

As she hurried down her road she could see no sign of Matthew. She was over half an hour late and there was no reason to imagine that he'd wait that long. She let herself into the silent house, hoping for a note but the doormat was bare. What should she do? Should she go straight back to Sam's? She made herself coffee while she thought about it. Two minutes later the doorbell rang and it was him.

"Matty, I'm so sorry."

"It's fine. I've been with your neighbours." He gestured next door. "Tweedledum and Tweedledee."

"You've been with the Jims?" she said, horrified. What on earth would he have told them? Fat Jim as an interrogator made Jeremy Paxman look like a pathetic amateur.

"May I come in?"

"Of course. Sorry." He followed her into the sitting room, shrugged off his jacket and flopped on to the sofa. She went into the kitchen, slipped a dish of penne carbonara that she'd made earlier into the microwave and laid out the salad.

"Nothing could bother me this evening," Matty called

through. "Mr James Hargreaves – 'Call me Jamie, dear boy' – has come up trumps and I've got an audition for a film on Tuesday. Part of the great renaissance of the British film industry."

"Fantastic. So he's worth his weight in gold."

"Perhaps not *that* much.

She stood in the archway which linked the kitchen to the sitting room, waiting for the ping of the microwave. "Is it historical?"

"No, contemporary. Romantic comedy set in Dorset, provisionally entitled *The White Cliffs*. Lovely scenery and a famous American TV actress to help export sales. It's not *The Full Monty* but it's a sweet little comedy and it might take off. The part's the hero's best mate, a handy device for him to pour his heart out to. There's going to be a lot of competition."

"I'll keep my fingers crossed for you."

"I couldn't wait to tell you. When I got no reply I thought I'd hang around for a bit and hope you'd come back, so I sat down on the doorstep."

"I got called out to a friend, an emergency."

"I thought it must be something like that as you're always so considerate. Anyway, this fat bloke came out from next door and asked me if I wanted to wait in there and, as it was starting to drizzle, that's what I did."

"Dinner," she said as the oven pinged. He got up and came into the kitchen and she dished up. She took an open bottle of Chablis out of the fridge and poured them each a glass.

"So." She sat down opposite him. "You've been interrogated by Fat Jim?"

"He's good," Matthew admitted with a grin. "I'd put him in the same league as Mrs Moss, my primary school headmistress. She had a secret weapon though: she used to grab your ear lobe and twist. Hurt like hell and left no tell-tale marks. As Fat Jim didn't have that advantage, he learned nothing I didn't want him to know." A faint puzzlement crossed his features. "Do I look like a taxidermist?"

*   *   *

For Love or Money

It was only after he'd gone the following morning that it dawned on her that in the fuss over Sam the previous evening she hadn't given him the habitual white envelope full of twenty-pound notes on his arrival.

83

A need for caution

It was almost a week later, a Thursday night, and Zoe had just come in from an evening at the FILO office. Her new client's father had died of a heart attack at the age of sixty-two, without warning, and he'd had to cut short his family holiday in Tuscany and fly home with his disappointed wife and sullen children. This, above all, was what seemed to obsess him. He mentioned it in every other sentence, as if his father had been incredibly thoughtless and inconsiderate, as if he should have hung on for another fortnight if he'd had the slightest respect for other people.

A year ago she would have been shocked, but she'd learned with experience how people had to focus on something, maybe some tiny thing, to mitigate their grief. And anger towards the unexpectedly dead was something she understood.

She was microwaving peppermint tea when the phone rang.

She picked up the receiver in the kitchen, lodging it under her chin as she prodded the teabag with her spoon. The caller began to speak before she could say hello or give her number, but that was the only sign that he wasn't completely calm. "Is that Mrs Kean? Zoe?" She thought the voice sounded familiar but couldn't place it. She agreed that she was Zoe Kean and he identified himself as Paul McIver. "Matthew Grove's flatmate. We met at his first night, in Kew, a few weeks ago."

"Of course."

"I didn't know who to turn to for help," he said, ominously.

"Has something happened to Matty?"

"He's been arrested."

Zoe sat down on the stool at the breakfast bar. The teabag slithered out of the mug and lay, creating a shallow grey puddle, on the surface. She took a deep breath. "I'm listening."

"We were in a pub in Hammersmith and got raided by the police an hour – hour and a half – back. Unfortunately Matt had a tiny bit of cannabis in his jacket pocket – only enough for the two of us to smoke a couple of joints over the weekend."

He wasn't embarrassed or defensive, merely matter of fact.

"Then they'll caution him," Zoe said briskly. "Slap his wrist and tell him he's been a naughty boy and not to do it again."

"Normally," Paul agreed. "Trouble is when they searched him they found an envelope in the inside pocket of his jacket with four hundred pounds in cash in it, so now they're saying he was dealing and the stuff he had in his pocket was all that was left from a hard night's trading."

"Oh, my God!" Zoe felt cold all over, as if some terrible Nemesis was knocking on her door, a wrathful figure in a Grecian robe. She had to remind herself that she'd done nothing illegal.

"And Matt wouldn't say where the money came from," Paul went on, "and I wondered if you knew anything about it, if you could help, if you maybe had friends in high places." When Zoe didn't answer he went on, "It could just as easily have been me with the stuff in my pocket and there'd be no problem. I'd have taken my caution with a 'Sorry, Massa' and been home by now."

She wondered how much he knew, if he and Matty laughed together over their clients, assuming that Paul was in the "extras" business too. "He wouldn't say where the money came from," she repeated dully.

"No. Got quite heated about it."

"It's a pity you happened to be in the sort of pub the police raid," she said rather tartly.

"Well we went there specially to score," Paul replied

reasonably. "We don't go there otherwise. They don't keep the beer well."

"Where's he being held?"

"Hammersmith."

"Has he got a solicitor?"

"No. We don't know any."

"They'll get him one if he asks."

"And what good will he be?"

"Not much, probably." She paused, thinking what to do for the best. "I'll get along there and see what I can do."

"Only he's looking at a custodial sentence. They'll say he sold four hundred quid's worth of grass this evening and that's a lot of grass."

"I said I'll go."

He said, "Thank you," and rang off without another word.

Should she call her solicitor? After a moment's consideration she decided that it would be better to go to the police station first and see what the situation was. She could call Geoff Majors at home later if necessary. She could see the look on his forty-year-old-schoolboy face if she told him she wanted his help in getting her much younger lover off a drugs charge.

She abandoned her tea and went out into the hall, glancing in the mirror, tidying her hair with her hands. She looked presentable enough as she always made an effort for her counselling. She put her smartest jacket on to be on the safe side, went next door and rang the Jims' bell. No one answered but she could hear Trefor barking and knew that he was never left home alone so she rang again, keeping her finger on the buzzer.

After a moment Fat Jim answered the door wearing nothing but a purple hand towel round his ample waist.

"You're a shocking spoilsport, Zoe Kean," he said.

"Can I borrow your car? It's an emergency."

"Sure."

Fat Jim wasn't mean with his possessions, however expensive. He said they were never as valuable as friends. He turned back into the hall to find the keys. The towel didn't meet at the rear and she was treated to a view of two dimpled pink bolsters jockeying for position. When he bent over to open a drawer she could look no longer and turned her back.

"There," he said, jangling the keys behind her. "Drive carefully."

"I owe you."

"What are friends for?"

She hurried round to the garage Jim rented in Friar's Lane, got into the Chevrolet, adjusted the seat forward and backed the car out carefully. It was a much bigger car than she was used to, not to mention a left-hand drive, but she couldn't worry about that now. It was a quiet night on the roads and in little more than five minutes she was clear of Richmond town centre and heading along the dual carriageway towards Chiswick Bridge, attracting a few glances, mostly admiring, some appalled, from other drivers. At least the car was an automatic which meant she could concentrate on steering the damn thing.

Paul McIver saw her as an establishment figure, as someone with power, power which he and Matty lacked. She'd never thought of herself in those terms but she could see his point: a rich older woman, a sugar mummy, a – ugly word – punter.

"I keep telling you – that money was a gift from a friend."

Inspector Henry Dacres leaned back in his chair in the interview room and stared at Matthew with curiosity. Did he really look so stupid that he was expected to swallow this story? Or was it so unlikely as to be true?

"In cash?" he queried. "In an envelope? Four hundred quid's worth of it?"

He was prejudiced against young men as beautiful as this one. They made him feel old, although he was only forty-three, and ugly, although he wasn't. Groves was well-groomed too which was something he despised in a man. At least, he had been when they'd booked him in: no one looked like a male model after an hour and a half in a cell.

He was aware of his prejudices and made allowances for them; he was a fair man.

87

"Yes, why not?" Matthew was saying. "I was given it last night and forgot it was there."

Sergeant Bilton spoke up, a tall, tough-looking man in his mid-thirties with a London accent, a former athlete now running to fat, his shirt pulling free from the too-tight waistband of his slacks. It was a humid July night and there was sweat in the hollows at the base of his neck. He said, "Wish I had so much money that I could be blasé about all those notes in my pocket."

"I shall need the name of this friend," Dacres said.

"I'd rather not give it."

"Oh, you'd rather not give it?"

"I want her kept out of this."

"Oh, you want her kept out this?"

"Is there an echo in here?"

"I don't think you realise how much trouble you're in, sonny, or you wouldn't be cracking feeble jokes."

"No. Sorry."

Matthew knew it was stupid to provoke this tight-lipped, unhappy-looking man who had so much power over him, but he'd been trying to make himself feel a bit less bloody scared. The sergeant bothered him not one whit, thug though he might look: he could see who was in charge here and Dacres had the look of the puritan in his eye.

He still didn't quite believe this was happening: one minute he was sitting in the pub with Paul and a pint of Fuller's best bitter, and the next someone was shouting that no one was to leave the premises until further notice. One or two people had made a break for the back but the noise of them being roughly apprehended had been clearly audible in the lounge bar and he and Paul had sat motionless and in glum silence, not looking at each other, while the uniformed policemen worked their way round to their table.

Dacres could smell Matthew's fear and wondered what it meant: was it the fear of innocence or of guilt? He had all the time in the world to find out. He grinned; it wasn't reassuring. "At least we've established that your generous friend is a woman."

"Look." Matthew reached out and fingered the envelope full of money that lay on the table between them, riffling the stiff notes. He still thought he could talk his way out of this. The man Dacres was quietly – even civilly – spoken and surely not beyond the reach of reason. "If I'd been dealing, these would be used twenties, not—" he checked – "consecutive new ones."

"That proves nothing," the sergeant said. "You sold your whole stock on to one other dealer. Care to give us a name?"

Matthew gave up: he leaned back and folded his arms. "I have nothing more to say. What's the point?"

"Right." Dacres got up. "Then you can not say it to the magistrates in the morning."

"I don't suppose they're going to listen either."

"They hear enough bullshit, son."

The door opened and a uniformed policewoman put her head round. "Have you got a minute, sir?"

"Take him back to the cells till I'm ready to charge him," Dacres said to Bilton, and followed the young woman along the corridor out of earshot.

"There's a Zoe Kean in reception," she said in a low voice, "about Matthew Groves. Says she can account for the money you found on him. Does that make sense?"

"I'm sure it does," Dacres said. "Groves' bit of totty come to lie his way out of here. Let's have a look at her."

Matthew sat in the cell on the hard bed ledge and put his head in his hands, trying not to cry. He could see his career disintegrating around him within weeks of it seeming finally to get off the ground, like a plane that takes off smoothly and then explodes in mid-air with no survivors. What was his agent supposed to say if he was offered any of the parts he'd been for lately? "Sorry, Matthew can't take the job. He's serving a six-month stretch in the Scrubs for drug offences?"

And people would be reluctant to employ him if they found out. It wasn't that drug use wasn't rife in the film and TV world, it was, but getting arrested for dealing, let alone sent down for it, was another matter and it made it difficult to insure you, as the besuited men in the insurance companies saw you as unreliable, even dangerous.

He might as well have flushed his whole future down the lavatory.

Holier than thou

D acres stood in the doorway scanning the waiting room. It was moderately empty for this time of night. There were three women: Diana Mainwaring, a tart who'd been plying her trade outside the Palais since the Kennedy assassination; a composed and elegant woman who looked in her late thirties, who'd probably had her bag stolen; and a stroppy-looking teenager with stringy hair who was biting what was left of her nails.

He was about to address this last when the desk sergeant caught his eye and indicated the second woman with a barely perceptible inclination of her head. Dacres raised his eyebrows in query but she nodded confirmation and he shrugged and went up to her.

"Mrs Kean? I'm Inspector Henry Dacres. I believe you've come about Matthew Groves." He stood with his hands on his hips looking down at her.

Zoe saw a man a little older than herself, of middling height and thin build, good-looking without being obvious about it. He had the cautious, vigilant eyes of his calling, difficult to read. A pale complexion for a man with black hair and eyes, she thought, too much time spent indoors. He wore a suit, grey with a darker stripe, not new, blue shirt, no tie.

She rose and offered him her hand and, after a moment, he shook it.

"I understand there's some query about where Mr Groves got a sum of money found on his person," she said, wondering why she sounded so pompous all of a sudden. She'd never subscribed to the view that you dealt with the police by talking like something out of a nineteenth-century novel and addressing them as "Officer", but here she was doing just that.

"Maybe." Dacres's manner was polite but wary. She was well-spoken, a respectable taxpayer on the surface, and he needed to learn more about her before committing himself.

"Well is there or isn't there?" she said sharply.

"Who told you?" he asked. "Mr Groves declined to make his phone call."

There seemed no reason not to tell him. "His flatmate, who was with him when he was arrested."

"I see, and are you a relative?"

"No, a friend."

"Uh, huh. The generous friend?"

"I beg your pardon?"

"Come with me please."

He led the way along the shabby corridor to a spare interview room and they both sat down. He made a note of her name and address, glancing up at the latter, recognising an expensive road. When he was ready he put away his pen and said, "You can shed some light on the provenance of this cash, you say?"

"Certainly. I gave it to Mr Groves yesterday evening."

"Why?"

"A gift."

"Four hundred pounds? That's a lot of gift."

"I'm a rich woman," Zoe said, neither boasting nor apologising.

"I need something better than that, Mrs Kean."

Zoe looked at him for a moment. She could see intelligence in the circumspect eyes, intelligence and interest. Dacres found her attractive and was trying to hide it because he thought it unprofessional. The realisation made her uncomfortable and she felt her cheeks begin to redden. He's got a bloody nerve, she thought irrationally. He was a man who divided women into ladies and slags, she'd be prepared to bet on it. Well, she'd soon show him which side of his arbitrary line she lived on.

She said coolly, "Mr Groves works as an escort. I use his services in that capacity from time to time."

"An 'escort'?" Dacres knew what that word usually meant, along with "model", but he couldn't believe that this self-possessed woman could mean it in inverted commas.

"Can we get this straight, Mrs Kean, because I don't want us to be talking at cross purposes. Are you telling me that Matthew Groves is a prostitute?"

"Yes." She wasn't going to argue over terminology.

"And you are his client? Or one of them?"

"Yes."

"At four hundred pounds a time?"

"That was two payments. I forgot to pay him the previous time." She looked straight at him, defying him to despise her, amused at the comical expression on his face.

Dacres was genuinely stunned. He raised his eyebrows, aiming for cynicism but missing by a wide margin. "Never knew a tart who didn't get payment up front before."

She ignored that. "So Mr Groves wasn't dealing this evening. He'd gone to the pub to obtain a small amount of cannabis for his personal use."

"Still a criminal offence."

"I know, but a very minor one surely."

"His personal use," Dacres repeated, "and yours?"

"No."

"You don't indulge? Or not in that particular vice?"

"I was once in a room where people were smoking dope, over twenty years ago. It made me feel nauseous, so trying it myself didn't seem like a good idea. I've never had any reason to revise that decision."

"What form did your payment to Mr Groves take?"

"Twenty-pound notes in an envelope. A white envelope." She drew him an oblong in the air. "This size."

"Used notes, I assume?"

"No, why? I'd got them from the bank yesterday and they were new ones. In fact there were two lots: the two hundred I got the previous time and forgot to give him and the two hundred I withdrew yesterday morning. Two lots of ten consecutive notes." She was gaining confidence. "Can you look me in the eye and tell me that wasn't what you found in his pocket?"

Dacres sat and regarded her for a long time. "I don't get it," he said finally. "You're an attractive woman. Lots of blokes would go for you. What the hell d'you want to pay for it from a bloke like that for?"

"A bloke like what?"

"Like . . ." He was lost for words of description. "Like *him*."

"What? Young, handsome, well-dressed, charming. Good in bed. Not carting a ton of emotional baggage about with him. A bloke like that? When there are so many men asking me out: paunchy, balding, middle-aged men, who spend the whole evening slagging off their ex-wives and moaning that they never see their kids, then need a dose of Viagra to get it up. You're right: I must be mad." She smiled to herself. "I was remembering something I read in the *Sunday Times* a few months ago," she explained, seeing his quizzical expression. "Do you remember when Todd Herschey, the Hollywood actor, got arrested for kerb crawling? Beautiful young man, pin-up for millions of girls and women all over the world."

"I remember. It was on the front pages for days."

"And people said, 'Why does he do that? As if he'd have any difficulty finding a girl to go to bed with him', and he said, 'I don't pay women to have sex with me; I pay them to leave when I'm done.'"

"And is that how it is with you and Matthew Groves?"

"Perhaps, but that's hardly your business. I happen to know that prostitution isn't a crime."

"Yes, it is; it just isn't illegal." Dacres got up. "I'm half inclined to charge him with dealing if only to have the pleasure of hearing you repeat this in the magistrate's court tomorrow morning, Mrs Kean, in front of a couple of bored reporters from the local papers, who will soon cease to be bored, who will think Christmas has come early this year. I can see the headlines."

"If you've got nothing better to do with your time, Mr Dacres."

"But your story checks out, since the notes match your description, and I *have* got better things to do, as it happens. I'll caution him for possession and let him go. This time."

She followed him back out into the corridor and he said, "Want to wait? Could be an hour or more."

"I'll wait outside. Don't forget to give him his money back."

"So long as you don't expect me to give him his dope back."

"No, I daresay you'll keep that for yourself."

He laughed. "It isn't very good stuff." Halfway along the corridor he turned and yelled after her. "I reckon he owes you a freebie."

"Two hundred quid?" Sergeant Bilton echoed incredulously. "Has he got two, or something?"

"Unbelievable, isn't it?"

"She must be a right old boot."

"That's the bizarre thing. She isn't. Nice-looking woman – late thirties, I should think. Bright. Elegant. Cultured."

"You'd give her one for free, 'Enry?"

"If she asked me nicely."

"I'm in the wrong game," Bilton said. "If I charged two hundred quid a time for it I'd be earning . . ."

"Two hundred quid a month," Dacres said unkindly, "judging by what your old woman says."

Matty was too numbed to be impressed by a Chevvy, even a custom-sprayed lime-green one with purple wheels. He followed her meekly out as if he was still a prisoner and she his jailer, merely taking over from Inspector Dacres for the night shift.

"I am so sorry," he said when he was safely installed in the passenger seat with his belt done up. "I don't know what to say."

"I gather you wouldn't give them my name."

"Paul shouldn't have called you. He had no right. I'd've pleaded guilty and gone to jail rather than let them drag you into it."

"Chivalrous, Matty, but unnecessary. As if I care what a man like Henry Dacres thinks about me with his pathetic bourgeois morality. Now, where's your flat?"

"Overstone Road. It's sort of the other side of the one-way system." He gestured vaguely. "Off Glenthorne Road."

"I know it. Let's get you home. You probably need a hot bath to wash that place off you." She pulled out into the

95

traffic and waited for the lights to change. "I hate Hammersmith Roundabout; cars seem to come at you from all directions, even at this time of night."

"I thought you didn't drive."

"I didn't say that. I said I didn't keep a car. This belongs to Fat Jim."

"I should have guessed."

She left the roundabout and drove quickly along an almost deserted King Street, turning right and right again, then left towards his flat. He pointed to a three-storey Victorian house in a terrace of ten or twelve and she drew up outside and shut off the engine.

"I quite understand," he said into the silence, "that you won't want to see me again."

"Oh, get over yourself. You've spent a few unpleasant hours under arrest. Think how useful that will be when you get a part in *The Bill*. Just as sitting in a police station waiting room for an hour and a half in the middle of the night is grist to a writer's mill." He looked pathetically young for a moment and she added, "Be more careful next time, because I think Dacres is out to get you. You bother him."

"There won't be a next time. It isn't worth the risk."

She leaned over and kissed him companionably on the lips. "Goodnight, Matty. I'll call you tomorrow."

"Goodnight, and I can't ever thank you enough."

He got out. She restarted the engine and drove off, leaving him on the pavement looking after her.

The top-floor flat was in darkness when Matthew let himself in. It was past one a.m. but Paul was usually up that late and he was hurt that his friend hadn't kept vigil for him.

The front door opened straight into the sitting room and he switched on the table lamp by the armchair. It was a typical rental, the furniture a miss-match, though not so old and shabby as it would have been in the days before landlords had to observe strict rules on fireproofing. The fitted carpet was cheap and the colour of sludge, the walls a cream darkened by generations of young men passing through, many of them heavy smokers. You could see where posters had hung by the sticky tape marks.

He'd lived in places like this since leaving the parental home at eighteen, except for the three years when he'd bought his own flat in West Acton with Mary, and he was getting fed up with it. Would he ever again have somewhere he looked forward to coming home to? Somewhere and *someone*? Was that so much to ask of life?

He went into the bathroom, pulled the cord to put on the light and began to brush his teeth. His face in the shaving mirror looked tired and squashed and he tried not to look at it.

At that moment he disgusted himself.

The room was small and functional, the grouting between the white tiles black with grime. The uncurtained window was eighteen inches square, below the gable. A hundred years ago this had been a maid's room, some country girl alone and lonely on the fringes of London, working twelve hours a day to build the fires and wash by hand and sweep and peel.

He felt rather than heard Paul come in behind him, barefoot and bare-arsed, his big body almost shining in the fluorescent light. He looked round, feeling crowded by the tight muscles of his friend's shoulders, stomach and thighs; Paul would spend money on his gym subscription but never on pyjamas. Matthew had got used to him wandering around naked over the past year and had taken an early decision not to look too closely.

"Thought you'd gone to bed," he said.

"Did she bail you out?" Paul asked.

"No need. I was cautioned for possession and that's the end of it."

"So you got a result."

He turned back to the sink and continued his bedtime routine. "Yes, I got a result."

"She explained the money?"

Curtly, he said, "Yes."

"I thought so." Matthew could see Paul smiling in the mirror. "I thought so when I met her at the pub in Kew that evening. You said you didn't do that, Mr Holier-than-thou."

"I don't."

"Four hundred; you could ask more than that."

"That's my business. And *you* had no business calling her."

Paul protested, hurt. "But I did you a favour. Is she mad at you?"

"Not so's you'd notice." Matthew held his head beneath the tap and swilled out the peppermint taste from his mouth, reaching for a towel to wipe with, finding none.

He spat frothily into the basin several times, then walked out of the room, switching the light off as he went, leaving his friend in the dark.

Keeping your hat on

"I gather you know Sam Lincoln," Zoe said.

Joanna glanced up. She was making toast for their lunch and, since her toaster was broken, this involved keeping a close eye on the grill. "His Annie and Adam are in the same class. Best friends one day, pulling each other's hair out the next. They'll probably get married. Who did you think recommended FILO to me? Who did you think recommended *you* to me?"

"Oh. I didn't know."

"Maybe he thought we'd hit it off." She pulled the toast clear of the grill as it started to smoke, placed the slices on the waiting plates and ladled baked beans from a jug hot from the microwave. "And he was right." She put Zoe's plate in front of her and sat down opposite.

"Knives and forks?" Zoe hazarded.

"Well, if you're going to be fussy." Joanna checked her cutlery drawer without success, took some utensils out of the dishwasher and rinsed them, wiping them on her T-shirt to dry them. They started eating.

"When you've got young children you soon give up anything fancy," she said, "you lose heart. All they'll ever eat is burgers, chips and beans; sausages, chips and beans; pizza, chips and beans. Preferably eaten with their fingers off their laps in front of the telly. Believe it or not there was a brief period in my twenties when I was civilised."

They munched in silence for a while then Joanna asked, "He a close friend of yours? Sam?"

"Probably my best friend these days."

"Seems strange to have a man as your best friend."

"Not to me. Oliver was my best friend for so many years

99

that it seems natural to have a man to confide in."

"But he is just a friend?" Joanna persevered.

"Yes. Why?"

"Well, he's attractive, intelligent and sensitive for a start, and how many men can you say that about? I know at least a dozen mothers from the school who'd happily throw their hats over the windmill for Dr Samuel Lincoln, and not all of them are single."

"Including you? Is that what this inquisition is about – you're asking my permission to have a go at him? Well, be my guest."

Joanna shook her head. "I'm not a masochist. It's obvious to me that he's not emotionally available. It's like he's shut up shop, closed for business."

"Then are you warning *me* off?" Zoe wondered aloud.

"Warning you, not *off*."

"No need. We're like brother and sister."

"So long as it's not like brother and sister in a small town in Alabama."

Zoe said, "On the principal that we fall for the same type of person over and over, if Sam's ever back on the market, he'll be looking for someone who wants to change the world and that ain't me."

"Nor me. Trying to keep my small universe from descending into actual chaos takes all my time and effort. I didn't know . . . what was her name?"

"Christine. Chris Granger. They never actually married, didn't see the point, and then it was too late."

"What was she like?"

"I didn't know her well. In those days she and Sam were just a couple we bumped into here and there, the way you do in Richmond. I only really got to know him later." She stopped to think, resting her knife and fork on the edge of her plate. "Christine Granger: she was earnest, took the world very seriously, including herself. No sense of humour, no grasp of the little ironies of life. Could hold forth for hours on the iniquitous and exploitative relationship between the West and the developing world, which we weren't allowed to call the Third World."

"I can't imagine it. Sam has a lovely sense of humour."

"Yes, he used to make very affectionate fun of her sometimes, but I don't think she realised. She was the sort of person who wouldn't accept a cup of coffee without checking where it came from. The first time she did that to me I was so taken aback that I blurted out 'Waitrose'." Joanna snorted with derision. "And after that she always spoke to me slowly and clearly as if I was a bit lacking."

"I'm not surprised."

"And the strange thing was that she was beautiful, drop-dead gorgeous. Like a red-headed Marilyn Monroe."

"Why is that strange?"

"I don't know. Just that earnest women are usually plain and sort of stringy, and you assume that's *why* they're earnest. Chris never gave a moment's thought to her clothes, or her hair, never wore make-up, but men used to turn round and stare after her in the street."

"Doesn't seem fair, really," Joanna said. "Nature should give beauty to people who'll appreciate it."

The back door banged at that moment and Joanna's two sons came in from the garden, the elder carrying a football. They were wearing Fulham football strips and looked hot and cross which was hardly surprising given the amount of football you could play in a patio fifteen feet square.

"Say hello to Zoe," Joanna said primly, determined to fight the battle for good manners, however hopeless, so nobody could say she hadn't tried. They grunted something that might have been a greeting. "Go and change your shoes and wash your hands and I'll get your lunch."

They went upstairs without another word as Joanna put more bread under the grill. "What's wrong with them?" Zoe asked.

"Generally or specifically? Generally, they're small boys. Specifically, I won't let them stay up till ten on school nights to watch the World Cup so I'm the Monster Mother From Hell. They'll get over it."

"Don't tell me, let me guess: their friends are allowed to stay up?"

"Until you ring *their* mothers and find out all the boys

conspire to tell the same story. They keep whining that it's only once every four years and I say that's good because then they'll be old enough to stay up next time round."

Zoe said, "I was barely aware there *was* a World Cup."

"Oh, the joys of a household without a man in it. Oh, God! I'm sorry. What a bloody crass thing to say."

"It's all right. Oliver wasn't interested in football, anyway."

"I still can't believe I said anything so grossly insensitive. Anyone would think I was a bloke."

"It's all right, Jo. Really."

Stevie, the ten-year-old, came skidding down the stairs at that moment and unwillingly held out his hands for inspection on demand. He was dispatched to the downstairs cloakroom to wash them properly. Adam could be heard prophylactically rewashing his in there already.

"Can I have those Canadian stamps that came this morning?" Stevie asked, pausing in the doorway.

"I promised them to Adam."

"Aww! He always gets everything 'cos he's the youngest."

"Funny, he claims you get everything 'cos you're the eldest."

"Can we get on the Internet?"

"No."

"Why not?"

"Because I've heard what it does to people's phone bills."

"Don't you care about our education?"

"Certainly. There's this wonderful new invention. It's called books."

Stevie grunted with disgust and stamped down the hall towards the tiny cloakroom. A brief argument ensued between the brothers, not loud enough for the cause to be apparent. To Zoe, an only child, sibling relationships were a mystery. People often actually seemed to hate their brothers and sisters and yet they never quite broke off contact with them.

"You really are the Monster Mother From Hell, aren't you?" she said.

"Tell me about it."

After a pause, Zoe said, "Canadian stamps?"

Joanna flushed. "I was hoping you hadn't heard that."

"Why? So you've changed your mind? That's your prerogative."

"I decided a few discreet enquiries in Calgary could do no harm. It occurred to me that Valerie was actually entitled to a half share of my mother's estate, such as it is. Also, if I can locate her I can write and tell her exactly what I think of her. Whenever I need cheering up I start mentally composing that letter."

"You could write it anyway," Zoe suggested, "even if you can't track her down. An explicit letter, detailed, cruel, even barbaric. You don't have to send it. It can be therapeutic."

"Now that's not a bad idea. And I might write one to my husband while I'm about it."

Uninvited guests

Zoe said, "Who can that be?"

It was eight o'clock on Sunday evening and Matthew had only recently arrived. They were nestled side by side on the sofa, sipping whisky and catching up on their news, when the front doorbell rang in a way that was not going to be ignored.

More than two would most definitely constitute a crowd tonight and whoever it was was going to get short shrift, she thought.

She went along the hall to answer it, not bothering to use the chain or the peephole since she wasn't alone, pulling the door open wide. The doorstep was surprisingly full: Henry Dacres stood there with six young men around him, all taller than he, so that he looked like the piggy in the middle, all dressed in jeans, their hands in the slant pockets of their bomber jackets, except for the one who was restraining the hyperactive Alsatian.

Dacres said, "I have a warrant to search these premises for controlled drugs, Mrs Kean."

He handed her a sheet of paper, an official-looking form.

Zoe stared at him rather than at this paper. "You're not serious."

"I'm afraid so." He stepped forward, making her take an involuntary step back, and was over the threshold.

"You'll find nothing here," she said. She watched the young men stream into the house without shame at their intrusion. They looked disreputable. If she'd seen them in the street she'd have crossed to the other side. "Unless one of these has brought it with him."

"We don't do that. This isn't television."

104

"Should I call my solicitor?"

"I can't stop you."

She shrugged, deciding to make the best of it. "This is absurd but you'd better get on with it. And that dog better be house trained."

She heard the youths fan out, half going upstairs, including the dog handler, two going into the kitchen, one into her study. She returned to the sitting room, realising only as she got there that Dacres had followed her.

"Mr Groves," he said, "how nice to see you again."

Matthew didn't reply. His eyes were dull with grief. He drained his glass, went to the cupboard and helped himself to another.

"Drink?" Zoe asked Dacres. "The only drug I stock."

"Why not? I'll have whatever you're having since Mr Groves seems to like it so much."

Surprised at his agreement, she poured him two fingers of the malt. She went into the kitchen, ignoring the young men who straightened up and looked at her suspiciously, and fetched ice to put in it. Henry Dacres sank into an armchair by the empty grate, tasted the whisky then used his fingers to fish out the ice cubes, dumping them with a little thought and an absence of ashtrays into a vase of roses.

"You don't put ice in malt," he explained to no one in particular, "specially not of this quality. Women don't understand these things."

She sat down next to Matthew, indicating solidarity. He was hunched forward, his eyes fixed on the carpet. She could feel his dumb misery and laid a hand on his shoulder to comfort him, her thumb rubbing rhythmically on the coarse cotton of his shirt. "This must be expensive," she said conversationally. Dacres didn't answer, sipping his whisky like a man who appreciated it. "Six constables and an inspector, wasting what? A couple of hours each? What do they budget your time at? And on a Sunday evening."

He leaned towards her, speaking quietly. It was him and her against the young constables and Matthew might have been a piece of furniture. "Mrs Kean, I want you to know that this wasn't my idea."

"Really? I thought inspectors had a lot of autonomy."

"Up to a point."

"And surely this isn't your – what's the word? – manor?"

"Not a term I use myself," Dacres said politely. "It's a joint operation with Richmond."

The youth who'd gone to her study came into the room at that moment, sounding pleased with himself. "Found this, boss." He held out a syringe in his gloved hand, six inches long, blackened at the end of its thick needle. Dacres reached out to take it and the boy exclaimed, "Careful, sir."

"I'm always careful." He took the syringe by the blunt end and examined the tip minutely. "If you're shooting up with this, Mrs Kean, you must have track marks like Cheddar Gorge." His glance slid deliberately along her slender golden arms.

"It's for my ink cartridges," she said, half amused.

"Sorry?"

"I use it to refill my ink cartridges. For my printer. Look." She took the syringe from him and the constable let out a warning cry.

"You're too jumpy, son," Dacres told him. "Mrs Kean isn't about to stick the business end of a diseased syringe into me, are you, Mrs Kean?"

"Don't tempt me. You suck the ink up, then inject it into the top of the cartridge. Costs a fraction of the price of a new one."

"Yes," Dacres said gravely, looking at Matthew, "one should look after the pennies." He returned the syringe to his constable. "Put it back where you found it, Bates." The man went off, looking disappointed.

From the kitchen they could hear bottles and jars being emptied, the contents checked and returned. They were even rifling through the freezer.

"Nice garden." Dacres stood up and crossed to the French windows. "Nice house in a nice road."

"Well, drug dealing's very lucrative, you know. You should see my yacht and my villa in the South of France." Matthew frowned at her as if to say that you couldn't expect policemen to have a sense of humour.

But Dacres knew she was joking. He drained his glass and turned back to face her. "Where's Mr Kean?"

"Mortlake Crematorium."

"Oh. Sorry."

"Are you always this crass?" Matthew demanded.

"Oh, you can still talk then? I was beginning to wonder." He examined the shelves on either side of the chimney breast. "You've got a lot of books by this Rosalind Tate. You must really like her stuff."

"Yes, I do."

Dacres ran his finger along the spines and Zoe shuddered for her babies. "Translations too. German, French. Is that Spanish?"

"Portuguese."

"How come?"

"I *am* Rosalind Tate."

"Oh, I get it. A *nom de guerre*." She was surprised that he should get the term right. He picked one book out of the run at random, opened it and read the blurb, said, "Hmmm," and looked at the picture of her on the back of the jacket, then at the live Rosalind Tate.

"Very glamorous," he said.

"That photo was taken some years ago."

"So I see."

"Here's Master Bates back," Zoe said coldly, "no doubt having found more drug paraphernalia." She saw Matthew looking up at Dacres as at some surprising new species of insect.

"There's a safe in the study, sir," Bates said. "In the floor. You need to know the combination."

"A common arrangement with safes," Dacres agreed. "Mrs Kean?"

"You'll find nothing in it but the deeds of the house and a few share certificates."

"Perhaps you could show me."

She sighed and got up, leading the two policemen down the hall to the room she thought of as most specially hers, or had until now. The room where she sat when she was sad or lonely, doodling on her computer. The room that even Sarah didn't enter to clean. A den, the Americans called it, which seemed right, a place for a wounded animal to hide.

Bates had been neat but the room had been violated.

She punched a five-number code into the safe, shielding the number-board from the two men. She didn't want to have to memorise a new code and saw no reason to trust these two merely because they were policemen. The safe came open with a sigh and the lid sprang up. Dacres squatted and removed the sheaf of papers, checking round the edges of the hole in the floor, finding nothing.

He glanced briefly at each piece of paper: house deeds, share and unit trust certificates, bonds. As she had said.

"Fine," he said. "You can lock it up again."

She entered the code a second time and pushed the door to. With a faint clicking it settled into place and she put the rug back over it.

They were there for two hours. She saw them examine the talcum powder in the downstairs cloakroom, dipping a damp finger in it to taste then spitting the cloying stuff into the sink. Half of her wanted to giggle. The dog dragged its handler about, sniffing here and there, oddly quiet.

Finally they were assembled in the hall and Dacres said blandly, "Sorry for any inconvenience."

"Can I expect this to be a regular event?"

"Oh, I doubt it. As you say, it's expensive. Goodnight, Mrs Kean." He looked down the hall beyond her. "Mr Groves. Sleep tight."

They filed out, Dacres last. He pulled the door to behind him but she pushed it anyway to be doubly sure, shot the bolts viciously and pressed herself against it.

"Bastard!" she sobbed. "Bastard."

"I'm so sorry. This is all my fault." Matthew's arms were round her, holding her tight, his face buried in her neck.

"Stop it." He abruptly released her, jerking away, his eyes startled. She pulled him back and laid her head on his shoulder. "I didn't mean stop doing that. I meant stop blaming yourself. He's to blame: that smug git Dacres who judges everyone by his own . . . antediluvian standards."

He moaned, "Zoe!"

They were pressed very close together, his body burning hot through the thin cotton of her T-shirt. His lips were in her hair, then on her face, her eyelids, her nose, finally reaching her waiting mouth, urgent, passionate. It was the two of them against the world. He was pushing her into the wall, ferociously strong now, his hands slithering her skirt up over her haunches, his fingers inside her pants, as if he would take her there, standing.

She could hear panting and thought for one wild moment that they'd left the Alsatian behind them before she realised that it was she who was breathless with desire. She was frenzied now, clawing him free of his clothes as if she couldn't wait another second to suck him into her, hearing a button from his shirt ping off and skitter away on the parquet flooring. She unzipped his jeans and released his erection, rolling it between her palms until he begged her for mercy.

He pulled her pants down her thighs, over her knees, freeing them from one leg only, leaving a rag of silk and lace dangling from her calf. She slid her arms round his neck, her legs round his hips, bracing herself against the wall. Their faces were touching, as if melting together with their sweat. He groaned. My God, he *was* going to have her here.

She opened her eyes and looked straight into his, croaked, "Yes!" and he was inside her.

At dawn, still exhilarated from the almost ceaseless passion of the night, she wanted to do it doggy fashion. Afterwards she lay on her left side, finally sated, with him close behind her, one hand curled round her upper breast, his lips hot on her neck.

"Was that good?" he asked when they'd both got their breath back.

"Mmm, that was lovely." She giggled. "Think how seriously pissed off Henry Dacres would be if he knew how his visit had affected us."

"I never want to see or speak to that man, or hear his bloody name mentioned again as long as I live."

"Hey, calm down."

After a moment, he asked, "You like that position?"

109

"For a change." She twisted her head to look at him. "Don't you?"

"It's just that you could be anyone like that, on your knees with your bum stuck up in the air." He kissed her shoulder. "And I could be anyone pumping away behind you. It's so impersonal."

"But that's half the point. Christ, Matty, if ever there was a night of sheer, blissful, meaningless sex . . ."

"OK."

"You don't want to do it that way again?"

He said, "It's up to you," and she remembered the way he'd said, "You're the boss," that evening in the restaurant and she turned over on her stomach and drifted into sleep.

On being entitled

"I don't think you should have any *more* biscuits, sweetheart."

Her voice would have sounded solicitous to a disinterested listener, the caring mother, and Zoe, who'd had two plain biscuits with her coffee, knew that this was an argument she had no hope of winning. She said, "No, Mum. I don't want to spoil my lunch. Do I?"

She'd been overweight as a child and had carried it badly, not wearing her curves with pride the way Joanna did. It really had been puppy fat – that sop offered to many a pudgy teenager – and had faded away by the age of twenty to reveal a slender, almost rangy body, but her mother had gone on monitoring and criticising what she ate for years and now that annoyance had come back.

Daphne Tate had been a beauty in her youth and had taken the fact that her only child didn't match up to her as a personal affront. She'd been expecting a boy too, a fine sturdy lad to be called Reginald like his father. At least, Zoe thought, her non-existent brother had been spared that. There had been only miscarriages after Zoe, as if she'd damaged something on her way out, presumably out of spite.

Oliver had been welcomed into the Tate family like a saviour, the son Daphne had spent her married life waiting for. Other mothers thought their daughters' boyfriends not good enough for them but there was no danger of that when Ollie came a-courting. The public school accent that he'd tried so hard and so unsuccessfully to lose in his late teens, along with the comfortable family trust fund that awaited him on his twenty-fifth birthday, made him the ideal son-in-law. She'd been charming and flirtatious from the start, attentive,

111

amusing, and Oliver had liked her which Zoe had felt was a sort of betrayal.

Her mother had started planning the wedding at once.

"Not white, darling. It's not your colour, makes you look sallow. Even if you *are* entitled, which few brides seem to be these days."

On her mother's lips the assumption of her virginity seemed not a tribute but an insult, as if no man had wanted her.

In fact, she'd had two lovers before Oliver. There had been Peter in the sixth form at her grammar school, two fumbling virgins pretending they enjoyed what was more scary than erotic, an almost dutiful coupling so as not to be left behind by their more insouciant classmates. Then there was Max at her first job, older, patient, enlightening. A twice-divorced man with monstrous alimony payments who'd nevertheless managed to retain his belief in romance, in its pure and healing power. He was short, fat and balding but had the most beautiful eyes and the sweetest smile, so that you soon forgot his shortcomings in their joint radiance.

Her mother had met Max once and referred to him always thereafter as "That Jew in your office."

Zoe looked at her mother dispassionately, remembering the perfumed butterfly of thirty years ago. She recalled the firm skin, now not only lined but sunken. The full mouth, always smiling at men then, collapsing now into the space where her real teeth had once supported it like the frame of a house – white, even teeth. The bright blue eyes were dulled by drugs and confusion. The once proud bosom was a low-slung shelf. She'd been disappointed when Zoe's breasts failed to swell beyond a bud, pinching and tweaking at them as if this painful assault would urge them into life. Now, in middle age, Zoe saw how bigger women sagged in changing rooms and was glad to be small.

Was there – had there ever been – *love* on her side? And yet it seemed to her that often the colder and harder mothers were, the more their offspring loved them, longed to please them; while warm, devoted mothers who sacrificed themselves for their children were taken for granted.

"No Oliver?" her mother asked as usual.

"Oliver is dead," Miss Young yelped. Zoe and her mother stared at her, spellbound. Zoe felt a flush creep up her neck. "Oliver Cromwell, 1599 to 1658," she concluded.

"Barking!" Mrs Tate said in a stage whisper and added, as if she had never said it before, "Can't even keep herself clean."

The young gardener Zoe remembered from her recent visits came in through the French windows at that moment, and walked towards them, carrying a wicker trug full of cut flowers in one hand. She saw that he was older than she'd previously thought, more like twenty-five than twenty. He took off his baseball cap with a gallant sweep and handed two buttonhole roses to her mother and Miss Young.

"For my two favourite old ladies," he said, and winked at Zoe.

"Dickie!" Miss Young exclaimed. "You are a naughty boy. You shouldn't have." She slotted the white rose into the top buttonhole of her cardigan and reached across to help Daphne who was fumbling with her red one. "York and Lancaster," she said.

The young man said to Zoe, "Hello there. I'm Tom Myerson, Myerson Landscaping."

"So I see." She'd read the two words printed in large green letters on his purple sweatshirt: no community service here. "I'm Zoe Kean, *her* daughter." She pointed at her own old lady, as if it mattered which one.

"I won't shake hands." He held his free one out for inspection, a long sinewy hand caked with soil. "Too mucky."

He continued his round. Where there was no buttonhole he would place a flower lovingly into thinning hair, creating for one dizzying second a Spanish dancer. The old women laughed with him, coming alive for two minutes of the dead day. One patted his pert bottom and was told to behave amid shrieks of mirth.

On his way back he donned his cap again, remarking to Zoe, "Hot out there today. I need to protect my neck from the sun. Worst place for a burn."

"Nice meeting you," she called after him, as he went out the way he'd come, leaving a mist of happiness behind him.

The thing that puzzled Zoe most about this place was that some of the senile old ladies weren't senile or even especially old. Some of them looked no more than sixty, although perhaps they just wore their years well. Sprightly women, immaculately dressed, who played bridge together and went for walks, forming their own impenetrable clique apart from the bewildered hordes.

It was as if they'd volunteered to go to prison for life.

How could they live with the daily reminder of what they would become?

Tide turning

A distant clock was striking eleven as Zoe left the house a few days later. She walked down to the river, stopping with annoyance but almost without surprise at seeing Henry Dacres sitting there on a bench on the towpath, his legs in denim jeans stretched out in front of him, crossed at the ankles. She noticed that he had small feet. She marched over to him and he glanced up and his eyes were widely startled.

"Got me under surveillance?" she asked, folding her arms defensively across her chest.

Recovering, he said, "We keep everybody under surveillance, all the time. Didn't you know?"

"You do know there are laws against stalking?"

"Funnily enough, I do know the law. There's no law against me sitting on a bench by the river enjoying the sunshine when I've got a free morning. How about you?"

"I was up working at six," she said, "I decided I deserved coffee out today."

She turned from him and began to walk towards Richmond Bridge. She heard a scuffling noise on the gravel behind and in a moment he'd fallen into step beside her. "Where are we going?"

"*I* am going to Tide Tables."

"I'll come with you."

"Well, I can't stop you drinking coffee in a public café. I thought you were based in Hammersmith."

"I am, but I live in East Sheen so my social life – such as it is – is more out this way."

They walked in silence for a while, negotiating the cobbles in front of the boat-houses, still slippery from the early high tide, the faintly putrid smell of the intruding river in their

115

nostrils. His hand shot out to help her as her foot slithered momentarily but she ignored it, regaining her balance.

Henry said, "No Mr Groves to give you a reason to stay in bed this morning then?"

"You can't get over that, can you?"

"I suppose it'd get a bit expensive if he came every night – no pun intended. Assuming he does. Come, that is."

"What *are* you talking about?"

"Male prostitutes usually fake it. I mean, why should they waste their energy on a punter, keep their real girlfriend short? Or boyfriend."

"You are a very sick man, Henry Dacres, and I pity you."

"Does he do anything by way of gainful employment, other than preying on rich, lonely women?"

"Dear God, what a stereotyped view of the world you have."

"Stereotypes are stereotypes because they're true."

"He's an actor, as it happens."

"Oh, an *actor*. I might have guessed. Any good?"

"Yes, actually."

"He'll have no trouble faking it then."

She stopped, belligerent, her hands on her hips, her face thrust into his. "Who is it you despise, Dacres, me or Matty?"

"Matty! What sort of a girly name is that?"

"There's nothing effeminate about Matthew, I can assure you. He's every inch a man and I ought to know." The memory of their love-making after she'd last seen Henry Dacres came back to her – frantic, lustful, almost brutal – and she felt herself begin to blush. Whatever the policeman said, she'd been left in no doubt of Matty's pleasure that night. She turned abruptly away and walked on, her faithful police dog still at her heels.

After a moment he said, "I read one of your books last night, borrowed it from the library."

"Glad you didn't waste your own money."

"Had to sit up till gone two to finish it. That's the problem with reading. Don't get as much time for it as I'd like."

They passed a well-dressed man in his early thirties pushing one of the three-wheeled buggies that had become so popular lately to the point that you hardly saw a four-wheeled one any more. It contained a small girl decked out from head to foot in Baby Gap, chattering nineteen to the dozen as they went along. Zoe had noticed in the last two or three years how much more common it was to see a man out with a pushchair in what were normally thought of as working hours.

"Unstable," Henry remarked.

"Who is?"

"Those pushchairs. Got to be. Like a bloody Reliant Robin."

They arrived at the café, tucked away under the arches of the bridge. There was a short queue and Henry said, "Why don't you grab a table outside, Zoe? What do you want?"

"Decaf cappuccino and I think I've earned one of those fruit slices."

"I didn't know you had to *earn* them."

The queue moved slowly and it was ten minutes before he appeared in the riverside garden with a tray, but she was contented, watching the passers-by on the towpath, the water fowl. It wasn't as if she was gasping for his company. He unloaded two cups of froth and two plates and stowed the tray down the side of his chair. "I got you proper coffee," he said. "No one can function on decaf, especially when they've been up since six."

"You're a bully, Inspector Dacres. I bet you wish you were an American policeman so you could carry a Really Big Gun."

"I'm assertive – masterful."

"And some women like that, I know, but I'm not one of them."

"I'll go and get what you want if you insist, but the queue's got a lot longer, so if you have any pity in you, you won't insist."

"Leave it." She pushed the foam back with her spoon and drank a small mouthful of the dark, bitter coffee. "What do you want from me?"

"You fascinate me, Zoe Kean." He leaned forward but spoke still in a conversational tone so that for a moment she thought she must have misheard him. "I want you."

"Well, that's direct."

"The only way I know how to be."

She said mockingly, "You *want* me, even though I'm the sort of contemptible person who consorts with prostitutes?"

"I didn't say it wasn't against my better judgment." While she was sorting through these negatives, he added, "If you had a proper lover you'd soon forget about him."

She looked at him for a moment and her face gave nothing away. He was an attractive man, she thought, wearing early middle age well, his hair still thick and curly, his figure trim, his bare arms muscular and strong. She read character and intelligence in his face, in his dark eyes. Had they met in other circumstances she might have felt drawn to him.

He was a man for women who liked "difficult" men, she thought.

"So you're not such a puritan after all," she said in the end.

"Aren't I?"

"You want to screw me and puritans don't do that."

"I expect they do. They just like to keep quiet about it. In any case, there are verbs I might prefer to 'screw', of which 'make love to' is one."

"If you're fond of euphemisms. So what's the deal?" she went on. "I sleep with you and you stop persecuting Matty, is that it?"

She wanted to offend him, to make him angry, to shoo him away like an importunate goose. She realised that insults to a serving police officer must be like water off that same goose's back, but this shouldn't roll off his greasy feathers so easily.

It didn't.

"Jesus! What sort of a man do you think I am? As if I were some sort of *rapist*. Jesus Christ!"

The shock in his face was clear to behold, genuine and pained, and she relented. She said, "All right. I stepped over the mark. I'm sorry."

"I should think so." He was silent for a moment then muttered, "No, I just can't believe you said that."

"All right! You'll grow old waiting for another apology from me."

She turned from him, towards the river, her quiet smile waxing radiant as she saw the Harbour Master's launch chug past.

"What's so funny?" he wanted to know, his shock subsiding.

"My friend's little girl, Annie, she's eight. She announced the other day that she wanted to be Harbour Master when she grew up, 'more than anything in the world'." Henry laughed. "You can see her point," she went on, "talk about lord of all you survey." She turned to him. "What do your friends call you – if you have any – Harry? Hal? Hazza?"

"My friends call me Henry, or in some cases 'Enry."

"If *you* could have one thing in the world, Henry, what would it be?"

He answered at once. "To have Hammersmith Bridge reopened so I can get to work quicker."

"Well! At least your goals are modest."

"If you will ask daft questions . . . What am I supposed to say: no more war; an end to world hunger; a cure for cancer; personal happiness? Too unrealistic."

"The first three, maybe, but not the last. Have you got children?"

"Speaking of happiness. Two boys."

"Do you see them?"

"Oh, yes. All the time. I'm on good terms with her. We didn't fight when we split up."

"Drifted apart?"

"Not even that. I suppose we both married the wrong person. You know how it is."

"No, I married the right person."

"These fruit slices are good. I must come here more often." Dacres drained his cup. "Don't you realise how dangerous it is, Zoe?"

"Huh?"

"Prostitutes are lazy and dishonest, they're liars and thieves and manipulators. Maybe they don't start out that way but that's how they end up because they feel used and grow bitter. The myth of the good-hearted tart is just that, a myth. I've met a lot in my time, professionally."

119

"Yours or theirs?" It was a cheap shot, but she couldn't resist it.

He replied equably. "Mine. Two years in vice at West End Central, two years being as much as any sane man can stand. The number of girls I've talked to – not just in order to arrest them but as informants, some even as friends in a strange sort of way – it must run into hundreds."

"They do say a lot of men like talking about it."

"I can't begin to tell you the contempt in which they hold their customers."

"And have you never come across a perfectly normal young girl who's run up debts and wants to turn a few tricks to get herself out of a hole?"

"Some of them start out that way, sure. Ten years later they're still flogging their bodies on the streets because it's a lot easier to get into than it is to get out of. Even if they haven't got a pimp and haven't acquired a bad drug habit in the meantime – and I'm not talking about a bit of grass here – there's always the temptation to do a few more tricks, to pay that big gas bill or buy that new winter coat."

She would have interrupted but he had a speech to make and he was going to make it.

"Sometimes they get out of the business for a while but they find they're earning three quid an hour saying 'Do you want fries with that?' and paying tax and national insurance on it to boot, so soon it's back to the street corners and the massage parlours and the cards in phone boxes and, OK, you think your Matthew's on a higher level than that but when push comes to shove he's having sex with you for money and he despises you the way all whores despise their punters."

He stopped, temporarily out of breath, and looked resentfully at his empty coffee cup.

"You're impassioned," she murmured, impressed by his eloquence. She shoved her cup towards him. "Here, you can finish mine."

"Thanks." He sipped and went on, "And then he could blackmail you."

She laughed in disbelief. "How d'you make that out?"

"You're a successful author. People know your name. There

are plenty of papers would be glad to print a juicy little story like that."

"Sure, then everyone who read it would rush out and buy my books, my agent and editor would open the champagne and my income would double overnight. You never heard the expression 'There's no such thing as bad publicity'?"

"And when your parents read it?"

"My father's dead and my mother's too senile to read the papers or to understand what was going on if she did."

"I'm sorry. I didn't know. But then there are your friends—"

She stopped him. "Henry, there are very few people in this world whose good opinion I care about and you, I might add, are not one of them. Perhaps there are only two, and I think Sam and Joanna love me enough not to judge me." She'd forgotten about the Jims, she realised, who weren't friends but guardian angels and guardian angels didn't pass judgment on you or get angry, only sorrowed over your shortcomings.

"Sam and Joanna," he repeated, taking them for a couple. "My ex-wife's called Joanna."

He turned moodily away to watch two swans glide by with five grey-brown cygnets and she looked at his side view thoughtfully. Joanna? No, it was too ridiculous for words. The world was full of Joannas, even divorcées with two sons. And yet it was somewhere in the back of her mind that she'd once – and only once – heard Joanna refer to her ex-husband as Henry. She wasn't going to ask.

She noticed that he had a handsome profile, distinguished, a tiny flush of white hair above each ear like a wing tip.

Neither of them spoke for a while, although the silence wasn't oppressive. She looked up at the tree above her, one of two with massive trunks, a good twelve feet in circumference, whose branches intertwined to form a canopy, protecting the terrace from the elements.

"Under the spreading chestnut tree," she murmured.

He didn't turn round. "They're sycamores."

"Dramatic licence."

"Dramatic licence? What does that mean? That you pretend something is other than it is because it suits you that way?"

"Something like that."

He turned back, as if he'd been seeking his resolve in the shining water. "Will you go out with me one evening?"

"No."

"I'll take you to dinner, or to the theatre, whatever you want. No strings. What have you got to lose?"

"A few hours of my time."

"I know we got off to a bad start but I grow on people, I really do."

She realised that she didn't dislike Henry Dacres at all, found something appealing in him even, but she shook her head.

"I'm well suited, thank you."

"Paying someone who'll promise to leave in the morning? Yes, you said. I couldn't make that promise, Zoe, because I might want to stay forever." He finished her coffee, pushed the cup back towards her and got up to leave.

"I shall ask again."

"If you don't mind being turned down again."

Unscheduled intimacy

The waiting room at the health centre was only a quarter full when Zoe arrived. She noticed Annie sitting in one corner, on a red plastic chair which was too tall for her so that her feet swung loose beneath it. She was absorbed in *Upper Fourth at Mallory Towers* but glanced up at the clack of the door closing behind Zoe and gave her a wave.

Zoe waved back, wondering what she was doing there; she knew Sam wasn't on duty on Monday mornings.

The receptionist was a young Asian woman called Meena who spoke with a Scottish accent. Zoe had seen her around town in western dress but for work she wore a sari, plain jewel-like colours, with her black hair in a heavy plait down her back.

"Mrs Kean," she said with a smile. "I'm afraid Dr Cheney's gone down with this summer flu. Her husband rang to say she can hardly crawl out of bed. Dr Sam's seeing her list this morning. Do you want to reschedule?"

"That's no problem," Zoe said. "I'll see Sam."

Meena lowered her voice. "Only with the nature of the appointment . . ."

"That's okay." Zoe had come for her smear test. She was "good" about these things: dentist every six months, optician every two years, smear test every three. She checked her breasts for lumps every month right after her period and flossed morning and night. With a following wind, she would live forever with clear eyesight and all her own teeth.

"Right," Meena was saying, ticking off her name on the list. "He was a bit late starting so there'll be a fifteen minute wait."

"I'll have a chat with Annie." She went over to sit with

the little girl. Most of the waiting patients were women and children. One fat, middle-aged man, leafing through a tattered copy of *Woman's Realm* without much satisfaction, was the only adult representative of the male sex.

"Sam had to work," Annie said, a little redundantly, "and we couldn't get a sitter. I said I'd be fine on my own but he wouldn't let me. Don't you think I'd be fine, Zoe?"

"I don't think it's legal to leave a child your age at home on her own," Zoe said tactfully. "You wouldn't want your dad to get into trouble, would you?"

She shook her head and assumed a grown-up voice. "School holidays are such a nightmare."

"Aren't you off to Somerset soon, to Gran and Grandpa Granger?" The child nodded. "That will be nice. For you and for them."

"You must promise to keep an eye on Sam while I'm away. Will you?"

"Of course I will."

Christine's parents had tried to lay claim to Annie on her mother's death. Since Sam hadn't been married to Chris he hadn't the automatic rights of a legitimate father and there had been a time – with the sudden and, as they saw it, shameful death of their daughter – when they'd talked about applying for custody through the courts. Bitter words had been exchanged on both sides but wiser counsels had prevailed and, the first shock dying down, the Grangers had backed off and a lasting peace treaty was signed.

Annie spoke to her grandparents on the phone every week and spent a month with them each summer and a few days at Christmas and Easter. It did make things easier for Sam in the school holidays. They had a roomy detached house near the sea outside Minehead and kept an old pony which Annie rode when she was there. Sam was terrified she would decide that she preferred living with them full time but Zoe knew that the little girl saw her father's happiness as her sacred trust and would never abandon him, not even to go to Mallory Towers.

"Sam's taking me down on the train from Paddington on Friday night," Annie said. "Gramps will meet us at Taunton in his Jag-you-are. He says mummy never approved."

"Of the Jaguar? No, I don't suppose she did."

"'Gas-guzzling status symbol.'" Annie giggled, then looked more solemn. "I don't remember her so I can't miss her . . . Only sometimes Gran and Gramps, and even Sam, talk like I must miss her terribly."

"That's because *they* do and they're projecting their feelings on to you."

"Is it wrong not to miss her?"

"Of course it isn't wrong."

Reassured, Annie was her cheerful self again. "And Sam's staying two nights. He can see me ride my pony. I can do little jumps now."

"Mrs Kean," said a voice distorted over the intercom, "for Dr Lincoln."

"That's you," Annie said and went back to her book.

Sam looked up and smiled as she came in. "Zoe, how nice. What can I do for you?" She explained and he looked nonplussed. "You wouldn't rather wait till Liz Cheney gets back?"

"No, why? Were you absent the day they did smear tests at medical school?"

"Of course not, but . . . well, with us being friends, it's a bit . . ."

"So much the better. Warm your speculum." Sam still hesitated and she kicked off her pumps, dropped her knickers and got on the couch. She lay on her back with her legs wide spread like a Playboy centrefold. "I'll do without a chaperone if you will." She knew that doctors liked a chaperone for intimate examinations, for their own protection against loopy patients.

Sam shrugged and took a pair of disposable gloves from the packet on his desk. "Actually I'd prefer you on your side," he said, "knees drawn up to your chest."

"Whatever turns you on, doc." She moved as instructed, her hands joined under her head as in prayer. "Cunny is a nice word. Don't you think?"

"I beg your pardon?"

"Cunny."

"Is that like 'cervine'?"

125

"Cunt is so aggressive with that plosive at the end. Cunny sounds round and warm and soft."

"Oh, I see. Now relax."

"I am relaxed. Oh! I told you to warm it."

"How am I supposed to do that? Okay. Still now." His voice sounded muffled between her legs. "All done." He removed the speculum into a dish of disinfectant and tore off his gloves, throwing them into the sanitary bin. "I shouldn't ring for the results for at least two weeks but that's the healthiest looking cervix I ever saw."

"You say the nicest things to a girl." She climbed down, pulled her knickers back on and resumed her seat.

Sam was writing on her notes. "When was your last period, Zo?"

"Ooh . . . let me see." She took a pocket diary out of her bag and leafed through it. "That's funny. According to this it was five weeks ago. I must have forgotten to note the most recent one down."

"So you've just had one? Just finished one?"

"N-n-no."

He stopped writing and looked up at her. "Are you usually regular?"

"Ish. Not clockwork."

"Ever been a week late before?"

"No."

"Well you're a bit young for the menopause, although it's not unheard of."

"There could be lots of reasons surely: stress, if I've got a bit run down . . ."

"A bit run down? I've seldom seen you looking better. Certainly not since . . ." He ground to a halt.

"Since Oliver died?"

"No. I mean, yes. Since then." He leaned back in his chair and folded his hands across his stomach. "The most common cause of amenorrhoea in a female of child-bearing years is pregnancy."

"That's impossible."

"Is it? So you haven't had intercourse since your last period?"

"Not without a condom."

He sighed. "Zoe! Condoms burst and they leak, not often but enough. They're a good idea to help prevent disease but you need some sort of backup by way of contraception."

"Yeah? It's not something I've had to think about for years."

"I'll do a test."

"It's just late. Leave it another week."

"All right, but if you are pregnant I need to know about it as soon as possible. A first child at your age needs close monitoring."

"Or early termination."

"Yes. In which case you can see Liz."

"I know your views on abortion, Sam. It's all right."

He sounded apologetic. He knew that his views weren't acceptable to most of the women in his social circle. "It's just that life is precious, and I've counselled so many women over the years who've shown all the symptoms of bereavement months, years, even decades after a termination . . . I don't mean to preach, especially to a sensible and strong-minded person like you. I accept that the decision is yours, especially if the father is a . . . ship that passed in the night."

"I'm sure it won't come to that. I don't *feel* pregnant. I haven't been nauseous or anything like that." She got up. "Shall I take Annie home till you can collect her?"

"Oh, Zoe, bless you. She's so good sitting out there with her book but it must be boring for her."

"Well, I can't promise diversion as I have work to do, but she can at least sit in the sun on my terrace and drink Coke."

Sam began to write on her notes again. "I've got Liz's house calls to do so I won't be able to fetch her much before one."

"Fine. I'll rustle us all up some pasta."

"You're a saint."

"What are friends for?"

Annie skipped into the house ahead of Zoe then stopped abruptly and turned back to face her. "If you and Sam got married, you'd be my mum, wouldn't you?"

"Well, sort of. Stepmother."

127

"And then I could be your bridesmaid. Only you and Sam get on so well. Don't you?"

"We get on very well, dear, but—"

"And I'm going to be away for the next month," the child hurried on, "so that'll leave the field clear, won't it? I wouldn't be a raspberry."

Zoe laughed. "The expression is *gooseberry.*"

"Oh."

"Only there's a bit more to it than getting on well together, Annie."

"You mean sex," she said matter-of-factly. "I know about that from school."

"That's part of it."

"Don't you want to have sex with my dad?"

Zoe, at a loss, said, "I . . . um—"

Annie retreated, having made her point. "OK. I just thought I'd mention it. Can I go next door and play with Trefor?"

Zoe hesitated. "I think they're out." Trefor instantly began to bark on the far side of the party wall and Fat Jim yelled at him, making a liar of her.

"No, they're not," Annie pointed out.

Zoe didn't know what to do. It was shaping up to be one of *those* days. The fact was that Sam had become distinctly puritanical since Christine's death and he considered gay men to be instrumental in the spreading of Aids. He didn't like Annie to spend time with the Jims and she didn't feel she could go against his wishes, however much she disagreed with them.

"Tell you what," she said. "I'll go next door and see if Trefor can come round to us for an hour or so. OK?"

"OK!"

"You get yourself something to drink from the fridge and I'll be right back."

She returned three minutes later with a happy Trefor tucked under one arm and his favourite ball in the other hand. Soon Annie and the puppy were running in the garden, yapping, screaming and chasing the ball, with Trefor breaking off occasionally to dig out imaginary foxes.

Zoe, having made basic preparations for lunch, left them to it and retired to the peace of her study till Sam arrived.

128

White pinks and other paradoxes

"And this German woman said to me, 'Pliss, vot iss dat flower?' and I said, 'It's a pink' and she gave me this really dirty look and said, 'It iss vite' and I said, 'Yes, it's a vite – I mean white – pink' and she said something in German to this other woman and they both glared at me as if I had two heads and stalked off."

"Well, you've confirmed a racial stereotype for them," Zoe said, laughing, "that all English people are mad."

She was in the sitting room of Joanna's house. It was the afternoon of the following Friday, both mother and sons now being liberated, like Annie, from the daily grind of school, and Jo was recounting a visit made to Kew Gardens that morning with her boys. It was a beautiful summer's day and Stevie and Adam were taking full advantage of it by playing with their computer games upstairs, the curtains drawn to stop the glare of the sun on the screen.

"At least they got a bit of fresh air this morning," Joanna concluded, "however reluctantly. And they're going out with their father on Sunday, to Bedfont Lakes, where they can apparently do all kinds of water sports. With luck he may drown them."

Ah yes, Zoe thought, their father. "What does your ex-husband do?" she asked casually.

"Henry? He's a policeman. An inspector."

"You never said."

"Didn't I?" She grinned. "No, well, people can be funny about it. Even perfectly law-abiding citizens get jumpy around a copper, or even a copper's estranged wife."

"I suppose. Like when you're driving along at a respectable speed and you see a police car and automatically hit the brake."

"Exactly. Built-in guilt."

"Is he stationed here?"

"No, in Hammersmith."

"Not Henry Dacres?" She tried to sound surprised.

Joanna either really was surprised, or faked it better. "You know Henry?"

"I've met him a couple of times, in passing."

"And – don't tell me – you didn't take to him."

"I wouldn't say that."

"No need to be tactful. Henry takes a bit of getting used to."

"No, really, I do like him, although I know what you mean. It never occurred to me, with your name not being Dacres . . ."

"I went back to my maiden name after we split up. Henry was a bit put out. He's something of a macho man, like most policemen. I suppose he still thought I was his property. He said it would be confusing for me to have a different name from the boys. Hang on."

She began rummaging through a drawer in the Welsh dresser. "There it is." She pulled out a photo and passed it to Zoe. Henry Dacres, ten years younger but unmistakable, proud as King Henry VIII, cradling his newborn son, his face rosy with joy, his eyes red from the camera flash, making him diabolical. "That's Stevie in his arms," Joanna said. "He wasn't there when Adam was born. Big drugs raid."

"Did you mind?"

"Not really. With Stevie he stood there saying 'Push. Push, woman, push' and if I hadn't been wired up to all those monitors I'd've got up off the bed and throttled him."

"I'm sure he meant well." Zoe examined the picture carefully. The baby had that raw-offal look peculiar to newborns. She handed it back.

"He's all right, Henry," Jo said. "A good man, if a difficult one. He hates criminals and perverts and anybody who hurts other people and he can take it all very personally at times like he's on a single-handed crusade. He dotes on the boys and he does his share of taking care of them. We've become friends since we separated, which I don't think we ever were before."

"Strange to marry someone who wasn't your friend," Zoe blurted out. "I mean isn't that the bedrock of a relationship?"

"In an ideal world, perhaps. He seemed so confident when I met him, so *masculine*, and at that point in my life I needed someone who would take charge. I'd been dumped by a man I thought was *the* one, Mr Right, the man I'd spend the rest of my life with. I thought my heart was broken beyond repair. Then Henry was there, appearing out of nowhere. He was strong and he wanted me. He said that to me, straight away. 'I want you'." Zoe laughed. "What?" Jo said.

"Nothing. It's a good line. I bet he uses it on all the girls."

"I suppose I should have thought 'bloody nerve'," Joanna went on, "but I needed to be wanted at that moment and David – 'Mr Right' – had made it clear *he* didn't want me. And Henry's a surprisingly tender lover." She looked as if she'd astonished herself by this revelation and laughed a trifle uncomfortably. She hesitated, trying to decide if their friendship had reached a certain level of intimacy, concluding that it had. "In fact when he brings the boys back he usually stays for supper. Then, when we've put them to bed . . . well, he sometimes stops the night."

"You still sleep with your ex-husband?" Zoe was incredulous.

"Not my ex, in fact. We've never divorced."

"Oh!"

"No. When I left him I had no grounds to divorce him and he had no intention of divorcing me and, as time passed, it didn't seem to matter. I suppose if either of us wanted to remarry . . . but I can't see that happening."

"He hasn't got anyone else then?" Zoe asked after a moment.

"Not that I know of. Every few months he begs – no that's not fair; Henry's too proud to beg – he *asks* me to give it another go."

"Really?"

"And sometimes, when I've had a hard day and the boys are playing up and all I've got to look forward to after I've put them to bed is a lonely evening in front of the telly, I'm

131

tempted. I really am. Then I remember how many lonely evenings I spent in front of the telly while Henry was out making Hammersmith safe for decent people to live in."

"It seems so strange," Zoe murmured.

"Perhaps, but sometimes I need the warmth of another body next to mine and not many men want to take on a fat and forty single mother. And I know Henry – he was part of my life for twelve years, still is – and I know he isn't a psycho, or diseased. It's one of the good things about being married, really, that you can be old and ugly and still have someone prepared to give you a shag."

"You're neither old nor ugly."

"Who said I was talking about me? Cheek!"

Zoe ran into Sam and Annie outside the station on her way home from Jo's, Sam carrying a big suitcase for Annie and a backpack for himself.

"Did the visitor you were expecting arrive?" he asked in a low voice.

Zoe stared at him, uncomprehending, and then the penny dropped. Grandma is visiting. "Yes," she said. "My visitor arrived in a rush during the night. Made a bit of a mess."

"Oh!" Sam looked relieved. "Good."

Annie danced round them both. "Have you got a visitor, Zoe? Will you bring him to meet us? He can make as much mess as he likes in our house and no one will know the difference."

"I'm afraid my visitor will be long gone by the time you get back from Somerset, Annie." She bent and kissed the child. "Have a lovely time."

"And don't forget what I said," Annie hissed in her ear.

Sam looked at the both, bemused. "So much whispering. Race you to the platform, Annie." He sprinted four steps with his suitcases then collapsed in mock exhaustion.

Annie giggled, "You are silly." She raised her eyes to the heavens in complicity with Zoe against male idiocy, and set off after him.

Building a fire

It was shortly after ten and Zoe was working in her study. She was wondering whether to save her files and settle down with a mug of cocoa and a bit of TV, but TV was crap on Saturday nights and she couldn't bring herself to make the move into the lonely sitting room. She sat in the dark, nothing but a yellow spotlight and the glow of the screen for illumination, grateful for the friendly, familiar shadows around her.

In normal circumstances when she was feeling gloomy she would call Sam, suggest taking a bottle of wine round to his place, but Sam was in Somerset. Besides, Annie's words had preyed on her mind and Zoe was afraid that she'd said something similar to her father, lighting her candle at both ends. She didn't want Sam to think that she was interested in him that way.

Dammit, she thought. There had never been any awkwardness between them. They'd been as sexless as the angels. What a pity that Annie was so obviously in want of a mother figure.

The doorbell rang. She ran the possibilities through her mind without reaching a conclusion. She'd have to go and look. Circumspect, she switched on the porch light as she peered through the peephole of the front door. Matthew stood there, startled by the sudden illumination.

"Oh, God!" She glanced in the hall mirror. "I look like a bag lady."

She pulled off the headscarf she was wearing and ran her fingers through her limp hair. It needed washing, something she'd scheduled for the morning. She wore no make-up and she thought her face looked blotchy and too pink. She'd had a bath a couple of hours ago and was now in sweat pants and a T-shirt, which had shrunk in the wash, and no bra. She was wearing the glasses she needed for staring at a computer screen, square black frames that did nothing for her.

The bell shrilled again. She took the glasses off, shoved them on the hall table and tweaked her hair one last time. There was nothing more she could do, short of pretending she wasn't home and that the porch light came on automatically whenever anyone had the termerity to ring her bell.

She opened the door and glued a smile to her face. "Matty, I wasn't expecting you till tomorrow, was I?"

"No." He vibrated unease. "I need to talk to you, Zoe." He seemed to lose heart. "I expect you're working. I'll go."

She said, "Don't be silly. You're here now," and stood aside to let him in. "You know the way to the sitting room. Help yourself to a drink. I'll back up the files I've been working on to disc and be right with you."

He went wordlessly off towards the back of the house. She felt cold in the pit of her stomach. What was this about? The terrible fear sprang unbidden to her mind that he'd tested positive for Aids and had come to break the news. She could think of no other explanation for his sudden appearance, his nervous demeanour.

Condoms, she thought. They'd been diligent in using condoms. She could be in no danger. Unless one had burst. She remembered what Sam had said a few weeks ago, and again when she'd had her pregnancy scare, that there was no such thing as safe sex, not a hundred per cent. Condoms burst and they leaked, not often but often enough.

Or had he come to tell her that their relationship – if that's what it was – their *arrangement* must come to an end? That must be it. He'd met some sweet, pretty girl of his own age. He was in love and couldn't do this any more, for *her* sake, whoever she was.

She realised, and it was a painful realisation, that she'd almost rather it were Aids.

She went back into the study and switched off the computer. She stood for a moment trying to compose herself. She slipped into the kitchen, took a freshly laundered shirt from the ironing basket, smoothed out the creases as best she could, and put it on over the skimpy T-shirt. Then she took a deep breath and walked through the archway into the sitting room.

He was in his usual place on the sofa but hadn't availed himself of her invitation to take a drink. He was leaning forward, his elbows on his knees, his chin resting on his fists. He reached into his inside pocket when he saw her, drew out a bulging envelope and held it out to her.

"Here's the money you've given me over the past few weeks. Three thousand, six hundred pounds. Count it."

"I don't want to count it. In fact I don't want it." She felt a flush of something very like hostility. "What is this?"

"I've fallen in love with you, Zoe."

She sat down with a bump in the armchair since her legs would no longer hold her. Whatever she'd expected, it wasn't this and for a moment she could hardly breathe.

"I can't keep this money," he went on. "I want to be with you because . . . well, because I want to be with you." He held out the envelope again.

She said, "Keep it."

"Take it."

"I don't want it."

"Well neither do I! Can't you see? Can't you see . . . how impossible it is for me to keep this, how unbearable?" His eyes were full of pain. "Maybe you're going to throw me out of the house any minute but I still can't keep it."

He was thrusting, jabbing, it at her, and she took it and tossed it over her head, over the back of the armchair. It hit the drawn curtains and slithered to the floor, splitting open, the notes splaying out over the carpet, paper that was like no other. She said, "There. I've taken it."

"I've got a lot of things to say to you. Will you listen?"

"All right, but I need a drink if you don't."

She got up and poured herself a large whisky. She held the bottle up to him but he shook his head. "Maybe later. If there is a later."

She sat down again, cuddling the glass against her chest. "I'm listening."

"That first night I really liked you. Do you remember when

135

we were sitting in that wine bar in Knightsbridge?" She
nodded. "I was thinking how attractive you were, how much
I'd like to see you again away from the artificial relationship
of escort and client, but there was nothing I could do about
it. I couldn't ask you for a date and risk you taking offence
and complaining to Jean and having her sack me."

"No, I suppose not."

"Then you asked me to . . . to spend the night with you
and I thought, 'It must be my birthday: not only do I get
to have sex with this fascinating woman but I get paid for
it too.' But I made a mistake that night, the biggest mistake
of my life. I thought I'd been nothing but a one-night stand, a
cheap thrill, and for days after I walked around like a zombie.
I was ashamed. But then Jean rang to say you'd asked for me
again and I was so happy going to Chiswick that night."

He smiled for the first time since his arrival, the smallest
upturn at the corner of his lips, remembering.

She said, "Go on."

"Well, as the weeks went by I tried to forget that you were
giving me money, and it helped that you were discreet about
it, tactful. I think that's why I forgot I had that four hundred
quid in my pocket until the police searched me that night at the
pub. And you were so nice about that too. I couldn't believe
how kind you were after I'd made such a mess of things. I
think that was one of the reasons – one of the many reasons
– I fell in love with you."

He looked intently at her, his gaze demanding some response.
She took a mouthful of whisky so she wouldn't have to answer
and, after a moment's silence, he continued, "You came to help
me that night. You didn't leave me to rot there and no one would
have blamed you if you had. You humiliated yourself to those
policemen . . ."

"Of course I did what I could. I would never have left you all
alone there, when I knew you hadn't done what they said."

"And then that bastard pig Dacres came and searched your
house and I thought our relationship could never survive that,
but you took it so lightly. You seemed amused by it."

"I think I was. It was a little adventure."

"I felt so close to you then and yet all the time there was this bloody money like a wall between us, which is why you've got to take it."

"I have done. Did you have to borrow to pay me back?"

"Some. I still had a couple of thousand. I borrowed the rest from Paul."

She drained her glass and placed it carefully on the table at her side. "And how will you pay him back?"

He waved the question away. "It doesn't matter. He'll wait. I'll do more escort work, bar work, whatever I can get, if only we can start again, you and me, on a different footing." He slid forward on his knees before her, his face serious. "Do you care about me, Zoe? At all?"

"Oh, Matty! Of course I do." She wrapped her arms round him, drawing him into her, holding his head against her breasts. "You've given me such a shock, that's all. I've felt close to you too, but I'm much older than you and you're so beautiful and talented—"

"But so are you." He sounded bewildered that she should see any difference in their comparative beauty and talents. "You're wonderful. The most wonderful person I ever met."

"Bless you, darling. I . . . I suppose I've been trying not to allow myself to care, to think about it even, given the way that we met. I didn't dare."

"Yes, I know," he said grimly. "It's taken me so long to pluck up the courage to say something, in case you laughed in my face, but tonight I was sitting at home alone and thinking about you, about us, and I couldn't stand it any more and I had to come, I had to *know*. Know where I stood. Anything was better than the uncertainty."

"Yes, anything's better than that." She smiled bravely. "So I'm not just another punter?"

"And that's another thing." He got up and sat next to her, on the arm of the chair, his cheeks flushed. "I let you think that I'd done that before, gone home with a client for money. I hadn't. I swore to myself when I began this escort nonsense that I'd never sink to that level, that I'd never sell myself, no matter what. You were the first and the last."

"But . . ." Her voice was a little cold because the honesty

that had been between them seemed to be slipping away. "You knew all about it – what to say, what to charge."

"Because Paul does it. He likes to tell me about it, boast about it, all the details. I think he gets off on it. He's called me a fool more than once for not taking the 'easy money' it offered, only it wouldn't have been easy, not for me . . . Besides." He smiled faintly. "I didn't actually charge you the going rate."

"You didn't?"

"No."

"You mean I got a discount?"

"If you like."

"Oh."

"Don't you believe me?" She didn't say anything, lowering her eyes, and he took her hand and squeezed it till she almost winced. "Why did you think I didn't have any condoms on me that first night? Why did you think we had to stop at that garage and buy some?"

"You said you'd run out."

"I know what I said . . . You don't believe me, do you? It's the truth, Zoe. Please say you believe me."

"Yes," she murmured, although she still couldn't look at him. "I believe you." She would believe him because she wanted to believe him. "I thought that there must have been so many women who would . . ."

"I'm not saying I haven't been propositioned plenty of times. I have. I've always told them politely that I have a fiancée, so as not to hurt their feelings or humiliate them."

She said, "I'd never done anything like that either."

"It never occurred to me that you had."

She looked up at last and smiled: as a loose woman she was clearly a hopeless failure. He stroked her hair back from her face lovingly and bent to kiss her on the temple.

"You were so nervous that evening," he murmured.

"You can say that again."

"I was afraid you were going to change your mind and send me away."

"I almost did, many times."

"But thank heavens you didn't and it was so good that night, the best it had ever been for me."

"Yes, for me too."

"You told me what you wanted from me and I liked that. Usually women expect men to be mind readers."

"I think that was more . . . the nature of our relationship. I'm not usually so forward."

"Well, it was wonderful. But there've been times since when I've felt ashamed, disgusted with myself. Times I despised myself."

"And me?"

"No. Yes. I don't know."

"You don't know if you've ever despised me?"

"I'm trying to be completely honest. There've been days when I felt cheap. And I resented that."

She was shocked. "Surely I never treated you like that."

"Are you sure? I seem to remember a morning when you said something about sheer, meaningless sex and that made me feel . . ." his hand fell away from her ". . . I don't know. I only know how much that hurt."

She remembered. "But I didn't mean it like that. Surely the most loving couple have nights of . . . nights of pure, animal lust."

But she remembered, too, the way she'd spoken about him to Henry that night at the police station, about how she paid him to leave without quibble in the morning. Part of it had been bravado, to see the look on Henry's face, but she couldn't entirely acquit herself of thinking of him as an object of purchase, or of behaving as if she did.

"Do you think we can start again?" he asked. "Put the mistake behind us. I know I'm younger than you are and just starting out in the world, but I believe that I have something to give you too, that it won't all be one-sided."

"I know you have," she said. "You've so much to give me. I don't know how easy it will be, or how hard, but we can try."

He said, "I think it will be as hard or as easy as we make it."

But is it all an act?

"Thank you for having dinner with me."

"Lunch, Henry. It's lunch, not dinner. An altogether different matter."

"We called the midday meal dinner when I was growing up."

"Let me guess: a two-up-two-down slum with no bathroom and the lavatory in a hut at the bottom of the garden."

"Now who's stereotyping, you infuriating, adorable woman? It was a perfectly nice three-bedroomed semi in Guildford with two toilets, a garage and a gazebo, but we still called it dinner. Anyway, whatever we call it, thanks for coming, even if you did drag me all the way out to Marble Hill."

"I like it here. I like to see the park while I'm eating, and the river in the distance. I find it relaxing." It was also cheap and she didn't want to be beholden to Henry, especially as she knew that he was finding the rent for his own flat as well as paying the mortgage on the family home for Joanna and the boys. "And I could see you were never going to take no for an answer," she concluded.

Henry looked relaxed, casual in khaki chinos with a black polo shirt, open at the neck, his small feet encased in black plimsolls. His skin was starting to tan now, taking the colour naturally and evenly. She thought his eyes looked tired and felt a surge of affection for him. She could understand why Joanna still wanted to feel his warm body next to hers.

He read the blackboard with the day's specials with some doubt. Most of them had a large V next to them, like a teacher's tick for good work. "You're not a vegetarian as well as a decaf drinker, are you?"

"No, and it's not all vegetarian food. In fact—" she glanced up as a young man in a voluminous green apron came, smiling, to take their order – "I'm going to have the sweet and sour chicken with noodles."

"Me too," Henry said.

"And could we have some water?" Zoe called after him.

"We're really pushing the boat out," Henry said.

"I don't like drinking at lunchtime, it leaves me disorientated for the rest of the day."

Henry drummed his fingers on the wooden picnic table till she thought she was going to have to stop him forcibly, then he said, "It's only in rich countries that people can afford to be picky about their food, to refuse perfectly good meat on a point of principle."

"I don't think you should overdo the boorish policeman act, Henry."

He grinned. "Unfortunately, after twenty-five years I'm not sure it *is* an act any more. All I'm saying is that in most places in the world they're glad of something, anything, to fill their bellies."

"Are they? Surely there are plenty of devout Hindu vegetarians in India, and Muslims in Pakistan and the Middle East?"

"Mmm." Henry knew when he was on a losing wicket.

"And a Jew or Muslim would rather starve than eat pork," she added.

"All right, already!"

She laughed. "It's no fun arguing with someone who's such a bad loser."

"I'd have thought it was *more* fun."

A bunch of boys, perhaps fourteen or fifteen years old, were playing five-a-side football in the park beneath them with spare garments bundled up for the goalposts. In fact, only one side had five players, the other four, but nobody seemed to mind. They had the crested ties of one of the local private day schools knotted round their unlined foreheads as headbands, although it was now the holidays.

Some act of defiance, she supposed.

She realised that she wouldn't be young again, not at any price. Teenagers had so much to fear these days: insecurity in their work prospects, callousness in their relationships, Aids. Surely no one could marry these days, as she had done seventeen years ago, without the spectre of divorce at the marriage feast.

"Do you think schooldays are the happiest days of your life?" Henry asked, as if reading her mind.

"God, no."

"So we have something in common. I knew it."

"When you're a kid, people keep telling you what to do all the time."

"They do that when you're grown up too, though."

"Who?"

"Your boss. Your spouse. The taxman."

"Policemen?"

"If only."

"I'm self-employed so I haven't got a boss, and I deal fair with the taxman so he deals fair with me." And the thought of sweet Oliver telling her what to do almost made her smile.

He said, "You don't know how lucky you are."

"I think you're either one of nature's self-employed or one of her employees and if you find yourself in the wrong category by mistake you're doomed to misery. You deliberately chose a profession with a rigid hierarchy of power, Henry, so that must be what you like."

He chuckled. "When you set foot on the lowest rung of the ladder, you envisage the view from the top, not getting stuck halfway up with someone's size twelves on your fingers."

"But why did you choose that job? Something you always wanted to do, demanding a toy helmet for your fourth birthday?"

He shrugged. "Nothing so definite. I left school. I was eighteen. The only thing I was sure of was that I didn't want to do any more studying. One of my best mates decided to join and I thought 'Why not?' I didn't want to be stuck behind a desk all day and it sounded interesting. And worthwhile. Now I'm mostly stuck behind a desk all day. Or all night this week."

"Solved many juicy murders?"

He shook his head. "We're specialists in the Met. Someone commits a murder anywhere in London and, unless it's

142

totally cut-and-dried, they put together a murder squad out of experienced officers. It plays hell with your home life. Me, I did five years on the beat, then two years in Vice at West End Central, as I think I mentioned, couple of years as a sergeant in charge of the crime squad, last few years in drugs."

"You certainly gave Matty a nasty fright that night." She had to find a way to tell him about her and Matthew, to make it plain. That was mostly why she was here.

"I don't want to talk about him. If he's learned his lesson, well and good."

It wasn't the moment, she thought. Coffee was the right time. "Is it so dreadful? Surely alcohol causes more crime, violence and premature death than illegal drugs do."

He looked at her earnestly. "If you had kids the way I do, Zoe, you'd be scared shitless. Mine are still at primary school and things haven't got that bad round here yet, but when they go on to the comprehensive they're going to see drugs all around them, their mates will be urging them to give it a go, mocking them as cowards if they say no. And paying through the nose for a posh private school like that one—" he nodded at the footballing lads – "won't save you either. Most parents manage to keep their heads in the sand and say 'It isn't that bad at our school' and 'My Kevin's too sensible to do drugs' but I don't have that luxury because I *know*. Heroin is cheaper than booze now and teenagers like to get out of their heads. I know I did, though on beer in my case."

Two plates were placed in front of them at that moment, skinless chicken with red and green peppers, lemon sauce, cream-coloured noodles. It was like an abstract painting and it seemed a shame to disturb it but Zoe found she was hungry so she picked up her fork and began to twirl the strands onto it. Henry leaned forward slightly and shovelled a mouthful in.

"Not bad," he said thickly, chewing. He picked up the jug of water and poured for them both into tumblers.

They ate quietly for a while then she said, "Can you look me in the eye and tell me you've never so much as puffed on a joint, Henry?"

After a moment spent deciding how to answer this, he said,

"I could and I'd be very convincing, but I will not lie to you, Zoe."

"Hypocrite."

"Society runs on hypocrisy. Clearly things are different on your planet." He cleared his plate. "Pudding?"

"Want to share a slice of home-made coffee and walnut cake?"

"If that's what you want."

The waitress brought the cake, two forks and two cups of coffee. Their forks met across the plate, advancing and retreating in a little dance. She ate more cake than he did.

"What did your husband do?" he asked.

"He was an economist. He did models, forecasts."

Henry tried to look intelligent and she laughed. "No, well it's pretty obscure except to other economists. Basically you ask what will happen in the economy in eighteen months time if interest rates are eight per cent, unemployment is two million and growth is two per cent. Then you lower your interest rates to seven and three-quarter per cent, or add a hundred thousand to the dole queue and see what difference that makes. And so on."

"I see. But isn't that sort of thing done by computer nowadays?"

"Certainly, but somebody has to know how the computer must do its calculations, what the consequences of the variables are."

"And who pays to know that?"

"Banks, insurance companies, investment managers. Even the government. Especially the government. They pay through the nose because the information is vital."

Henry said, "Not a fly-by-night, Mr Kean."

"No, Oliver certainly wasn't a fly-by-night." Now was the time. "I suppose you think Matty is."

"Well, it's not much of a basis for a relationship, is it?"

"Things have changed, Henry. You need to understand that. Matthew and I . . ."

He misunderstood. "It's finished?" And there was hope in his eyes. "You've come to your senses at last?" She thought how good Henry was for her ego with his almost puppy-like longing for her.

"No. On the contrary. I mean, I was never out of my senses." She explained as best she could while he fiddled with his coffee spoon. "So you see," she concluded, "there was never a monetary transaction between us."

"Oh yes there was," he said sharply. "There was at the time. Still, it's an interesting philosophical point: can prostitution cease to be prostitution retrospectively if the whore gives the money back?"

"So that's how it is, Henry. I wanted you to know so that you wouldn't waste your time –" He stifled a yawn. "Am I keeping you up?" she asked.

"Well, yes, as it happens. As I say, I'm working nights this week and I'm going to bed the minute I get home and," he added, in case she thought he hadn't been paying attention, "I don't consider it a waste of time."

"Then let's go."

He paid the bill and they walked along the footpath to the narrow lane that ran down to the river, neither of them speaking. The boys' football came hurtling towards them at one point and Henry jumped into action, circling neatly round the ball and booting it back with one clean kick. His success clearly made him happy and she thought how easily men were pleased, how uncomplicated they were.

"Are you parked here too?" he asked, wielding the remote control to unlock his Rover.

"I don't run a car. I walked here."

"You *walked*?"

"It's only a mile or so, along the river."

"I'll drop you home. Get in."

"Thanks, but I'll cross at the ferry and walk back on the other side."

"Oh." He looked crestfallen and she realised that the meeting had been a disappointment to him, that he'd got his hopes up. She shouldn't have let him get his hopes up, should have made the purpose of this lunch clear from the start. The last thing she wanted was to hurt him.

He was standing with the driver's door open, half in and

half out of the car. She was on the other side and he had to speak up for her to hear him. "I meant what I said. I want you, and I don't mean only in a sexual way."

"I'm sorry, Henry. I explained—"

"I heard you but he's not the man for you and I don't give up so easily."

"On your head be it. Don't complain that I gave you any encouragement."

"I can't bear to see you made a fool of like this, Zoe. I can't bear to see you taken in. Above all I can't bear to see you hurt."

Her ego plummeted back down. She felt desolate. "Is it so impossible that he should love me?"

Henry had painted himself into a corner; he couldn't tell her she was unlovable when his every word and gesture contradicted it. She was infinitely lovable but not to a man like Groves. He grimaced. "See you then," he said and got into the car. He leaned across and wound the passenger window down to add, "And thanks again."

"Bye, Henry." She hesitated then added, "See you."

When Irish eyes aren't smiling

The following night Matthew took Zoe to a jazz pub in Barnes, a lively jangling sort of place. It was their first real date and she felt almost nervous walking through the quiet streets hand in hand with him.

It wasn't crowded when they arrived and he grabbed a table in the corner and left her there to repel invaders while he went to the bar. She sat looking round. Not a young crowd, in general. A clientele, mostly male, in their comfortable years when waistlines thicken and hair thins. They were animated, though, freed of their daily cares for a couple of hours on a Wednesday evening, full of the spirit of beer and music.

A soloist was playing "Summertime", interjecting too many redundant notes. He reached a crescendo of superfluity at the end of the second verse and wound down to sporadic, only polite, applause.

Matthew, arriving at the bar, was accosted almost at once by a man of about fifty on an obvious intercept mission. He was much the same height as Matthew but had the wasted look endemic to those who are losing the struggle with the bottle, as if one flick of the finger would be enough to floor him. His clothes were darkly if shabbily expensive – Oxfam branches in the smarter areas of town – but they weren't clean.

"Matt. Long time. How are you keeping?" His accent spoke of a long estrangement, perhaps an exile, from the Emerald Isle. He was already drunk but only in the way that alcoholics keep their levels topped up all day, steady of foot and voice. His Irish eyes smiled. He nodded at the soloist. "Tommy will never learn that less is more."

"Septimus. I'm fine." Matthew gave his order to the barman. "Can I get you one while I'm in the chair?" He knew that you

147

shouldn't buy booze for a boozer but if he didn't someone else would.

To his surprise, Septimus refused the offer. "I'm set up for a bit, but come and join me."

"Thanks, but I'm with my girlfriend."

"Oh?" Septimus leaned companionably on the bar next to him, taking the opportunity to move closer. "Only I heard on the grapevine that you and Mary split up."

"That's not something I want to talk about."

"Thought you might have come to your senses at last, realised how much more fun sex is without women and their endless nagging and moods and periods and babies. Their nasty, floppy little titties."

Matthew laughed good naturedly, although the older man spoke in earnest. "I've told you a hundred times, Sep, I'm on the other bus."

"Don't knock it till you've tried it." He laid a hand on Matthew's arm and leaned into him and his breath was a little sour, his teeth yellow and uneven. "You are still the most beautiful thing I've ever seen, you know, Miss Groves. You drive me crazy."

"You're too kind." Matthew pocketed his change and picked up his beer and Zoe's glass of wine.

"Which is yours?" Matthew nodded to the corner and Septimus looked Zoe over carefully for a moment. "What's she got that I haven't got?"

"I'm sure you don't need a basic anatomy lesson."

Septimus shrugged and went back to his seat, so near the dais that you'd expect the trumpeter's spit to drop on his head.

Matthew rejoined Zoe and she said, "I thought your friend wanted to buy me, he examined me so minutely. I was half expecting him to come over and inspect my teeth, maybe run a hand up my fetlocks."

"Oh, he wouldn't do that." Matthew took a long drink of his beer. "Wouldn't lay a hand on a woman if he could avoid it. But he's harmless. Septimus O'Faoloin – Sep All Forlorn. I've known him for years."

"Septimus? That's not a name you hear much these days."

"I guess not many people have seven sons any more, even in Ireland."

"Is he the seventh son of a seventh son? That's supposed to be lucky."

"If he is, it hasn't worked for him."

"No, I can see that. He looks like a doctor who got struck off in 1962 for doing illegal abortions and has never got over it."

"I suppose he does a bit. He's a competent session musician who makes about enough money to keep him in whisky. Bit of a sad case."

"Looks like he might have been handsome in his youth."

"Mmm, maybe. That black Irish look with sooty hair and blue eyes. What a terrible warning to us all about the transitory nature of human beauty."

"He seems to be on his own. You didn't ask him to join us?"

"When he's sober he's charming and witty but it's not a blue moon tonight as far as I know, and he can be downright unpleasant when he's steaming. Also he's gay and it can get irritating."

"Some of my best friends are gay."

"Sure. I don't mind that as such but he's one of those gays who insist that everybody is gay and that the ninety-eight per cent of the population who say they aren't are just in denial."

She laughed. "I know the type. I can honestly say that I've never fancied making love with another woman. And you can take that look off your face."

"What look?"

"That glazed look all men get at the thought of two women making out."

He grinned. "Guilty, m'lud."

She was soon enjoying herself. She liked the atmosphere of cheerful mania, the wit of the music, the happy chatter which gave way to reverent attention when the band played. After an hour the musicians took a well-earned rest, heading for the bar like engineers on furlough from Saudi Arabia. There was an open-mike slot while they were gone and Septimus O'Faoloin was first on stage.

149

For a moment it looked as if he was too drunk to stand, let alone sing, but two men from the audience got up to shouts of encouragement from the rest and held him up to the microphone, a hand under each of his armpits.

"Birds gotta swim," Septimus began, unaccompanied, "and fish gotta fly."

A man in a lumberjack shirt called out, "Shome mishtake, surely," but was shushed.

"I gotta love one man till I die." Septimus lowered his head and his baritone rose from deep in his chest. "Can't help loving that man of mine."

His voice was so richly beautiful that Zoe felt tears starting in her eyes and Matthew, noticing, said, "Yes, it's such a waste."

He finished to ecstatic applause, was helped down from the dais and came lurching over to their corner, a tumbler of whisky, apparently conjured from nowhere, in his unsteady hand. He was visibly pumped up from his triumph. Matthew said, "Oh, dear," but more in sorrow than in anger.

Septimus stood swaying in front of their table for a moment, then said loudly, "Thought you said you were here with your girlfriend, Miss Matilda Groves, not your mother."

Zoe felt her face redden but she was nowhere near as red as Matthew. Now he *was* angry. He got to his feet and she saw his hands form fists, although he kept his voice calm. "That's enough, Sep."

"She must have money. That must be it."

"I said enough! I think you should go home before I feel obliged to punch your scrawny little face in."

One of the barmen came hurrying across and put his hand on the drunken man's shoulder, his voice soothing. "You're out of order, Sep. Come on. You don't want to go bothering these nice people."

"All right. I'm going." Septimus shook the man's hand off, looked Zoe up and down one last time and sneered, "Christ, she must be fucking loaded, that's all I can say," then staggered out of the bar. The barman shrugged an apology and hurried back to his clamouring customers.

Everybody was staring in their direction, enjoying the little scene, glad that they were not the objects of Sep All Forlorn's notice tonight. Matthew said, "Show's over," and sat down. Conversation gradually resumed at the other tables until the band began their second set. "They all know what Sep's like," he said. "Do you want to go?"

"No, don't let him drive us away." She put her arm through his and hugged it to her side. "Let's enjoy the music."

He took her free hand and kissed the back then, more intimately, the soft hollow of the palm.

Hush, little baby, don't you cry.

That night, as they lay in the tranquil minutes between orgasm and sleep, he said, "What are you thinking?"

"I was thinking how much nicer it is to make love with you every day and not have to wait what seems like ages till the next time."

"We're good together, don't you think?"

"I do think."

He blew softly on the hairs on her forearm, causing goosebumps.

First sign of madness?

"Can he love me, Ollie? He's very convincing but I know how good an actor he is. Can Henry be right and I'm just making a fool of myself?"

She examined the much-loved face in the photograph, with its regular but undistinguished features, the laughter lines around the mouth. Why did she find it so hard to believe that she was loved? She'd had no difficulty in believing that Oliver had loved her seventeen years ago, no moment of doubt in their years together.

So why not Matthew?

Because the money was there, still, a barrier. The one insistent fact: that she was a rich and lonely woman and he was a poor and charming man.

She could hear her mother's voice, gentle but unrelenting down the years: "Come here, Zoe. Let me do something with your hair, if I can . . . I wouldn't wear shorts, dear, not with those legs . . . Here's your birthday money. Don't go wasting it on books, buy yourself some mascara, some lipstick, something to make yourself look nice . . . You don't do yourself justice." And Septimus O'Faolin's voice, merging with her mother's: "She must be fucking loaded."

The truth was that she didn't think she could win the love of a handsome man, that she could deserve it.

The money. It was still lying where she'd left it on the sitting-room carpet. She fetched it and put it in her bag. She had a use for it.

She was surprised how many detective agencies were listed in the *Yellow Pages*. Were the good people of Surrey continually investigating each other? There were six in Richmond itself and she finally settled on Mason and Brownlow, ordinary

152

English names that reassured. Their office was near the town centre and perhaps the Paradise Road address was a good omen. She could drop in there on her way back from Waitrose, as if by accident, as if she wasn't really going to do this distrustful thing.

For the same reason she didn't ring to make an appointment. If they were there then they were there. If not . . .

She paid most of the cash into her bank, the assistant not flinching at the heap of twenties placed before her, counting them twice to be sure with a rubber tip on her finger. Zoe kept back six hundred and bought two days' groceries, then shortly found herself standing at a peeling black door leading to an office above a travel agent's, a brass plate announcing in three neat lines:

Mason and Brownlow
– Private Enquiries –
Please ring.

She pressed the bell, hearing it buzz somewhere above her head. For a few minutes it seemed there was going to be no reply and she picked up her two plastic carrier bags and was preparing to depart, telling herself that she'd been spared the temptation after all, when she heard heavy footsteps heading her way. The sky was full of grey cloud and the large, middle-aged man who opened the door had a furled umbrella in red, yellow and green stripes, a raincoat hung over one arm.

"Yes, love?" he said.

"Mr Mason?" Zoe hazarded. "Or Mr Brownlow?"

"Both long gone, I'm afraid." He looked her up and down. "Will I do?"

"You're going out."

"No, I answer the door like this, then if I don't like the look of the client I'm going out and if I do I'm coming in."

"I'm flattered. I think."

He gestured up the stairs. "This way."

She followed him up the steep, narrow staircase. He didn't offer to help her with her bags. At the top he pushed open a door to the left, into his office, and gestured her in. An open door to the right revealed a galley with a kettle, mugs and a half-used jar of instant coffee. She could see a bottle of Tesco's own-brand washing-up liquid squeezed flat in an attempt to get out the last of the detergent, and a carton of milk, the lip torn roughly open, yellowish mucus in the gap. Beyond these, behind an open concertina door, stood a lavatory pan with no seat.

"I'm not here much," he said, following her gaze, "so there's no point in making it nice. Anyway, people expect private detectives to be a bit seedy and I hate to let them down." He was now behind his desk and stretched his hand across. "Jerzi Topolski. No relation."

Ordinary English names, Mason and Brownlow. She shook his hand and said, "I didn't suppose you were."

"That's one of the nice things about Richmond: no one ever says 'No relation to who?' or 'Whom?' Which is it? I never know."

"Whom."

"Yes, you looked like you'd know. Sit down, Mrs . . . ?"

"Kean. Zoe Kean."

She sat down. So did he. He was younger than she'd first thought, maybe forty-four or -five, taller too. His bulk made him appear shorter in proportion, but he must top six feet. He had a weathered face with a nose that looked as if it might have met more than a few fists.

He said, "Now, what can I do for you?"

"Have you been in business long, Mr Topolski?"

He nodded approval. "Check my credentials. Quite right. I was in the police for twenty years, starting as a cadet at eighteen, quit six years ago because I couldn't take the bureaucracy any more." He touched his face. "And I was too old to keep getting my nose broken by vicious little gits not old enough to vote. So I bought out Mason, who was retiring. God knows what happened to Brownlow. Maybe I should investigate. Sadly I can't give you references since my clients' affairs are confidential. You a good judge of character, Mrs Kean?"

"Not really."

"Interesting. Most people think they are, get indignant if you question it, like you'd accused them of lacking a sense of humour. 'I like to think so', that's what most of them say." He spread his big hands. "Either you trust me or you don't. Otherwise try one of the big firms with branches in Paris, Frankfurt, New York and Tokyo. I give the personal touch. I'm also a lot cheaper."

"All right." She found herself liking him, although she was now a famously poor judge of character. "I want to make a few enquiries about a young man of my acquaintance."

"Yeah? I had you down as a divorce."

"I'm a widow."

"Sorry. Me and my size twelves. What sort of enquiries? I can do the basic – criminal record and a credit check – within twenty-four hours. Is that what you had in mind?"

"A bit more than that."

"You want him followed?"

"Not exactly. Ask around, find out what you can about him, what he does with his spare time, how he lives, if he's got a girlfriend."

Jerzi Topolski drew a clean sheet of paper towards him and scrabbled about for a pencil. "Name? His name, that is."

"Matthew Groves."

"Address." She gave it to him. "What sort of car does he drive and what's the registration?"

"He doesn't."

"Okay. Have you got a recent photo?"

"No."

"I'll take a decent description then."

"He's thirty-two, five foot ten or eleven, slim, blond, blue eyes."

"Hmm. Okay. I don't need to know why you need this information, so long as you can assure me that it's legal and above board."

She felt herself blushing. His eyes held hers, intelligent and shrewd, and she felt as if she'd been dragged up in front of the headmaster to explain her conduct. "My daughter," she said at last. "She's only seventeen and she's been seeing him. He seems nice – charming, good looking – but I'm worried that he's too old for her and that he might be a . . . fortune hunter."

Topolski began to laugh, then stopped abruptly. "You're serious, aren't you? Is there a fortune?"

"Enough for most people. She's an only child. Rachel." She was pleased with her little fiction. Rachel: a pretty dark-haired girl with eyes like jet, hovering on the threshold of womanhood, sitting her A levels next year, her mother's pride and joy. As Sam said, an alternative life came in handy.

Topolski shrugged. "Fair enough, but if she's well smitten you'll only make things worse by interfering and she won't believe anything bad you say about him because she's in *lurve*. Still, if he is a fortune hunter you can always offer to buy him off, something for which I'm willing – or at least *prepared* – to act as intermediary. I charge by the day and my expenses. If you'd like to give me, say, three hundred to be going on with."

She took the envelope out of her bag and began counting and he raised his eyebrows. "Come prepared, Mrs Kean?"

"I happened to have the cash."

"Sure, you did. Give me your phone number and I'll call you when I've got anything to report."

She handed him one of her cards and he laughed.

"What?" she said.

"When you paid cash I assumed you'd given me a false name and didn't want to pay by cheque."

"I told you, I happened to have it. A loan repaid."

He said, "Give me a week. Maybe two. I'll be in touch."

A matter of allegiance

They were getting to know each other, the way couples were supposed to do in an ideal world *before* they started sleeping together.

She took him to a reading by some young English novelists at the Voice Box on the South Bank and he sat in rapt attention and asked her perceptive questions afterwards. They went to the theatre and differed amicably about the play all the way home. They sat on the sofa, twined together, and watched monochrome movies on TV late at night.

She hired a car and they drove out to the Chilterns and ate lunch at a pub in Wendover and walked up Coombe Hill and down again through the beech woods, past Chequers with its grazing sheep and along a sheltered hollow called Happy Valley.

He insisted on paying his half of everything and she had to let him.

He was doing three escort jobs a week, to Jean's delight, to pay his debts, and Zoe tried not to think of him on those evenings. He would come to her afterwards, however late, as if he needed to prove that he wasn't going home with these women. He tried to arrange the work around her evenings at FILO as far as possible.

He was doing as much bar work as he could get at lunchtimes too, mostly holiday reliefs, and Zoe was astonished at how pitiful the pay was, often as little as twenty-four pounds for a six-hour shift.

She didn't introduce him to her friends, mainly because she wanted him to herself. He didn't introduce her to any of his either. She didn't give him a key and he didn't ask for one.

They bathed together and dried each other and made love

while still damp, but she didn't tell him that she loved him. It was too soon and she wasn't sure yet how she felt. He told her almost daily that he loved her but when she didn't respond in kind he was prepared to be patient.

One Sunday afternoon she went to watch him play cricket for the Putney Peculiars. They were late arriving, South-West Trains having been subject to inexplicable delays, and he rushed off to change as his team was fielding.

She set off to walk round the boundary and soon realised, to her mild surprise, that the man occupying one of two deckchairs under a shady tree was Paul McIver. He was wearing a cricket sweater over a black T-shirt and black denims. He raised a hand in greeting and, although she had no desire to sit with him, she thought it would be pointedly rude not to do so.

"Is this seat taken?" she asked hopefully.

"No. You make yourself at home, Zoe." She sat. After a pause he said, "I love this sedate game, I could spend all summer sitting in the shade watching, maybe snoozing. You?"

"I think it takes the English to invent a game where you play for days and one side is beating the crap out of the other and then they call it a draw on a technicality." He laughed. "The teas are always good, though," she added, "for some reason." Her father had been a keen player, later a keen umpire, and she'd spent many a childhood Sunday afternoon in the pavilion, wolfing down food away from her mother's strictures.

"Ah yes," Paul said, "mahogany tea from the urn, sandwiches made from Mother's Pride, as if wholemeal bread had never been rediscovered, slices of cucumber and slimy processed cheese, iced 'fancies', and it tastes like nectar. All those loyal wives and girlfriends or, in the case of two of this team, boyfriends."

"Really?"

"Why do you think they're called the Putney *Peculiars*? Mind they don't brainwash you, Zoe, into their weird cult."

"I think I'm quite safe. Which team do you support?"

"Middlesex and England. So I pass Norman Tebbit's test of Britishness."

The former Conservative cabinet minister had once said that immigrants could prove their loyalty to their adopted country by supporting England at cricket rather than the West Indies, India or Pakistan. As asinine remarks by politicians went it probably made the top ten.

"Did you grow up round here? she asked.

"Born and raised in Harrow, hence my lifelong devotion to Middlesex. At cricket, that is. I'm not talking about my personal life."

"Not an old Harrovian?" she asked, expecting the answer to be no.

"Yes, actually." His chameleon voice was suddenly upper class, utterly convincing just as it had been as a Jamaican drug dealer. "Following in the footsteps of Winston Churchill and Mark Thatcher." Seeing her surprise, he went on, "My family was well off in those days. Dad lost everything at Lloyd's ten years ago."

"Oh, no! Everything?"

"Pretty much. When you've had money and lost it, that comes hard."

"I know. I mean, I can imagine."

"Can you?" He looked at her over his sunglasses again, his eyes almost as opaque as the lenses. "Can you really?"

She found him unnerving. She said lightly, "As a writer there are few bounds to what I can imagine."

"The day my dad realised what had happened, that it was all going to have to go, he took a plane out to our holiday place in Antibes. He just adored that villa. I think it was his favourite place in all the world and losing it was more than he could bear. He loved to swim there but this time he left his clothes on the beach and walked out into the sea until he drowned."

She didn't know how to respond. The conventional murmurs of condolence seemed inadequate. Instead she put her hand on his arm and squeezed the flesh through the coarse cotton ribbing of his sleeve. He laid his hand over hers, his fingers caressing, the skin firm and silky and unexpectedly pink. He took his sunglasses off and looked deep into her eyes and smiled a sad smile.

"It was ten years ago," he said, and they released each other and she felt a little foolish.

To her relief the players came out onto the field at that moment to sporadic applause. Paul put his fingers between his teeth and whistled a long, vulgar blast. Matthew was fielding at the far side. The visitors began to make runs but slowly and rather dully. Amateur cricket did not demand close attention from its spectators and they were able to carry on a conversation without missing anything crucial.

"Did you get that TV part you went for a while back?" she asked Paul.

"No."

"I'm sorry."

"I felt like Dustin Hoffman in *Tootsie.* Remember?"

"All I remember is when he first dresses up as a woman and his flat mate says, 'Whatever you do, don't play hard to get'."

"But at the beginning he goes for an audition and they say they want someone taller and he says, 'I can be taller', so they say they want someone older and he says, 'I can be older', and finally the producer in exasperation snaps, 'We want someone *else,*' and *that* was what happened to me last month."

She said lamely, "I'm sure something will turn up soon."

"What I keep telling myself."

After half an hour Matthew was put on to bowl and took two wickets in two overs. After the second one he turned a graceful cartwheel to celebrate and Paul and Zoe both snorted with mirth.

They came in for tea ten minutes early, the visitors all out for eighty-nine. Matty bounded up to Zoe and fell to his knees in front of her, heedless of the grass stains on his well-pressed flannels, pushing into her lap like an eager puppy.

"You were brilliant, darling," she said, and leaned forward and kissed him hard on the mouth.

"You wait till you see him bat," Paul drawled.

Two sorts of people

W hen Zoe got back from her walk by the river the next morning she saw that there was a message on her answering machine. When she pressed the play button a voice boomed out, the sort of person who shouts on the telephone on the grounds that his interlocutor is some distance away.

"Jerzi Topolski here, Mrs Kean."

Topolski. In the ten days since she'd been to his Dickensian office, she'd managed to expunge him from her conscious memory.

He said, "It's Monday morning at ten thirty. I've got the information you wanted. I shall be in my office for the rest of the day—" he groaned – "doing my VAT returns, so stop by if you like, if you get this in time. Otherwise call me to make an appointment."

Half an hour later she was ringing his bell.

"Come in, Mrs Kean." He ushered her up to his office. The desk was covered with receipts: garages, taxis, stationers, electrical suppliers. "Do *you* have to do this every quarter?" he asked.

"Yes."

"But I suppose you have some tame accountant."

"No, I find if you keep proper records as you go along, then there's no problem."

He grunted. "Which proves that there are two sorts of people in the world. Sit down, if you can."

She moved a stack of ledgers from the chair and, seeing nowhere else to put them, laid them neatly on the floor.

"Matthew Groves," Topolski said. He picked up a buff folder full of loose pieces of paper of various shapes and sizes and she thought she could see photographs in there.

161

"He has no criminal record except for a recent caution for possession for a laughably small amount of cannabis, but I gather you know about that."

"Oh. How did you . . . ?"

"I told you I used to be with the police. I have a number of contacts I can call on for these sort of enquiries, find out if a name means anything to them."

"Contacts called Henry Dacres?"

She was dismayed. Henry was the last person in the world she wanted to know that she didn't completely trust Matthew.

"Henry and I go back a long way," Topolski said. "We were at West End Central together when we were still wet behind the ears. We watched each other's backs for a long time. He lodged with me and my missus for a few years before he got married."

Talk about of all the gin joints in all the towns in all the world. Could she have picked a less suitable detective to protect her own privacy? Or were they all Henry's old mates?

She said, "Isn't it illegal for him to give you confidential information?"

"It would be," he agreed, "if he did a computer search on my behalf, say, but I wouldn't abuse our friendship by asking him to do that and he'd tell me to go to hell if I did. No, Henry was one among many people I asked if they'd heard of a Matthew Groves, or knew if he had any previous."

"And how much did you pay him for his information?"

"Oh, he'd be hurt and wounded if I offered him money. I expect we'll have a drink together soon but we'll both buy our rounds. Henry was specially curious as to why I wanted to know about Groves, seems to take a friendly interest in you, Mrs Kean."

She didn't answer and he continued leafing through his file. "No serious debts – that's to say no county court judgements against him, no blacklists. Owes a bit on his credit cards, but then who doesn't? No family in this country that I can track down – parents emigrated to New Zealand three years ago. Was living with a woman called Mary Havisham till a year ago but they split up. Now shares a flat—"

"He was living with a woman?"

"Yeah. They were buying a place together in West Acton. He moved out in May of last year, after three years, transferred the flat into her sole name, although he had some equity in it. Sounds like she couldn't afford to buy him out and he didn't want to leave her homeless. Must have had a guilty conscience. Let's hope she's not sitting in the attic surrounded by cobwebs still wearing her wedding dress."

"Huh? Oh, Miss Havisham. I get it."

"As I was saying, he now shares a flat with one Paul McIver, another unemployed actor. Groves and McIver both do a bit of escort work for a woman called Jean Frobisher but the agency seems legit, as far as escort agencies ever are."

"Aren't they ever?"

"As legit as massage parlours. Maybe one in a thousand, depending on location. McIver escorts blokes as well as women, but Groves apparently sticks to the fairer sex. McIver is, frankly, a bit of a whore but Groves probably not."

"I see."

He handed her some photos of Matthew with a woman. She was in her late forties, Zoe judged, what the French called a *jolie laide*, elegant and rail thin, her grey-streaked hair pulled back into a ballerina's knot. They seemed to be having lunch, although it was hard to believe that the woman ever ate anything. In some of the photos they were laughing together but none showed them so much as touching.

"Alison Judd," Topolski explained. "She and her husband Maxwell run an independent production company making drama series and serials, the occasional one-off TV film, mostly for ITV and Channel 4. A strictly business lunch at the River Café, her treat, not even a bit of harmless flirtation. Your Matthew Groves isn't cheating on you, or not while I was watching."

"I beg your pardon?"

"Only you haven't got a daughter, Mrs Kean, seventeen or any other age."

She reddened and said stiffly. "I despise myself for lying to you, in fact. I wanted the information for myself."

163

"You're a good liar. I never doubted the existence of 'Rachel' for a moment."

"Is that a compliment?"

"Could be. Anyway, it's none of my business *why* you want this information. There's not a lot else. Matthew Groves is a law-abiding member of the community, give or take a few grams of grass and nobody cares about that these days, not even Henry." He turned another page. "Oh, yeah. You gave his age as thirty-two. Equity seems to think he's twenty-eight."

"Oh! But don't actors sometimes knock a few years off?"

"True, which is why I double checked at St Catherine's House." Topolski handed her a copy of a birth certificate. "Matthew Francis Groves, born in Camberley General Hospital on the first of January twenty-eight years ago. Happy New Year, Mrs Groves."

She took the piece of paper and stared at the year. Dear God. She'd been at big school by then, had had her first period and screamed herself into a fit when anyone mentioned Rod Stewart.

"And here," Topolski went on, "is my bill. The second sheet details my expenses."

She glanced at it. "You didn't stint yourself at the River Café, did you?"

"Should I have? I have to blend in, or I'd get thrown out." Zoe found it hard to believe that Jerzi would blend in at the River Café under any circumstances. "Settlement in one month," he said, "if you please."

"I'll pay you now." She took out her cheque book and wrote him a cheque.

He examined it carefully and handed her the buff folder. "Read it at your leisure. Pleasure doing business with you, Mrs Kean."

She stood up, stuffing the file in her bag and shook hands with him.

"I'll see myself out."

Making a fool of yourself

S he decided that she must introduce Matthew to one of her friends – that it was now time for him to become a proper part of her life – and she settled on Joanna. It was too soon for Sam, even if he was her best friend. She knew what it was like when you put a couple of good-looking young men together: the place suddenly turned into a chicken run with two roosters fighting over the available hens, even if the said hens were old and stringy and hadn't laid a decent egg for years.

So she arranged to meet Joanna and her sons at the open-air swimming baths one Thursday afternoon in August and went out and bought a new swimsuit. It was years since she'd swum and she tried on a dozen, torn between the obvious charms of the bikini and the welcome purdah of the one-piece with rara skirt. She settled on a red and white costume with wide diagonal stripes, spaghetti straps and a decent amount – in both senses – of cleavage. The swimsuit came with a matching cotton wrap that stopped mid-thigh and she treated herself to strappy sandals, a shady hat and some new sunglasses.

She'd previously thought of Joanna's children as a homogeneous mass, Stevadam, but saw now that they were very different in both looks and personality. Even as an only child she was familiar with the family ritual whereby one child is the clever one, another the pretty one, a third the joker and so on. Sadly at the moment all the desirable qualities seemed to have vested themselves in Adam, leaving Stevie to sulk on the sidelines.

Adam had his father's looks: tousled black hair and dark eyes, intense narrow face, thin build, his skin tanned a golden brown with the sun. He had his mother's outgoing personality, though, and soon ran off to join a group of boys his own age who were playing with a giant beachball, being accepted into the gang by them without question.

Stevie, meanwhile, had Joanna's fair complexion, his hair the dirty dishwater colour that charitable people call strawberry blond, his eyes a washy blue. His tummy was prominent above his loose bathing trunks. He presumably got his brooding, slightly irritable manner from Henry.

Zoe was reminded of the anecdote whereby Mrs Patrick Campbell had suggested to Shaw that they have a child together with her looks and his brains and he'd said, "But what if it's the other way round?"

Joanna had no qualms about wearing a bikini, and had clearly put on a little weight since buying it, but she settled on her beach mat, on display to passers-by, cellulite and all, with a breezy self-confidence that Zoe longed to possess. She plastered herself vigorously with sunblock and handed the tube to Stevie who said, "I'm not putting that on, it's for girls," in an angry growl, as if in training for his imminent adolescence. There was already a flush of red up his neck, something that threatened to become a rash.

"Well, I'm certainly going to have some," Matty said quickly, pulling his T-shirt over his head, releasing a pleasant whiff of fresh male sweat. And to Joanna, "May I?"

"Of course."

Both women watched as he oiled his face, neck, arms and torso. Zoe imagined that he was anointing himself with something sweet and sticky – jam, chocolate, golden syrup – especially for her so she could lick it off later. She realised with embarrassment that her tongue was sticking out in anticipation and retracted it.

When he stood up, unzipped his jeans and stepped out of them, Joanna took her sunglasses off to watch. His swimming trunks were plain navy-blue, neither skimpy nor voluminous, and Zoe realised that he didn't need to advertise. He rubbed sunblock generously on his legs then handed the tube to Stevie as if the boy had only been waiting for him to finish.

Stevie began to emulate the older man without further

protest and Joanna mouthed "Thank you" at Matthew over the boy's bowed head.

"Stevie," Matthew said, sitting down again, "your mum was telling me you're quite a diver."

"At my old school." The boy was unable to avoid looking pleased, though he did his best. "Won't be the same at the new place."

"You're off to secondary school next month?" He nodded. "That'll be exciting. The facilities'll be much better and you'll learn all sorts of new things. Make lots of new friends too, I shouldn't wonder."

"Mmm." The boy looked doubtful.

"How about you show me your diving?"

"All right." Stevie, shaking off his sulks, jumped up and Matthew followed him towards the diving boards.

"What a jewel," Joanna said. "Where did you get him? Adonises R Us?"

"Oh, I picked him up in a hotel bar one evening."

"You're kidding!"

"Yes, I'm kidding."

"Shame. I was going to head straight down there. It's Stevie's birthday tomorrow, his eleventh, and he wouldn't have a party, said he didn't know enough people to invite. I do worry about him."

"Children's parties are hell by all accounts."

"Yes, but it worries me that he can't seem to make friends the way Adam does. Adam's so easy by comparison, so much fun, and I have to make an effort not to like him better than Stevie. Anyway, I've made him a cake so you're both invited to partake of that when you've done enough swimming."

"So long as I don't have to eat jelly."

"Absolutely no jelly."

"Then I accept with gratitude."

After a while Joanna said, "We're off to Devon on Sunday, a week on the beach at Woolacombe."

"Is Henry going?"

"Henry? You must be joking. He hates holidays. That was one of the bugbears of our married life: when I finally persuaded him to get away somewhere he always wanted to know how soon we could come home again and I felt as if I had *three* tiresome children to keep amused. What about you – you going away?"

"No. Even when Oliver was alive we never went away during school holidays—"

"Ah, the luxury."

"And now . . . well, it's no fun on your own."

"It'd be fun with *him*." Joanna nodded her head to where Stevie was teaching Matthew to dive and Matthew was pretending he needed teaching. "I bet you could think of all sorts of things to do with him, even if it was raining. I know I could and I saw your tongue hanging out, lady, so don't think I didn't."

"Maybe next year."

"Okay." She was silent for a moment, then burst out, "What is it you're afraid of, Zoe?"

"I don't know what you mean."

"Yes, you do. If I had someone as nice as Matthew looking at me the way he looks at you, I wouldn't sit around saying, 'But' and 'What if'. Being hurt. That's what you're afraid of, isn't it?"

"I suppose."

"But that's a risk you take every time you set foot outside your front door. 'It's better to have loved and lost than not have loved at all.'"

"Never to have."

"Sorry?"

"It's better to have loved and lost than *never* to have loved at all."

"See, you agree with me. So what are you going to do? Bury your feelings so far down you need deep-cast mining equipment to find them again, the way Sam Lincoln does? Or are you going to take a risk?" When Zoe didn't reply, Joanna held up her hands in surrender. "Okay, it's none of my business. I'll shut up now."

"No, it's all right. Thank you."

Stevie really was a good diver, magically losing his clumsiness in the light run along the board, the jump, the arch, the jack-knife and the clean entry to the water. Boys gathered to watch and applaud, Adam loyally leading the clapping. Matty, following behind, did a belly flop that made both women wince and they could hear Stevie and the other boys laughing as he climbed sheepishly out of the water, rubbing his stomach.

"He did that on purpose," Joanna said.

"You think?"

"I'm sure of it. It takes guts to deliberately make a fool of yourself in front of kids, but it's something you have to learn to do as a parent."

When they were done swimming, they dried themselves in the sun and put their clothes back on over their costumes, then walked round the corner to Joanna's house for tea. She'd made a simple chocolate iced sponge with "Happy Birthday Stevie" in ragged white lettering and eleven candles distributed haphazardly round the edge. Stevie blew out the candles with one puff and cut the cake into large segments for everyone.

For the adults there was humous and taramasalata. "Don't know about you," Joanna said, "but I can only take so many sweet things."

She made Melba toast for the dips under the grill and – to her amazement and delight – Matthew offered to mend her toaster and, being provided with a screwdriver, did just that in a matter of minutes.

"Is it really fixed?" she kept saying, stroking her hands along the matt green sides of it as if it were a favourite pet miraculously brought back from the dead.

"It'll be fine. I hope. If we hear fire engines in the middle of the night, we'll know where they're heading."

Stevie insisted on showing his new friend his computer games after tea and Matthew dutifully went upstairs with both boys for an hour.

Joanna, who had registered "we" and "the middle of the night" said, "You lucky, lucky cow."

Matthew and Zoe strolled the short distance back to Zoe's house hand in hand. As they waited for the crossing lights at the roundabout in the evening rush hour he said, "I love you," and she opened her mouth to answer him in kind but then squeezed his hand instead.

"You're so good with kids," she said. "Even nerdy ones like Stevie."

"It's hard to know what to say to them," he said, "but think how much harder it is for them. I mean, we know what it's like to be a child, however deep in our psyches we've buried it, but they have no idea what it's like to be a grown-up. They're far more scared of us. We have all the power."

She said, "I never thought of it that way."

"I was like that at his age. He'll grow out of it."

She was surprised. "You were like Stevie?"

"Yeah, it's a terrible age. You've no confidence at all. You're wondering when your voice is going to break and whether it'll sound silly. And you've had your first erection and are worried about that, or else you haven't so you're worried about *that*. If you haven't got sisters then girls are like something from another planet and you can't talk to them without making a complete idiot of yourself. Everything your lovely parents do and say seems designed to humiliate you in front of your friends, especially when they have comical New Zealand accents, and—"

"Enough!" she said laughing, kissing him. "You're making me pity you and you're the least pitiable person I've ever met."

"Adam's a right little charmer but Stevie's the one I identify with." She wondered if he'd like the boys so much if he knew who their father was. "He's upset about his grandmother dying," Matthew went on.

"What?"

"It seems Joanna's mother died quite recently."

"Yes, I know."

"Well, Stevie's taken it very hard."

"Really? Has he said anything to Jo?"

"That's just it. He said she was so upset at the beginning that he didn't want to make things worse for her by going on about how miserable *he* was. I think he feels protective towards her, with her being a single parent, and him being the elder boy, he sees himself as the man of the house, poor little chap. Then he says she seemed to get really angry about something and he was half frightened to mention Grandma. Do you know what that was all about?"

"Yes, but I can't tell you. I was told in confidence."

"Fair enough, and then she went for some counselling – Oh, was that with you?"

She nodded. "That's how we became friends."

"Well, you must have done a good job because Stevie says that soon afterwards she seemed completely back to normal and he didn't want to raise the subject in case he upset her again."

"Oh, poor little boy. I'll find a tactful way to bring it up with her."

"That would be good."

"He really opened up to you, didn't he?"

"You can't be nervous of someone who's just done a humiliating bellyflop in front of half the kids in West London."

That evening, before supper, he was sitting in the armchair by the fireplace, faintly tired from the afternoon's exercise, warm from the summer day, completely relaxed. She went and straddled him, her knees on either side of him, her full skirt billowing to cover his thighs and belly and hips. She wore nothing underneath and the denim of his jeans was abrasive against her skin. She rocked back and forward on the roughness like a girl child innocently masturbating, because it feels good and no one has yet told her not to. His arms went round her, his hands sliding under the knitted cotton of her short-sleeved jersey, tracing the line of her spine with delicate fingers right up to the nape of her neck.

"No underwear at all," he remarked.

"Who needs underwear?"

His face tilted up to smile at her and she took it in her hands and kissed his mouth, teasing top and bottom lip. He was passive, giving her the lead, and was silent as she reached between them and unfastened his belt, pulling down his zip and freeing his erection.

She'd liked to make love to Oliver in this chair – *his* chair

– but he complained that it hurt his back. Matty was younger and fitter and had a strong back.

She took a condom from her skirt pocket, put it on him and took him straight into her without further preamble. He gave a little grunt and closed his eyes as she began to move up and down, very slowly. She ran her tongue over his eyelids, making him shiver.

She arched backwards, spine and head, feeling the sun through the open French windows on her hair and shoulders. His hands moved round to her breasts, circling the nipples as they hardened and grew. She could hear a crow cawing on the apple tree outside, raucous voices from the garden of the pub a hundred yards away, the sounds of a fine evening in summer, magnified in her mind, in her heightened senses, intense.

She kept her movements agonisingly slow until he began to buck upwards more urgently to meet her. Then she fell still, leaning forward again, wrapping her arms round his neck to steady herself.

His eyes were open wide now, the pupils huge, obscuring the iris. He wasn't looking at her, though, but at nothing.

"What's the rush?" she whispered. "You have a train to catch?" She stroked his hair back from his forehead, feeling drops of sweat at the hairline. She sucked them up, one by one.

He sighed heavily and she began to move again, circling on his lap for a minute or two until she felt him jerk as he climaxed.

"Sorry," he murmured, "too soon." And he reached a hand between her legs and fingered her quickly to orgasm. "I love you," he said, as she eased off him, holding the condom in place. She brought her legs round to sit sideways on his lap, tidying him away, dropping the knotted condom on the mantelpiece. She laid her head on his shoulder and buried her face in his neck with one long inhalation.

He wriggled to change position.

"Am I too heavy?" she asked.

"Not at all. It's just this chair – it's hard on the back."

An end to a perfect evening

Two more weeks went by: weeks full of sunshine and love.

One evening Matthew volunteered to cook supper, claiming that he knew how to make the best cheese soufflé in the world. Since Zoe had never succeeded in making any sort of soufflé that didn't stick to the dish to the extent that it had to be thrown away afterwards, she left him to it after token offers of help.

"You go and put your feet up," he said, "but –" he called her back – "I must have payment for the chef in advance." He pulled her to him and kissed her long and passionately until she was ready to forgo dinner altogether and go straight up to bed, but Matthew pointed out that he'd already separated the eggs.

"Now get out of my kitchen, woman, and let the artist create."

He'd borrowed her apron – a riot of pink pigs – and she experienced that moment in any relationship where the beloved is regarded for the first time not only with desire but also with a profound tenderness.

She sat reading in the sitting room, a white-wine spritzer – mostly soda – beside her, the French windows open to a perfect summer's evening, listening to the companionable sounds of cupboards being opened, dishes being clattered and vigorous chopping.

She stretched sensuously. Her body felt good to her, as if the more she gave it to her lover, the more completely it became her own.

He was singing softly to himself, the tune floating from the kitchen into the sitting room. It was a blues song, she thought, possibly about some woman who'd had wrong done to her by some man, although that wasn't a hard guess.

He'd been excited when he arrived, saying he had something to tell her, some great news, but that it must wait until dinner was served and the wine was ready for drinking toasts. He'd set up the slatted hardwood table on the terrace, with the flowers he'd brought her – sweet-scented carnations, white and coral – in a plain glass vase, and laid places for dinner including napkins, which he'd ironed. The terracotta pots trailing blue and white lobelia stood, a pair of sentries, on either side of the French windows.

The garden was beautiful and the book absorbing. She couldn't remember when she'd last felt so happy.

Then everything went quiet and she glanced up to see him standing in the archway from the dining area, his face a mixture of shock and fury. He was holding the buff file Jerzi Topolski had given her. She let out an exclamation and dropped her book. It fell splayed open on the floor, the bookmark shooting across the room.

He was struggling to keep his temper. "What the fuck is this?"

"Where . . . where did you find that?" She was trying frantically to remember where she'd left it. She'd thought it was safe in her study.

"I was looking for an egg whisk and I found it in one of the kitchen drawers," he said coldly.

She remembered now: she'd come into the house, the phone had been ringing and she'd shoved the file haphazardly into the nearest drawer as she answered it and never thought to look at it again. "Matty—"

"I can't believe this. You've been spying on me." He flourished the file at her. "Mason and Brownlow, private enquiries?" He leafed through it. "Here's a copy of my birth certificate, for Christ's sake! And photos of me having lunch at the River Café with Alison Judd. I don't believe this. I can't believe you did this. What sort of person are you?"

She felt ashamed and thoroughly in the wrong so she went on the attack. "I'm a rich woman. I have to be careful of fortune hunters."

"I'm not interested in your money. I thought I'd made that clear."

"That's easy enough to *say*. That man at the jazz club that evening—"

"Septimus? That pathetic old alcoholic? You can't be serious."

"He was just saying what other people *think* when they see us together. 'Look at that middle-aged woman with her toy boy. She must be loaded.' "

"No one gives us a second glance. No one but you thinks twice about it. As for Sep, he was being petty and spiteful because he was jealous, because he's infatuated with me and has been for years."

"I had to find out how many lies you'd told me—"

"What!"

"You're twenty-eight for a start."

"Yes." He looked bewildered. "I'm twenty-eight. What of it?"

"You don't deny it?"

"Of course I don't fucking deny it."

"You told me you were thirty-two."

"No, I didn't. When did I?"

She thought back. She must have got the idea from somewhere. "*She* told me, Jean, at Allsorts."

"Oh, I see. Did you say you wanted a thirty-two-year-old?"

"I suppose I asked for a man in his thirties."

"Well then. If you'd asked for a man in his forties, I'd've been a well-preserved forty-two, because that's the way Jean operates. What the customer wants is what the customer is told she is getting."

"Yes, you have to keep the customers sweet, I can see that. And I've only your word for it that I was the only one . . . the only one you went home with."

"Yes," he said after a pause, "you have only my word. I suppose I thought that would be good enough but why should you take the word of a whore? So what other lies am I supposed to have told you?"

"You didn't tell me about Mary Havisham."

175

This one hit home. He looked deeply defeated, and she thought she saw tears in his eyes.

"Am I not allowed to have had previous girlfriends?"

"No. I mean yes, of course . . . but you never so much as mentioned her, someone you lived with. For years."

"No. In the same way that you don't talk about your dead husband."

"I don't try to hide his very existence . . . I don't talk about him to anyone because it still hurts too much."

"I sensed that and I've respected it. And I didn't tell you about Mary because it was too painful for *me*. I loved her and she ended it. I thought we were going to be married, start a family, until she came home from work one day and told me it wasn't going to happen, that she'd met someone she liked better. She told me I was too *nice*, for Christ's sake, that she was bored with me. I packed my bags and pushed off that same night, left her everything, even the flat we'd chosen together, furnished together, for our life together."

So much for Miss Havisham, mourning forever in her rotting bridal gown. She murmured, "I'm sorry."

"I didn't so much as date another woman after that because I was hurting so badly – until you. I didn't think I'd ever be able to trust a woman with my heart again, but you seemed so straight, so honest, and that was one of the things I loved about you."

She noted with sadness his use of the past tense.

"But you're all the same," he went on, "deceitful, dishonest, untrustworthy. It's not a mistake I'll make a third time." He shook the file and emptied the photographs onto the floor. "And that lunch with Alison was pure business, by the way, something Jamie fixed up; she's a TV producer."

"I know."

"Oh! Well at least he's not incompetent, your private dick. You got your money's worth, and I know how important that is to you." He stood looking at her for a moment and his face was full of sorrow. "You asked me once how I managed to cry on stage when I needed to – remember? – and I said I thought of something very painful."

"I remember."

176

"I did it by thinking of that day when Mary broke my heart. Now I'll have something else to work with. Two strings to my bow. So isn't that fucking marvellous?" He flung the file down on the table in front of her. "Here. Take it and I hope it keeps you warm on long winter nights, Zoe, along with your piles of bloody money."

She couldn't speak, couldn't apologise, couldn't explain, could only watch as he tore off the apron, snatched his jacket from the coat rack in the hall and slammed out of the house.

She went slowly into the kitchen. He'd made a roux in a Le Creuset pan on the hob, yellow with freshly-grated Parmesan, smooth as thick buttermilk and dotted with coarse black pepper. A jug held the yolks of three eggs, waiting to be beaten into the mixture, a bowl their whites to be whisked stiff.

A dish of salad stood on the worktop – red Santa plum tomatoes from Spain, olives like shiny purple bullets, crisp green leaves, extra virgin oil and balsamic vinegar, mustard and fresh basil from the garden, the same basil he'd once licked from her fingers.

The bottle of *Châteauneuf-du-Pape* he'd brought with him had been opened to breathe.

The oven pinged to tell her it had reached the right temperature.

She emptied everything into the kitchen bin: pan, jug, bowl and all, and switched the oven off.

She poured the wine down the sink.

She was shaking.

She picked up the salad bowl to dispose of that as well, but began to cry into it instead – big, loud tears – until the lettuce was soggy and the olives greasy and grey with them.

Breathing space

M atthew was packing his bags.

One bag, in fact, though a large one. His room was small: a single bed, a chest of drawers and an ugly wardrobe fought for space. It was necessarily tidy and therefore easy enough to keep clean. He laid his suitcase on the bed and began taking clothes from the chest and wardrobe and folding them into it. Apart from the suits he'd bought for his escort work and which he wouldn't be needing where he was going, there weren't many clothes and it wouldn't take him long.

He went about his work with method, deliberately keeping his mind as empty of thought as possible.

The door into the sitting room was open and Paul appeared at that moment, holding out a plain white envelope with a handwritten address.

"This just came for you, man."

"Thanks." Matty took it, glanced at the handwriting, recognised it and dropped the letter on the bed. He wasn't going to read it while Paul was in the room but his friend showed no sign of leaving.

"You're not taking much for a month," he remarked.

"Just what I can carry. And before I forget." He stopped what he was doing and took a chequebook from one of the drawers in the chest, tore out the top cheque, already filled in, and gave it to Paul. "Two months rent, to be on the safe side, plus a bit extra for any bills that come in while I'm away."

"I won't sublet your room then," Paul said. "Want to talk about it?"

"About what?"

"Whatever it is that's given you a hump the size of the millennium dome."

178

"No."

"Coffee?"

"No thanks. I've got to get on. Plane leaves in four hours."

Paul finally took the hint and left. Matthew snatched up the letter and slit it open with his thumbnail. It was short and he took it over to the window to read where there was more light.

24th August

Forgive me, Matty.

I've been very confused lately. I feel like Catherine Sloper in *Washington Square* although, instead of an unloving father constantly reminding me that I can't possibly be loved for myself, let alone by anyone as special as you, I have a hyper-critical mother who remembers nothing these senile days except that I was and am a disappointment to her.

I'm not going to try to justify what I did. It was wrong and I am ashamed.

I love you. There, I've said it at last.

Please, please don't tell me it's too late.

Zoe

He stood looking out of the window for a moment, over the rooftops of Hammersmith, which were more dingy than usual in the morning sunlight. Then he folded the letter and tucked it into his suitcase.

He took a pen and a pad of writing paper out of the chest of drawers, sat down on the bed and began to compose his reply.

An hour later he was hefting his suitcase along King Street on his way to the tube, moving it from hand to hand to ease the strain. He stopped at a pillar box and dropped his letter into it. He stood for a moment, wondering if he was doing the right thing, knowing that it was academic as the letter was now beyond retrieval and he would be twelve thousand miles away by the time she read it.

Make or break time.

He could remember what he'd written, word for word.

179

25th August

My dearest Zoe,

I've decided to go to New Zealand for a month. My parents have been urging me to go for so long and it will give me time to think things over.

I know what you're thinking – Matty's running up more debts. I got that part in the film – that was the great news I wanted to share with you that night. It's not a fortune but it's enough to pay what I owe Paul and buy my airfare and leave a bit over, and Jamie says it's the start of much bigger things, but then he would say that, wouldn't he?

He waited only five minutes for a Piccadilly Line train to Heathrow. There was a vacant seat at the end of the row and he was able to keep an eye on his case as it bulged against the wall of the compartment.

I never lied to you, darling. It wasn't me who told you I was thirty-two – I didn't know you'd been told that – and letting you think I was a tart was a lie of omission, as was Mary.

Above all I wasn't lying when I told you I love you. I want to be with you for the rest of our lives. Money's not important to me the way it seems to be to you, because it can't buy happiness, cliché though that may be, and all yours ever seems to have done is come between us.

He checked in at Terminal Three in good time, surrendering the case with relief. He bought a copy of the *Independent* and sat, trying to read it, in the departure lounge while he waited for his flight to be called.

Please don't take my leaving as meaning that I don't forgive you, darling. I do. That is not the issue. If you can't trust me, if we can't trust each other, then perhaps I must walk away, take the terrible pain that will give me in the short term over the unending pain of knowing that you don't really believe in me.

Well, that's what I've got to think over. Location shooting

starts in Dorset on September 28th and I'll be back a few
days before that. I'll be in touch then. Take care.

The most difficult part of the letter had been how to sign
himself. He'd settled on:

Your loving Matty

As cruel as God

"Can I come in?"

"Have you got a warrant?"

"That's very funny." Henry walked past her into the hall. "You should put a bit more of your sense of humour into your books. White, please, no sugar."

"What's that supposed to mean?"

"That's how I drink my coffee."

"There's lots of humour in them."

"Black humour, maybe. You're hard on your characters. Why don't you let them be happy? It's like reading Thomas Hardy: the two of you as cruel as God to your creations."

He walked into the kitchen.

She began spooning coffee into the filter, not questioning his right to treat her house like a café. You couldn't dislike a man who read Hardy. She thought about what he'd said.

"I do let them be happy. Sometimes."

He sat down at the breakfast bar. "Let them be happy, Zoe. Let yourself be happy."

"What do you want, Henry?"

"I thought you'd like to know that Paul McIver has been asking questions about you."

"What!"

"Paul McIver, shares a flat with Matthew Groves."

"Yes, I know who he is. I've met him. Twice. What do you mean, questions? How do you know?"

"You didn't need to employ Jerzi Topolski to check up on Matthew Groves for you. I'd have done it for free, but then you're a rich woman, as you pointed out the night we met, and Jerzi could use the work. He and Marta have got six kids, all still at school."

"I don't believe you."

"Yes." He counted them off on his fingers. "There's Mikey, Roman, whose godfather I am, Eva, little Sophie—"

She yelled at him. "Henry!"

"Sorry. You do believe me, Zoe. You know you do. I wouldn't lie to you."

"I used to think West London was a big place; now it's like some gossipy village where everyone knows everyone else's business."

"I told you, we watch everybody all the time. Did you think I was joking? Anyway, even though you chose not to employ me, I decided to do a bit of snooping off my own bat, ask a few questions of people on my manor—"

"I thought you didn't use that term."

"Must have picked it up from you. Hope I don't catch any other bad habits. As I was saying, I asked around about Groves and, almost incidentally, about McIver only to find, to my surprise – or was it? – that *he* – McIver – had been asking questions about *you*."

"And what questions exactly has Paul McIver been asking about me?"

"Do you own this house? How many copies do your books sell and what does that translate to in terms of annual income? Was your husband well insured? Had he family money? That sort of thing."

"Jesus!" She sat down opposite him as the coffee machine began to gurgle, forcing water through the grounds. She felt as if someone had hit her hard in the guts with a medicine ball.

Henry said, "You look beautiful today." He reached across the breakfast bar and took her hand in both of his. He kissed it, his fingers stroking her wrist so lightly that it made her shiver.

"Stop it, Henry!" She jerked her hand away. "I . . . what the hell am I supposed to make of that?"

"Merely a tribute to a fascinating woman."

"If you don't stop wilfully misunderstand everything I say . . . well, I won't be responsible for my actions."

"You know what to make of it, my love. God knows, you're not stupid. Groves and McIver, they're playing for high stakes.

183

It's one thing Groves taking a bit of money off you for the odd shag, quite another the pair of them taking you for a ride for a third of what you have."

She repeated stupidly, "A third?"

"That's what the divorce courts would give Groves a couple of years down the line." She stared at him in disbelief. "You think no one is that calculating, don't you?" He shook his head. "I wish I'd retained my innocence that far into middle age, but I couldn't afford it."

"And I wouldn't be cursed with your cynicism at any price. I can assure you that I've no intention of rushing up the aisle with Matty or anybody else. For a start I'd lose the widow's pension from my husband's old firm. It's only ten thousand a year—"

"*Only* ten thousand," he mocked her. "How the other half do live."

"Six thousand after tax, but it's better than a poke in the eye with a sharp stick."

"Five hundred quid a month," he agreed. "So that's two and a half goes at Mr Groves, or was when he was still charging you for it. Is that enough?"

"Nowhere near."

"No, you strike me as a hot-blooded woman. I like that. Is it index-linked?" She didn't answer and he continued, "Groves is a bad lot and you know it. Why else did you set Jerzi on him?"

"I . . . find it hard to trust people nowadays."

"Sure you do. Everyone does. And why? Because people aren't trustworthy. The moral order is now the moral chaos and it's every man for himself. When Jerzi started out, not much more than five years ago, it was nearly all divorce work. Now he spends half his time working for single women who want their boyfriends checked out. It's like they're getting the divorce in before the wedding."

"Really? Lots of women do that?" She'd thought she was uniquely evil in what she'd done. This revelation was cheering.

Henry didn't think so. "What basis for a relationship is that? If you can't love someone, if you can't trust your instincts?

But you can always trust a policeman. Didn't your mother tell you that when you were little? Still, they're talking about making prenuptial agreements legally binding in this country. Did you know that?"

"I suppose I saw something about it in the papers."

"So that people like you can get married to someone you don't trust an inch in perfect safety. What a step forward. Marriage without the bother of true commitment, of sharing, of 'for better, for worse'."

He looked at his strong hands on the counter. "One puzzling thing: I take it you know Groves has left the country in something of a hurry."

"Don't be so melodramatic, Henry. He's gone to visit his parents in New Zealand. As for the hurry, as you call it, he had to fit the visit in before he starts filming at the end of the month."

"Oh." Henry was disappointed. "Filming," he muttered.

"Yes, an important part in a big British film."

"Isn't that a contradiction in terms?"

The coffee machine stopped spluttering. She resented his presence, wondering why she let him interfere in her life. She got up, poured coffee for him and added milk. She tried to slam the fridge door shut but the soft strip of insulation wouldn't permit it.

She said, "Drink it and go."

On the doorstep he grabbed her and kissed her.

She was about to struggle, then could see no reason why she should. He must really fancy his kissing technique if he was prepared to put it to this sort of test and there were better ways to punish him for his presumption.

And for bringing her such bad news.

She slid her arms round his neck, pressing her body closer against his and opened her mouth to his hard little tongue. She heard him give a grunt of surprise and he redoubled his efforts. It was not unpleasurable and she felt a spasm of desire shoot through her. She ground her pelvis into his, testing the size and strength of his erection against her belly.

Nothing there to disappoint a woman.

185

Which was one of those sentences which had two dia-
metrically opposed meanings, like the Lass of Richmond
Hill whose "charms all other maids surpass". The thought
made her giggle, which Henry appeared to mistake for an
encouraging wriggle.

When he released her, he looked into her laughing eyes and
said softly, "Damn it."

"Something wrong, Henry?"

"I shouldn't have done that. I've just made it harder for
myself."

"Yes, I can feel. So, why don't you take your hard-on round
to Joanna's, like you usually do."

She watched in amusement as several pennies dropped into
their allotted slots and for a second she thought he was going
to slap her, then he wheeled round and walked away without
looking back.

Anyone who took on Henry would have to be in need of a
sparring partner as well as a lover, she thought, as she stood
on the doorstep with her arms folded, watching him go up the
road and out of sight.

Send on the substitute

S he answered the phone that evening with a breathless,
"Hello."

"Zoe? It's Paul McIver here."

"Oh." Why was she too well brought up to demand answers
from him? Too frightened of confrontation, something she'd
backed away from all her life? Why have you been spying on
me? Does Matty know? Have you been doing it for him? Is
there a conspiracy, the way Henry makes out?

Feebly, she said, "Hello."

"I wondered if, with Matt away in New Zealand, you were
wanting a bit of alternative company."

It took a second for his meaning to register, then she was
speechless for a moment. Icily, she said, "No, thank you," and
put the phone down gently, lest she smash it in her fury.

She couldn't sleep that night, thrashing and turning as if she
was the thin-skinned princess and her mattress full of peas.
The room was too hot, too cold, too light, too dark. The bed
was too empty. The four a.m. blues Oliver had called it, usually
brought on by one glass of wine too many the night before. For
months after his death she hadn't needed alcohol to give her
sleepless nights, but since late April, since Matty, her sleep
had been long and dreamless.

Her head spun in a stream of words and images, conver-
sations and faces. Paul McIver and Matthew Groves. Matthew
Groves and Paul McIver. What Henry said was absurd, wasn't
it? That Matty was only pretending to be in love with her,
planning to win her trust and love, then take her for everything,
or a third of everything.

She could still hear Septimus All Forlorn's voice, shaky to

match his hands, as he stared at her with that damaged gaze and said, "She must be fucking loaded." Was that what Matty saw when he looked deep into her eyes – a load of pound signs like in a cartoon?

But she loved him. She longed for him to come back to her with a desperate, aching longing. Mightn't it be worth it, if he was prepared to give her a few years of happiness in exchange?

No. If he didn't love her then it could never be more than a worthless illusion.

She turned on her back and slid her hand between her legs, her fingers rubbing in rhythmic circles. Here at least might be relief, some chance of sleep. But ease was a long time coming, flirting with her, coming close then slipping quietly away again, and before long her hand grew tired and she realised that it wasn't going to happen tonight, not like this, not on her own.

She gave up and lay panting, gnawed by frustration.

Even the departure for New Zealand could be nothing more than a clever move in the game. Back away, make her think she was losing him, only to come in hard later and sweep her off her feet.

She wished she hadn't rung the escort agency that day, had never seen their advert. She wished Matty had been booked up that evening. She could have been escorted by some amiable young man who hadn't a hope in hell of getting in under her guard, because it had been a good guard.

She wished . . . No, she didn't.

She turned on her right side. Beyond the open window the garden was noisy – creaks, wheezes, things she'd never normally hear – and Trefor was barking as if a long way off. How was anyone meant to sleep with all that racket going on?

It dawned on her that Henry had started paying court to her only after he'd rummaged through her assets in the safe that evening, and had learned of her successful alter ego. Who could you trust? Not even a policeman. But then she realised – because she was a reasonable woman – that he hadn't had the *chance* to pay court to her before that, given that they'd only just met. Henry wasn't a gifted actor and the wanting in his eyes was unmistakable.

The safe. Surely Matty had heard her say that night that the deeds to the house were in the safe, so why would he need to ask if she owned it? Or had she mentioned the deeds only when she was in the study with the two policemen? She couldn't for the life of her remember.

And she only had Henry's word for it that Paul had been snooping. Henry had said at Marble Hill that he wasn't going to give up that easily, so what better way to foster the suspicions that he knew from Jerzi still haunted her? Could he be so devious, so ruthless in what he wanted?

Somebody was deceiving her. But who?

It nagged at her all the next day too, keeping her from either work or relaxation, and all evening until eleven. Then she caved in and phoned her usual minicab firm. The doorbell rang in less than ten minutes. She didn't recognise the driver, not one of her regulars, and got the impression of a sandy-haired man in his thirties, a beer belly and a cheery grin.

"Hammersmith was it, luv?"

"Yes please."

He had a London accent and wore jeans, T-shirt, trainers. He wasn't going to stand out in an identity parade. She got into the front seat – she liked to see where she was going – and fastened her belt. He drove at speed but more than competently and they were turning the corner into Overstone Road before half past. He drew to a halt and she paid the five pounds requested and added a pound coin by way of a tip.

She was about to unfasten her seatbelt when she saw a couple turn the corner from Glenthorne Road and pass under a street lamp. She froze in her seat, her hand poised over the release mechanism. It was Paul McIver with a woman. A woman who was neither young nor attractive. A punter, in other words, no doubt with an unsuspecting husband at home so that he had to bring her back to his place.

Paul had his arm round her shoulder and she was laughing, her pert face turned up to his.

He stopped for a second and kissed her and the woman's

hand uninhibitedly groped at his crotch. The overhead light illuminated his handsome face as the kiss ended and Zoe saw what his companion evidently could not: the look of distaste in the curl of his mouth and the proud flare of his nostrils.

She turned her head away as they came past the taxi in case they saw her, even absorbed in each other as they were, then said, "I've changed my mind. Could you take me back to Richmond, please."

He looked at her hard. "You're the boss."

She could cope with Paul on his own – she would have made herself cope – but not with this unknown and pathetic woman.

The driver did a three-point turn in silence and drove away. She was wrapped up in her thoughts but after a moment she glanced up and saw that he'd turned down a blind alley, a short road lined with garages, narrow with parked cars, devoid of lighting.

He stopped the cab at the far end, where it was as dark as it ever is in London on a cloudy and moonless night, and switched his headlights off. They sat with the engine smoothly ticking over, not moving. His silhouette was large.

"I don't think this is the way," she said as calmly as she could, although her heart was pounding.

"Nigger two-timing you?" he said it in a pleasant, friendly tone, as if he was commenting on the weather. That's what they're like."

"I beg your pardon?"

"You changed your mind when you saw the sambo with the other woman. You want to stay away from that type, luv. Get yourself a reputation."

"I don't like that sort of talk." Like all educated people she thought she could reason with men such as this one.

"Everyone knows what sort of white woman hangs around with niggers: slags, that's what sort. It's not true about them, you know. You don't want to swallow that myth." His hand was on her arm now, tight. He sneered. "You got a big mouth, come to think of it. Bet you can swallow it. Whole."

Horrified by the poison spewing from him and its implications, she managed to twist out of his grasp and wrench open the passenger door, only to realise that she still wore her seatbelt. He lunged across her to drag the door shut, and he was strong. It disturbed her how much stronger men were, even when they weren't particularly big or heavily built.

He said, "You want a proper seeing-to, darling? You got it."

His breath was hot on her neck, his right hand clutching her left breast, his fingers digging like talons into her flesh. She felt paralysed with fear but knew that she had to keep calm, to stay in control, that panic was the last thing she needed.

"Come on," he said, fumbling for the zip of her trousers. "It's not like you're fussy. Not if you'll do it with a fucking darkie."

She saw a car judder to a stop at the end of the road at that moment, perhaps twenty yards away. It extinguished its headlights and three young women got out, talking and laughing, shrill, happy, the passengers a little drunk. Zoe lunged for the steering wheel and blasted the horn in a long continuous roar. The girls turned to see what was happening. Then she pushed the door open with all her strength and screamed for help.

The driver swore violently, clicked her seatbelt loose and, with one brutal shove, had her out of the car onto her hands and knees in the road. He swung round, sideswiping a parked Volkswagen with a crunch that seemed to fill the night, put his headlights on full beam to blind, and charged back up the road as some instinct made Zoe roll out of his way into the gutter.

The three young women came running towards her as fast as their high heels and tight skirts would allow.

"My God!" the first one said. "Are you all right?"

"I think so." She examined her grazed palms, feeling oddly detached. "No permanent damage."

"What happened?" the second asked.

"Let's get her up before you start bombarding her with questions," the third said. She helped Zoe to her feet and Zoe promptly sat down again on the high kerb as her legs failed to support her. Girl Three, the most practical, crouched next to her and asked, "Do you need an ambulance?" Her tone was gentle, as if Zoe was very fragile.

191

She shook her head, realising that none of these women was more than twenty-five, almost young enough to be her daughters. She felt incalculably old. "Thank you so much," she said. "You've been very kind. I'm all right now."

"Did he get your bag?" Girl One asked.

"No, I didn't have one." She patted her jacket pockets, finding house keys and purse, as expected.

"That was lucky," Girl Two said. She was carrying a bag so huge it must contain most of her worldly goods.

"We're taking you to the police station," Girl Three said.

"Oh, I'm sure that isn't necessary."

"Don't be absurd." The third woman was brisk. "You're unharmed but he may try it with someone else. It's not far to the police station and we have our car here."

Zoe knew she couldn't resist – that it was, as her Good Samaritan said, her duty to report the incident to the police, however much she wanted to go home and forget it had ever happened. She allowed herself to be inserted into the back of their Renault Five and driven to the police station.

Girl Three, the organiser, whom she now knew to be called Esther, went in with her, leaving her friends to go home. There were no other customers and Zoe began explaining as best she could to the desk sergeant, a plain and capable-looking woman in her mid-thirties, what had happened, although she had difficulty knowing where to start and the police-woman kept patiently asking her to calm down and take it slowly.

"I'll deal with this, Penny," said a voice from somewhere in the nether regions behind the sergeant, a voice Zoe knew at once.

She exclaimed, "Henry! Thank goodness."

He came forward into view, standing behind the desk beside the woman, his hands in his trouser pockets, his expression unreadable. "That's not what you said last time you saw me."

"Not really your thing, sir," the sergeant said eyeing them both doubtfully. "It's an assault."

"Leave it to me. Get someone from Richmond round to the minicab firm right away. I want that scumbag in custody within the hour. Miss . . . ?" He looked with polite enquiry at Esther.

"Rosenblum, Esther Rosenblum."

"If you'd be good enough to give your address and phone number to the sergeant, Miss Rosenblum, someone will be in touch to take your statement, probably tomorrow."

He turned back to Zoe. "Let's get you cleaned up. It's all right. I'm trained in first aid."

She followed him meekly and he led her to a room marked "Doctor" and made her sit down. He didn't speak as he ran tepid water into a kidney dish and mixed in some iodine. He dabbed balls of cotton wool in the mixture and swabbed her hands clean of grit and gravel.

She flinched at the first touch of the disinfectant but said nothing and he said, "There's a brave girl."

"Thank you, Henry. It makes me feel heaps better being treated like a six-year-old."

And in an odd way, it did.

He held her hands under the light and peered at them, dabbing until he was satisfied they were clean. "They'll heal up fast enough in the fresh air," he said. "Bit sore for a few days." Then he knelt and inspected the rip in the left knee of her trousers.

"Very fashionable that," he remarked.

"On a teenager, maybe."

He tore more of the material away, careful where some had stuck to the blood of a small gash. "I fear these are ruined." He swabbed her knee and put a sticking plaster over the cut, without offering to kiss it better. Satisfied at last, he said, "Let's adjourn somewhere less antiseptic."

He led her through an open-plan office that was presently deserted. "I was just going home," he explained, flicking on strip lights as he went. They reached a cubicle cut out of a corner of the office with movable wall panels, the top halves clear plastic. "Not exactly private," he remarked, "they like to make sure I don't drop off to sleep in here."

He gestured her to sit on the black leather swivel chair behind the desk and pulled a hard chair up next to her. "Now," he said gently, "start at the beginning."

She explained about her sudden decision to confront Paul with what he'd told her. "I was in two minds. I'm not good at confrontation."

"You could have fooled me. You're bolshie enough when I'm around."

"But when I saw him in the street he had someone with him." Henry made no reply, waiting for her to continue. "A woman. A . . . a client."

"Oh," he said neutrally, "a client. You could tell."

"I could tell."

"One can. Some poor, depraved, desperate creature, no doubt."

She ignored this. "So I decided to go home, leave it to another day. I didn't realise the driver had turned off the main road until . . . I suppose I was lost in thought. He misunderstood what he'd seen and he started saying all these terrible things – racist, sexist things about the sort of women who went with black men, the kind of bigotry that you don't expect to hear on the threshold of the twenty-first century . . . I'm sure you know the sort of thing."

"I know it very well and hear it all the time, occasionally from my own men. Me, I've met a lot of very unpleasant black men in my years on the job and a lot of equally unpleasant white men. Your driver must have low self-esteem, not to mention a very small penis."

She snorted a laugh, the numb shock of the evening's events suddenly dispersing like mist in sun, to leave her shaking with mingled terror and mirth. "Thank God I didn't get to find out." She began to giggle. "Oh, no! He did say I'd be able to swallow it whole."

"Good job you got your fist to his horn."

And now they were both giggling helplessly in Henry's office, hanging on to each other like riders on a roller coaster. Their faces were very close together and for a second she thought he was going to kiss her, but he'd learned his lesson.

"Minicabs aren't safe," he said, pulling himself together.

"Rubbish! I use them all the time. I use that firm all the time. Though I won't again."

"You should learn to drive, much safer for a lone woman."

"I *can* drive. Why do people assume that anyone who doesn't own a car is some sort of a freak?"

He got up. "Well, I'll take you home. Unless you'd rather walk. It's only – what? – seven or eight miles along the river."

"No, not this time. Thank you, Henry."

"I'll need a full statement. Tomorrow will do, though."

At the front desk the sergeant known simply as Penny said, "No sign of the driver, sir, or the car. He could be fifty miles away by now. The minicab firm say he was somebody's mate's brother's mate and they took him on because they were desperate, what with being short handed for the summer holidays. They're not even a hundred per cent sure of his name."

"Surely they checked his driving licence, at least."

"Not so's you'd notice, apparently. They seem utterly mortified, kept saying what a good customer Mrs Kean is."

"Not any more," Henry said. "You could sue them for damages, Zoe."

"What would be the point of that?"

His Rover was comfortable with wide soft seats. As they drove along the A4 she said, "They're opening Hammersmith Bridge again next year, so you must be a happy man."

"I'll believe it when I see it. Anyway, I've changed my mind about that – about the thing I want most in the world." He glanced sideways at her but she wasn't going to ask. She already knew what he would say if she did. After a moment he said, "You never told me the one thing in the world you would wish for."

"For Oliver to be alive, I suppose. For him not to have been on that particular mountain on that particular day, to have set out five minutes earlier, even, or five minutes later."

"I meant something within the bounds of possibility," he said gently.

"Oh, then to be happy."

"I refer the honourable lady to my last answer."

"It is possible, Henry. It is. If you don't believe that then it's not worth bothering to go on." He didn't reply and after a moment she said, "I'm sorry about the other day."

"Yesterday?"

"Was it? It seems like ages. I'm sorry about yesterday."

"No, it was my fault. I'm not in the habit of grabbing women in that Me-Tarzan way."

"Only I'd like us to be friends."

"Oh, I just love it when a beautiful woman says that to me." They came down off the A4 onto the Chiswick roundabout and he said, "I didn't know you knew Jo."

"She came to me for counselling when her mother died."

"Ah! The dark family secret that seems so irrelevant to poor, insensitive, male me, as if it made Jo suddenly a different person. I didn't know you did that. Must be very worthwhile, helping other bereaved people."

"That's not why I do it. I do it because it helps me."

"Well, that's honest."

"It helps fill the long evenings, for one thing."

"Your evenings seem to me to be full of drama. This is your second appearance at Hammersmith Police Station in as many months. You're like a soap opera."

"I suppose you disapprove of counselling."

"No."

"Joanna didn't stay long in therapy, but we became friends."

"Small world," Henry said. "Damnably small world." They were crossing Kew Bridge now, heading towards Kew Green, the lights of West London gradually fading along the riverside as people settled to sleep. "For the record it's a good six months since I last slept with Jo and if she says different then that's just wishful thinking."

"It isn't any of my business."

"It could be."

"No, Henry, it can't."

He stopped outside her house and undid his seatbelt. "I'm going to see you safely inside and I don't want any arguments."

"You weren't going to get any. Thank you."

He saw her in, switching on lights for her until the place felt safe and comfortable, until there were no dark corners, until it felt like home. He refused the offer of coffee or a drink and turned to go. She felt very alone at that moment and wanted to ask him to hold her, but knew that that wouldn't be fair.

"Want to tell me the real reason Groves has left?" he asked in the hall.

"I told you—"

"I know what you *said*. I also know if I was him and everything in the garden was lovely it'd take all the wild horses in England to tear me away from you."

He was waiting for her to answer and there seemed no point in lying to him; indeed, no possibility of doing so. "He found out about Jerzi Topolski."

Henry said evenly, "That was careless."

"Well, I'm not practised in deceit."

"And he took umbrage?"

"Wouldn't you?"

"Certainly. So has he gone for good?"

"No."

Henry said, "Pity!" and left without further ceremony.

She went upstairs and showered, soaping herself over and over especially in the places the man had touched her. Her breasts felt swollen and sore. When she got out, she wrapped herself in a towel. She wiped the steam from the mirror and looked at herself. Then she showered again.

She still didn't feel clean.

Neighbourhood Watch

Henry got back in his car and started the engine. Then he switched off the ignition and sat thinking. What bothered him was that the scumbag minicab driver knew where Zoe lived. He hadn't wanted to mention this to her for fear of alarming her unduly, so he couldn't be sure that she was on her guard. Only a fool would come looking for more trouble with the charges this bloke was facing, but then he hadn't sounded like the brightest bulb in the box.

It was a warm night. He could stay here on sentry duty until it was properly light, then go home and get a few hours kip before turning up for work again at two tomorrow afternoon. He restarted the car, drove down to the bottom of the road to turn round and came back up, parking a few yards below her house where he had a clear view of it.

He reclined his seat a few degrees and lay back against the headrest, his face turned towards the house. A gentleman, he thought, doing knightly service for his lady.

What was it about her that obsessed him? He'd had his fair share of women over the years – probably a few other blokes' shares, come to that – but, until now, only Joanna had had anything like this effect on him. He thought about Zoe: that combination of toughness and vulnerability; the way her shining hair moved as she walked, falling like a heavy curtain to her bony shoulders; the way her dark eyes flashed anger at him.

Tonight there had been something like affection in her eyes. How would they look at orgasm, at that moment when, however equal the relationship in other ways, a woman gave herself up to her man?

Now he had an erection. Fat lot of use that was.

198

He realised that he hated Matthew Groves, not because he'd possessed Zoe's body – a man came reluctantly to terms with the idea that he'd had predecessors – but because he'd somehow taken root in her heart.

Zoe: he'd looked it up in the dictionary. It meant "life", probably as in life sentence in his case.

After about half an hour he saw the last of the lights go off in her house. No one had come up or down the road since he'd been here. He glanced at his watch, the dial illuminated. It was nearly two a.m. It would be light in four hours and he could go home with a clear conscience. What would she think if she looked out of the window and saw him sitting here? Decide that he really was a stalker, probably.

He knew that her bedroom was at the back, on the quiet side of the house with the view over the garden and into the deer park beyond, so there was little danger of his being spotted.

An offensively coloured Chevrolet came silently down the road at that moment, taking up most of the carriageway so that Henry feared for his wing mirror. But it stopped above him, outside Zoe's. He slid a few inches down in his seat, alert, and watched as a fat man wearing evening dress and carrying what appeared to be a puppy got out of the right-hand door – the passenger side, as Henry quickly realised – shut it without slamming, like a model citizen, and went into the house next to Zoe's. The Chevvy then reversed adroitly back up to the Green and disappeared.

Odd combination: evening dress and puppy. Strange accessory. Looked like a yappy little thing. Henry liked dogs that did things, earned their keep: rounding up livestock, sniffing out drugs and explosives, stopping blind people from bumping into him in the street.

After two minutes the fat man came out of the house again with the puppy on a lead and walked down the road towards the river, looking neither to right nor left as he went, his patent-leather evening shoes squeaking rhythmically as he passed the recumbent policeman. They were gone only a few minutes, returning in time to encounter an even fatter man, also in evening dress, at their front gate. The driver of the Chevvy, Henry deduced, its paintwork now safely garaged away from the ministrations of small and not-so-small boys with gouging implements and against the envy of less happier motorists.

The two men kissed gently as they stood on their front path under a laurel tree and the fatter one caressed the not-so-fat one's face with his sausage fingers. Henry thought they exchanged a few words but if so it was in an inaudible murmur. The puppy lifted its front paws hopefully up to the thinner one's knees and let out a soft yapping demand for attention. The fatter man picked it up and they all went indoors.

Domesticated queers, Henry who was no more than averagely homophobic thought. They seemed happy. He couldn't bring himself to envy them.

He'd been a Jack the lad in his twenties but he'd been faithful to Jo while their marriage lasted, even though he worked in a culture where fidelity meant not being found out. It hadn't been difficult, so perhaps he shouldn't pride himself on it. They'd been good together. They'd had rows, sure – what couple didn't? – but the day she'd said calmly that she thought it would be better if he moved out, she might as well have taken a knife and thrust it into his guts and twisted.

He'd been a good husband, by his own standards, by most people's standards, surely: working hard to support his wife and sons; doing his share of looking after them, given the demands of his job; loving them all. But on that horrible day she'd accused him of being obsessed with his work, of neglecting her and the boys, and he'd been too stunned to put up an effective defence so that the jury had found him guilty by default.

He'd dated a few women in the last two years, mostly because he thought he ought to, because he was too young to accept that his romantic life was over, but none of them had lasted, none had progressed beyond a casual meal in a pub or a trip to the cinema.

Then meeting Zoe, seeing her sitting there in the police station so cool and self-possessed, the sheer audacity of her explanation of the four hundred pounds, her defiance as she'd looked him in the eye and challenged him to despise her, there'd been the same sensation of falling off a cliff that he'd experienced the afternoon he'd met Jo at a carol concert at St Anne's on Kew Green.

Not that he would have gone to such a thing normally. Serendipity had guided his steps there. It had been one of those perfect winter afternoons just before the solstice, cold and crisp and dry, the sun a yellow disc dropping rapidly in the south-west. December 17th, a Saturday, a date imprinted on his brain. He'd set out after a late lunch to walk along the river from his digs in Putney as far as Kew. He'd intended to catch the train back from Kew Bridge but the Green had looked so beautiful in the distance as the day faded, he'd made a detour.

He'd seen that there was a carol concert on at the church. You had to pay but it was already half over and no one was checking tickets any more so he'd slipped in at the back, justifying it by telling himself that the church wasn't actually losing any money by it. He'd slid into a pew next to a plumply pretty woman with brittle hair, so blonde as to be almost silver, and she'd whispered, "I'm glad someone was even later than me."

He wasn't one to waste such an opportunity. He'd taken her for a drink at the Rose and Crown and they'd conversed in the steamy warmth under the noise of pre-Christmas jollity. She'd talked knowledgeably about music so that it actually made sense to him for the first time. She'd asked for a pint of beer and he'd never been out with a woman who drank beer before. He'd started out hoping for a one-night stand and ended up seeing her home, kissing her chastely goodnight on the doorstep and arranging to take her to dinner the following weekend.

They'd been married on Valentine's Day and his colleagues had crowed gleefully that Henry Never-Tell-'em-Your-Real-Name Dacres was tamed at last. He'd gone into this family-making business with a whole heart, bought the house in Kew Foot Road on what had been a crippling mortgage at the time, affordable only because the old lady who'd owned it for forty years had left it almost derelict on her death, if structurally sound.

They'd pretty much camped out in it for two years while

he did the necessary repairs and alterations himself, unable to afford to pay anyone to do it, fitting it in around the overtime he begged whenever possible. He hadn't begrudged any of it because it had been for her, Joanna, and for Stevie and, later, for little Adam.

He'd got her on the rebound, of course, when some Worthless Bastard had finished messing her about, but that had surely not been why the marriage failed, not after ten long years.

What was it with women and Worthless Bastards?

Stevie was the WB's child, but no one knew that except him and Jo, nor ever would – apart from Marta Topolski, who knew everything and said nothing. Jo told him she was pregnant on their fourth date, some time after New Year, explaining that was why she couldn't see him any more. He'd said, "I mustn't have been paying attention when my dad gave me that little talk about the birds and the bees: I got the impression I had to shag a woman to get her up the duff, not just hold her hand."

"Make a woman laugh," was what his father had actually advised, "and you'll be in her knickers while the good-looking bloke's still combing his hair." Jo had laughed that night and when he'd pointed out that if they got married soon everyone would assume the child was his, she'd found no way of turning him down.

She told him later that her flatmate had suggested she bed him and fool him the baby was his, but she was incapable of such deceit, horrified at the idea of it. He'd been indignant that anyone should think he'd fall for that old trick.

He'd been a father to Stevie in every meaningful sense, the other man nothing but a sperm donor. He'd been there when Stevie was born, supporting and encouraging Joanna, and cradled the newborn in his arms – the first baby he'd ever held – and had thrilled with love for him.

All these years he'd loved him no less than his own son. Indeed, he often felt he loved him more, since Stevie seemed so much more in *need* of love than Adam, who had a happy self-sufficiency about him.

Jo had been furious to discover recently that her mother and grandmother had lied to her about the circumstances of her own birth, and he hadn't been able to make her see that Stevie's was a similar case and that such subterfuges were born of love.

He was getting cramped, shifting in his seat to stultify other muscles, different joints.

Zoe had some spunk, he thought, going out to confront McIver like that late at night, even if it hadn't panned out the way she'd expected. He admired women who were strong and brave. He'd been furious when his chief inspector, reading his report on the pub raid, had said it was worth turning over this Kean woman's place as she sounded a dodgy article. He'd protested that it was a waste of time and money but had been overruled. He'd been boorish that night, deliberately so. Since this would clearly be the last straw for her, there had been no point in trying to make her like him.

But he'd come back a few days later, like a tongue probing a diseased tooth. He'd sat by the river a hundred yards from her house, pointlessly, as it had seemed, but she'd appeared within hailing distance in less than fifteen minutes. For a moment he'd been unable to speak, convinced that she was an illusion conjured up out of his imagination, there only because he so badly wanted her to be there. Then she'd marched over to confront him, very solid and very real, her arms folded belligerently across her flattish chest, and he'd followed her to the café because he was by that time incapable of doing anything else.

Pointless, it had almost certainly been.

He yawned widely. Not fatigue so much as boredom. Then shut his mouth abruptly as someone tapped on his window. He saw a uniformed PC peering in at him. He must have been preoccupied to let himself be snuck up on like that. Black mark, Dacres. He couldn't lower his window without starting the engine so he opened the door a few inches. The boy – he didn't look old enough to shave – jumped back and put a hand to his baton.

"It's all right, son," Henry said, showing him his warrant card.

"Sorry, sir," the boy whispered. "You on surveillance? Only I wasn't informed and one of the neighbours phoned in a report of a loiterer." He indicated the house next door to Zoe's. So the fat queers hadn't been as absorbed in each other as he'd thought.

"Get in." Henry jerked his head and the young man went round and concertina-ed himself into the passenger seat. He was at least six foot four and looked very uncomfortable, although he'd have made things easier for himself if he'd taken his helmet off. Henry pulled his own door shut. "You see that house?"

The boy looked, his neck dipping for a better view. "With the blue door?"

"I'd like you to keep a good eye on it for the rest of the night."

"All right. I mean, yes, sir."

"If you see a sandy-haired man approaching the house, looking suspicious, don't hang about, shout for help."

"Right you are."

This was the sort of subordinate Henry liked: the sort that didn't ask stupid questions. He said, "Off you go then, lad," and the constable got out of the car and stood looking up at Zoe's house as if expecting it to explode in a ball of fire at any moment.

Henry started his engine and drove off home to bed. On deserted streets it only took a matter of minutes to get there. Zoe would be all right: she always gave as good as she got. If the idiot minicab driver did show up, he'd most likely be the one in need of an ambulance.

A couple of months into the split with Jo he'd stayed late one night after bringing the boys home and they'd ended up in bed together and it had been great, like the early days of their marriage. For a year or more after that he had felt he was living in the best of all possible worlds: a family and regular sex in Richmond, his bachelor existence in East Sheen with all the spare totty he could lay his hands on.

Except that it hadn't worked out that way: there was no shortage of fish in the sea, just a disinclination on his part to reel them in. He wasn't sure why or how his attitude had changed but by the spring of this year it had come to seem like the worst of all possible worlds and, as he had truthfully told Zoe, he hadn't slept with his wife since.

He drew up outside his flat, switched off the lights and engine and got out, slamming the door because he could never remember not to. He must sort it out, settle things with Joanna, one way or another.

Shortly before lunch the owner of the minicab firm turned up on Zoe's doorstep with a vulgarly enormous bunch of flowers. She refused to let him in or listen to his apologies, but the flowers gave her an idea and she went out and bought white and yellow roses and left them soaking in a bucket of water for the rest of the day.

Early that evening she collected the flowers, wrapped them in some gold paper that she'd bought, and took her statement to Henry at his office. She went by tube, which dirty and noisy conveyance suddenly seemed the epitome of safety.

"Those flowers for me?" he asked. "You shouldn't have."

"You'd be mortified if I sent you flowers, Henry."

"Try me."

"This is for you." She reached in her bag and handed him a bottle of her special malt whisky.

"Ah, I thought of buying some of this after I had it at your house, until I saw the price. Thanks, I'll try not to develop a taste for it." He twisted the cap off. "Join me in one now?"

"Thanks, but I'm pretty much on the wagon at the moment."

He told her that the number plate of the missing minicab had been circulated to every police force in the country but that no sightings had yet been reported.

"People can't just disappear, can they?" she asked.

"They can and do. He could have slipped through the channel tunnel and be halfway across France by now. We may have to reconcile ourselves to not catching him, but it's early days yet."

"What will happen if you get him?"

"I shall be pressing for a charge of attempted rape which will mean a custodial sentence if he's convicted, especially if the judge thinks he's a danger to women."

"Is that likely?"

"No," he admitted, "the Crown Prosecution Service will probably settle for a charge of assault."

"And juries tend to acquit on rape charges, anyway."

"True, but you had witnesses, which is unusual. I have to be honest with you: the more time goes by the less likely we are to catch up with him, but we'll keep trying."

"I'd almost rather forget the whole thing, not have to re-live it in court."

"You look tired and pale, my darling. Tell me that creep hasn't broken your spirit."

"That creep hasn't broken my spirit."

"Good."

He gave her Esther Rosenblum's address and she took the flowers round to her with her gratitude. Then she went home and tried once more to shower the smell of that man off herself.

Spring cleaning in September

Zoe went to Tesco and picked up three two-litre plastic bottles of extra-strength bleach. She debated with herself whether she could manage a fourth and decided she couldn't. She would have to make more trips.

She felt itchy all over, as if insects were crawling on her skin where that man had touched her.

The Irish woman at the checkout beamed at her. "Spring claining? Don't you hate it?" and Zoe smiled back and nodded.

Sam rang the bell. When he got no reply he rang again. He stepped back, looked up at the house, then rang again. Still nothing. The adjacent door jerked open and Fat Jim peered over the fence. "Oh, it's you," he said without much enthusiasm, since he was aware of Sam's hostility towards gay men.

Sam said stiffly, "Hello, Mr McLaverty."

"She's in."

"She's expecting me for supper." Sam looked at his watch. "I'm a few minutes late even. I suppose she forgot."

"No, she's in," Jim insisted. "I saw her come in half an hour ago with some shopping, then I heard the bath running fifteen minutes later. I'd have heard if she'd gone out again. Her door sticks and she has to slam it shut."

Sam flourished a wrapped parcel he was carrying. "It's her birthday."

"I know. Jim and I did our barber shop quartet rendition of 'Happy Birthday to You' for her at lunchtime."

"Quartet?"

"We make enough noise for four." Sam pushed in the letter

box and peered through the slit. Jim said, "Maybe she's still in the bath."

"Then I'd hear something, surely. Movement. It feels like an empty house, you know, like where someone has . . . died." The two men looked at each other uneasily. "Oh, dear God!" Sam said softly.

"No!" Jim was more robust. "Not our Zoe."

"Should we break in?" Sam looked at the sturdy door doubtfully.

"I've got a key in case she locks herself out. Just hold your horses." Jim went inside and reappeared at once with two keys, a mortice and a latch. He tried the mortice. "It isn't double locked. More proof that she's in there." He wielded the flimsier key and pushed the door so hard that he almost fell into the hall behind it. "Zoe!" he bellowed up the stairwell. "It's me. Jim."

"And Sam," his companion added.

There was no reply, only a smell like twenty swimming baths at once, and Jim pounded up the stairs with a surprising turn of speed, Sam close behind him. Jim went straight through the master bedroom and into the en suite bathroom in a way that Sam hesitated to do and Sam heard him exclaim, "Oh, dear God!" He hesitated no longer but went in.

"What's she done?" he asked, half panicky. Her naked body looked horribly red and flaky and there were blisters forming in odd places on her limbs but the water was clear, almost unnaturally so, not as if she'd slashed her wrists.

"It's bleach," Jim snapped. "Must be gallons of it. Can't you smell it? Get the shower running, cold water." He used the back of his hand to wipe his eyes which were watering in the fumes.

Sam said, "I'm calling an ambulance."

"No! She'd hate that. You're a fucking doctor. If you can't treat her what fucking use are you?" Jim wrenched the plug out of the bath and bent to lift her. Sam tried to help but Jim barked, "Shower! Cold!" at him.

Sam, knowing the voice of authority, twisted the shower

taps, setting a gush of water free from the head. It was the hot side of warm and he prodded the controls at random until it ran cold. By now Jim had her, holding her beneath the armpits and manhandling her under the cold water, her head falling forward over her chest, his own clothes gradually soaking in the force of the shower.

"Ugh!" she exclaimed after a moment. "It's f-f-f-freezing."

"Tell me about it," Jim panted.

She opened her eyes blearily, red and sore. "Where am I?"

"Sweetie," Jim said, "you tried to take a bath in what must be practically neat bleach. Don't you remember?"

"I wanted to be clean," she murmured. "I couldn't get clean."

Jim and Sam swabbed her body down with the cold water until they were sure all trace of the bleach was gone. Her skin was a fiery red, puffy, and there were a few angry blisters but, "I've seen worse," Jim said, and Sam had to agree. They wrapped her in a bath sheet and Jim carried her into the bedroom and laid her on top of the bed. She wound her arms round his neck. "Never had a bloke strong enough to carry me to bed," she whispered hoarsely. "Always thought how nice it would be." And she fainted.

Jim cleared his throat. He was embarrassed, possibly for the first time in his life. "Well," he said roughly to Sam, "you're the doctor. What now?"

"We treat it like burns," Sam said. "Fresh air is the best thing. And time."

Fat Jim flung the bedroom window open and breathed deep of the railway line.

"I found this in the first-aid cabinet in the other bathroom." They looked round at Thin Jim who was standing in the doorway holding a bottle of calamine lotion. "Any good?"

"I'll put some on the red bits," Sam agreed, "but leave the blisters and the places where she's peeling. I don't want them infected."

Fat Jim went back into the bathroom and shook himself like a dog. Then both Jims watched as Sam anointed her body.

"Didn't know you were so far out, love," Thin Jim murmured, stroking the hair back from her face. "We thought you were just waving."

Sam, the bottle empty, placed the towel lightly over her, wanting to cover her from the Jims which was absurd, he knew, since neither of them had the slightest interest in looking at naked women. So perhaps it was from his own greedy eyes that he was protecting her.

"I think we all need a drink," Fat Jim said. "Sam?"

"I'll be down in a minute. I want to be sure she's going to be okay. I'll take her to casualty in a second if I think it's the right thing to do."

"Hours hanging about with a load of low-life," Thin Jim said.

"And we should know," Fat Jim said. "Nights we've spent there when some dickhead at one of the clubs has too much to drink and a bloody good fight. We'll be in the sitting room."

Sam joined them ten minutes later. The Jims had helped themselves to medicinal doses of Zoe's Clynelish. They looked at Sam expectantly.

"She seems to be sleeping easily now," he said, "breathing fine. You should get out of those wet clothes, Jim."

Fat Jim shrugged. He'd placed a sheet of newspaper on the carpet to drip on. "We can't leave her."

"We're not going to. The bed in the spare room's made up. I'll sleep there tonight."

"What about your darling little girl?" Thin Jim asked.

"In Somerset with her grandparents."

The Jims looked at each other then nodded. "That sounds like the best solution," Fat Jim said. "One of us will take over in the morning. Whisky?"

"Why not?"

"What do you think brought this on?" Thin Jim asked Sam, as he poured him a drink. "Problems with Matthew?"

"If this is down to him," Fat Jim burst out, "I shall tear him into little pieces. And then tear the pieces into littler pieces. And then eat them."

"Matthew?" Sam said. "I don't know any Matthew."

The Jims looked at each other again, the complicit glances of the established couple that said so much in such small ways. "He seems to be a boyfriend," Fat Jim ventured. "I mean," he went on a trifle apologetically, "what with us living next door we see most of the comings and goings. Seen him around here a good few times this last couple of months."

"Every day for a while but not these last two weeks," Thin Jim added.

"I had no idea," Sam said glumly. "She didn't confide in me."

"He seemed such a nice boy," Thin Jim said sadly. "Young. Pretty. She looked so happy. Like she hasn't looked since poor Ollie went and fell off that stupid hill."

"Figure they've had a falling out?" Fat Jim asked.

"I've no idea," Sam said.

"Dad?" A voice floated in from the hall. They'd left the front door open in their haste.

"In here, son," Fat Jim called, to Sam's immense surprise.

"I didn't know where you'd got to with both of you pounding out the house like that." A shy-looking boy of about seventeen poked his head round the door. He was tall and stringy with short red hair, gelled so that it virtually stood up on end, and a comically strong Glaswegian accent. His eyes widened at the sight of Fat Jim's wet clothes. "Fall in the river again, Dad?"

"Again!" Sam said.

"Just an accident with an overflowing bath," Fat Jim told his son.

Sam said, "You fell in the river?"

"I was drunk," Fat Jim bellowed, as if this constituted an explanation, then, more peaceably, "Sam, this is my son, my youngest." He put his arm round the boy proudly. "Young Jim. Jim, this is Dr Sam Lincoln."

"All right?" Young Jim said, by way of greeting, the last word sounding like "reet".

"Youngest?" Sam echoed.

"I've got five, three boys and two girls."

"Five?" Thin Jim began to giggle and Sam realised he must sound like the village idiot. "Sorry," he said. "I didn't know."

"Took me a while to come to terms with my sexuality," Fat Jim said comfortably. "Meantime I was being a good Catholic boy."

"The Pope can't sleep nights for good Catholic boys like him around," Thin Jim put in.

"What happened about your wife?" Sam asked.

"Oh, she got a Papal annulment on the grounds of my beastly depravity and married a rich bookie."

"Is there any other sort?" Thin Jim said.

"True. They've retired to Marbella now. Young Jim's just stopped off to touch base on his way there. Right, son?"

The boy let off a volley of what might have been fluent Spanish, although it was hard to tell, then lapsed into something resembling English, "Can I have a drink, Dad, if we're having a party?"

"No, you're too young. Anyway, we're going home now." He stuck out his hand to Sam. "We did all right."

"Yes," Sam took his hand and shook it vigorously, "we did."

Sam slept badly, cat napping for perhaps an hour at a time. Whenever he woke up he went to Zoe's bedroom to check on her, taking her pulse and listening to her breathing. He still wasn't certain that she wouldn't have been better off in hospital but by dawn the redness was beginning to fade from her skin and he thought that she couldn't have been in the bath long before Fat Jim hoiked her out.

At half past five she opened her eyes and said softly, "Sam?"

"I'm here." He sat down on the bed and took her hand in his. "Sweetheart, do you remember what happened?"

"Dimly."

"Why didn't you tell me you were near breaking point? I had no idea."

"Nor did I. Surely people are allowed to be depressed on their birthday?"

"That's a novel way of looking at it."

"I'm forty-two today. Yesterday."

"I know, but that's nothing these days."

"It is when you're only twenty-eight. It's old. Your thirties. They last a really long time."

"Who's only twenty-eight?"

"No one. I mean, lots of people are, obviously. It was just an example."

"You're as old as you feel."

"Oh, don't say that."

"Can you tell me what happened?"

She drew in a deep breath and let it out slowly. She told him about the minicab driver, the bare details.

"My God!" he said, when she'd finished, "why didn't you tell me?"

"I thought I was OK about it but I kept feeling dirty where he'd touched me and then tonight . . . I don't know what happened. I'd run out of bleach and I went to get some and for some reason I bought loads of it and then I thought I'd have a bath—"

"Did you forget I was coming for supper?"

"I must have done, and then I thought the bath wasn't clean and I started pouring the bleach in and somehow . . ."

"You're not trying to tell me it was an accident?"

"No, I'm not saying that. I knew what I was doing, at some level." She reached her free hand up and stroked his tense face.

He kissed her blistered fingers. "What are we going to do with you, Zoe?"

"I'll be all right now." Sam looked doubtful. "Don't you see. I've hit the bottom. The only way is up."

"The worst is not, so long as we can say, 'This is the worst.'"

But she had hit the bottom, she knew it, she just wasn't sure which bottom it was: the bottom of the long, steep descent from the death of Oliver, or the short, sharp tumble that was the departure of Matthew and the revelation of Paul McIver's double dealings.

She closed her eyes and he knew he should let her sleep but instead he said, as if reading her thoughts, "Zoe, who is Matthew?"

213

"Matty? He's . . . a man I know."

"The one-night stand you talked of? The ship that passed in the night?"

"In the beginning, perhaps. Not now. Not for a long time."

"Do you love him?"

"I think so."

"You think so? Is it like with Oliver?"

"No, but I don't think it has to be. I think that's the mistake we make of believing it'll always be the same as before, of rejecting anyone who isn't a carbon copy of our first great love. It can't be the same, because we've changed and grown older. I was very young when I met Ollie, very insecure, and needed someone like him, someone steady, stable, even a bit boring, to make me feel safe."

"And has this Matthew hurt you?" It came to Sam in a revelatory shock that, if so, he would hold him down while Fat Jim carried out his threat to tear him into little pieces and eat him.

But Zoe was shaking her head. "No, I hurt him. It was a betrayal."

"Betrayal is a big word."

"What else do you call an inability to trust someone who's offered you his unconditional love?"

"I call it real life."

"I'm a shitty woman who doesn't trust people any more, because I trusted Ollie not to go and die on me and leave me alone and he bloody well went and did it anyway." She began to cry and he hugged her to him and held her tight and she sobbed, "You're hurting me."

"Sorry." He let her go.

"My skin's so raw."

"That was stupid. Forgive me." He leaned forward and she thought he was going to kiss her, which he did, on the forehead. "So, where is Matthew?" he asked.

"New Zealand."

"New Zealand?" He raised his eyebrows and their old, familiar, joking relationship was back. "As far away from here as you can get without actually leaving the planet, in other words. Was it something you said?"

She laughed weakly. "He hasn't emigrated. He'll be coming back in a couple of weeks."

Though not necessarily to her.

Nothing underneath

"**D**ay shift." Thin Jim appeared on the doorstep at eight o'clock nursing another bottle of calamine lotion. "Guess what, we had some of this in our bathroom cabinet as well. Must be stuff you buy for no reason and forget about." He came in. "How is she?"

Sam said, "Okay, I think. People do silly things sometimes."

"You got that right. Young Jim said if you need any help spreading this stuff on her he'd like to volunteer."

"Guess he's not confused about his sexuality," Sam said.

"It's hard for Jim to come to terms with the fact that his favourite son's straight, of course, a blow for any father. You can't help wondering where you went wrong, but he tries to be open-minded." When Sam didn't laugh, he added, "That was a joke, by the way."

"Yes, I know. I have to be at the surgery at nine—"

"That's why I'm here. Is she awake?"

"She was a little while ago."

"I'll make her some breakfast. You get along."

Sam said, "I'll call round later. Lunchtime," and left. Jim went upstairs and tapped lightly on the bedroom door.

"Come in." Zoe was sitting at the dressing table in her blue and white Chinese robe, brushing her hair. "Jim, hello."

"You're up. I thought maybe you'd want to rest today."

"I have things to do."

"Is that a good idea? I was going to make you some breakfast, bring it up on a tray. I can fetch our portable TV, if you like."

"What, so I can watch *Richard and Judy*? You want to drive me mad?"

"Fair point."

"Breakfast is a good idea, though. Just some toast for me, and coffee. I'll be down when I've had a quick shower. Do I look like someone who's been in a house fire?"

He examined the bits of her that were visible. "Someone who's taken a touch of the sun, that's all. And your face is fine." He proffered the calamine lotion and she took it.

"Thanks. I don't think my face went in the bleach." She disappeared into her bathroom, calling, "I'll be down in ten minutes." Jim shrugged and went downstairs to make a fresh pot of coffee and some toast, as requested.

She came down dressed for a day out: a linen, teal-coloured trouser suit with a cream silk blouse, her discoloured limbs carefully covered, cream and teal slingbacks with a low heel. Jim made no comment but watched while she ate two slices of dry toast.

When she'd finished she reached across the breakfast bar and laid her hand over his. "You've been great, Jim, but I have a bit of business to see to now so I'll let you get back to your own life." He opened his mouth to protest but she went on quickly, "I've got to go and see someone, sort a few things out. If you love me, you won't try to stop me."

"Course I love you but . . ."

"Well?"

"Jim'll never forgive me if I let you go out. He'll yell at me. Then I'll yell back and we'll end up splitting up, after all these years, and there'll be a horrible custody battle over Trefor, and he'll be the product of a broken home and grow into the sort of delinquent dog who fouls pavements and bites people and shags their legs, and it'll be your fault and how will you be able to live with yourself?"

"Darling!" She kissed him to shut him up. "You and Jim are the most rock-solid couple I know. OK?"

"OK."

"I'll ring for a minicab." She glanced out of the window. It was a cool day, overcast with a visible breeze. "No, no minicab. I'll take the tube."

When she arrived at the house in Overstone Road she found the street door open and, seeing the names McIver and Groves on the top bell, made her way up the two shabby flights of stairs to the attic floor. A flimsy wooden door had the number 3 on it and no bell so she knocked with her fist.

"Hold on." After a minute or two the door swung open and Paul stood there. "Hey, Zoe. Change your mind about my offer?"

"No." She walked past him without waiting for an invitation. "I want to talk to you." She sat down carefully on an armchair; it looked as if the springs might be dodgy. She glanced round. Her first thought was that it was a dump. It was also her second thought. The flat smelled of sex and of a woman's perfume – Joy by Patou, expensive but rather heavy and old-fashioned. She got up, opened a window and sat down again.

"Make yourself at home," Paul said sarcastically. He shut the door and lounged on the sofa opposite her. "You look smart, businesslike. Going on somewhere?" He was wearing jeans so tight that she could be fairly sure he wore nothing underneath, topped by a red cashmere sweater. Bare feet. He was unshaven. "I only just got up," he added.

"I didn't think you were an early riser. You've been asking questions about me and I want to know why."

Paul reached across to the coffee table and picked up a packet of cigarettes and an old but clearly valuable gold lighter. "Don't suppose you do?" he said, offering her the packet.

"No, and I'm surprised you do."

"Yeah, well I ration myself to five a day and try not to have one before lunch, but today I'm starting early." He sucked a cigarette out of the packet and lit it, tossing the lighter back on the table as if it was worthless. He saw her looking at his taut thighs. "Sure you didn't come to take me up on my offer, Zoe?"

"Quite sure."

"You don't like dark meat? You a racist?"

"I don't like you. Disliking one man who happens to be black doesn't make me a racist."

He laughed and inhaled a long lungful of nicotine, blowing

it out through his nostrils. "That's blunt. I like that." He pushed his free hand up under his jersey and lazily scratched his stomach, making it a sensuous act. He inhaled again and she waited while he tasted the smoke to the full and let it out. He could do all the stage business he wanted; it wouldn't make her forget why she was here. "That's enough of that," he said finally, stubbing his cigarette out, half smoked, in a dirty coffee cup. "Those are nasty blisters on your hands, Zoe. How d'you do that?"

"I'm not leaving here till you tell me what I want to know."

In the thinking time the cigarette had allowed him, he'd decided to call her bluff. "Who says I've been asking questions?"

She called the bluff right back. "The police."

She'd shaken him. "The police?"

"As you guessed the night Matty got arrested, I have friends in high places." She looked him straight in the eye. "You've been asking questions about me, about my personal wealth and income. I find that sinister."

He leaned back against the arm of the sofa. "How old do you think I am?"

"I haven't given it much thought. Why would I? Thirty-five?"

"I'm forty-four."

"So you're wearing well. Congratulations."

"I'm getting old and tired and I want to settle down. After I met you in Kew, Matt let a few things slip about you, or maybe I pumped him – the nice house in the middle of Richmond where property prices are way high, the dead husband, no kids – and I thought you might be what I was looking for. Anyway, you smell of money."

She was incredulous. "I *what*?"

"Oh, yes. It's not a matter of diamond necklaces and Rolex watches and designer threads. It's a look in the eye that says 'I shall never be hungry or cold or homeless'. It says, 'I belong'. And it says, 'Fuck you'."

"If I smell of money I'm surprised you needed to snoop on me."

"I had to be sure, didn't want to put myself out for nothing."
He smiled faintly. "You looked as if you would be kind
to me."

"*Kind* to you?"

"Sure. You think I want to be bond slave to some miserable
harridan?"

Cruelly, she said, "Are you sure you're still up to the job at
your age? I mean, men are different from women, our stamina
doesn't flag the way yours does. Can you earn your keep?"

He replied without rancour. "I can satisfy one woman, as
much as she likes. Think about it."

"I don't need to think about it."

"Well, I thought you might be interested, specially with the
way you were coming on to me at the cricket match—"

"Hey! I was showing a bit of human sympathy over your
hard-luck story."

"Seemed to me like an excuse to paw me about."

"If you can't tell the difference between sympathy and
pawing then you must be a very warped man."

"I shouldn't be at all surprised." He might be forty-four,
going on thirty-five, but his eyes were a hundred years old.
"Anyway, I thought I could take you off Matt if I put my
mind to it."

"But he's your friend."

"No, he isn't. He's my flatmate. It's not the same thing.
He's the fourth white-boy actor I've shared with in the past
ten years. After a while they start to do okay and then they
move out, find somewhere nicer, maybe buy a place. But I'm
still here. Can you name one famous black actor? A British
one, I mean. There are one or two in the States." She thought
about it for a moment till he said, "You can't name a single
one, can you?"

"Not offhand."

"And I have to do gay escort work as well as straight. I
can't be fussy like cute little Matthew because the female
clients are all white and only a minority of them are prepared
to be seen out on the arm of a black trophy boy, even if
they'd secretly like to take him home." He paused, then
added, "I don't go home with the gay clients – maybe

220

a quick blow job in the back of the car if the money's right."

She grimaced. "That's none of my business."

"No, it isn't."

"How much of that stuff you told me at the cricket match was true? About your father losing all his money and killing himself?"

He paused, as if trying to remember what he'd told her. "A substantial amount of that is true. In essence if not in detail. There was money when I was a kid and now there isn't."

"But none of this gives you the right to become a . . . a leach."

"Marry for money? But women do it *all the time*. Well, don't they?"

"Some," she admitted.

"So what right have you got to look down on me?"

"You're just a cheap whore."

"Actually I'm an expensive one."

"And it was you who led Matty into escort work, into prostitution. I suppose it amused you to make him as corrupt as you are."

He looked at her for a moment and his lip curled with what might equally have been amusement or contempt. He said softly, "It's so easy to judge people, isn't it, Mrs Kean? So easy to be honest and decent and honourable when you can afford those virtues."

She was growing tired of his evasions. "Were you asking questions about me on Matty's behalf?"

"I look out for myself because nobody else does."

"That doesn't answer my question."

Now the contempt was unmistakable. "I don't have to answer your questions." He paused for thought. "All I will say is that Matt doesn't need your money. He's in a film, first name after the two stars in the credits. He's got a shit-hot agent – the sort of man who wouldn't bother to return my calls. He's being bought lunch by producers at the best restaurants in town."

"I must go." She got up.

When he didn't move, she added, "I'll see myself out."

221

Back on the street she leaned for a moment against the door, feeling as if she'd run a race. She could have saved herself the trip since she'd learned nothing.

Sam was drinking coffee in Zoe's kitchen when she got home. "You look smart," he said. "Got your business done?"

"In a negative sort of way. Not going to scold me?"

"I was going to bawl Thin Jim out for letting you leave but then I realised it's not as if *I*'d have been able to stop you."

"You were right about the strain of the last couple of years getting too much for me, even if your pressure cooker simile did suck. I didn't want to admit that I wasn't as strong as everyone thought."

"Welcome to the club." He picked up his parcel from the counter. "In all the hoohah I didn't get round to giving you your birthday present."

She took it with a smile of thanks. He'd given her presents before, on her birthday and at Christmas, as she had him. His were usually a book she'd expressed interest in, a new CD by a singer he knew she liked, impersonal tokens. This was too small for a book or CD; more like a jeweller's box. She unwrapped it and prized the box open. It contained an antique brooch, a narrow oblong of silver set with dark red stones.

"It's beautiful."

"Just something I saw in a junk-shop window as I was passing. Made me think of you, of how they'd suit your colouring."

"Sam, how frivolous." She almost added, "What would Chris have said?" but thought better of it. Christine had despised jewellery, except for the narrow gold ring she wore on the middle finger of her right hand, a non-wedding ring. She pinned the brooch to her lapel. It did suit her colouring. She put her arm round his neck and kissed him just below the ear.

He got up. "I must be going. Oh, there was something else I wanted to say. I was wrong about the Jims. They were wonderful last night, so calm and sensible."

"Hardly like a pair of screaming queens at all?"

"They're good people."

"Yes, they are. Although their singing would make a nun curse." She followed him along the hall. "Will you be around over the weekend?"

"No." He looked quietly happy. "I'm going down to Taunton tomorrow night and bringing Annie back on Sunday. Ready for school on Tuesday."

"Good. I've missed her."

"Me too."

"Give her my love and I'll see you both soon."

"You sure you'll be OK?"

"Yes, I have an important letter to write."

She was going to take the advice she'd given Joanna and write an angry letter that could never be sent because the recipient was dead. Maybe a couple of angry letters.

She shut the door behind him. She hoped Sam would open up for business again one day, soon, although she wouldn't be his first customer.

Saying goodbye

My darling Oliver,

I've torn up three drafts of this letter already. I set out to make you understand how angry I am with you, that you fell by the wayside and left me to struggle on without you, that dull John Morrow was the last person to exchange a few friendly and inconsequential words with you, to see your sweet smile.

But I find that I'm not angry after all, or not any more. So, this is to say goodbye and, for the last time, I love you.

Zoe

11th September

Dear Mum,

I should have had the courage to say these things to you years ago, while you could still understand them, but better late than never, even though you won't read this letter and would make no sense of it if you did.

If I had spoken, I can imagine your response: the stony stare, the denial that you had any idea what I was talking about.

So I wasn't the prettiest child in the street, not like you when you were young, but you could have told me I was, could have made me feel that way. You were always a pragmatist and I know you'd say that there's no point in telling an ugly duckling it's a cygnet when the sad fact is that most ugly ducklings grow up to be ugly ducks.

Didn't it ever occur to you watching Dad, how he'd play with me, tickle me, throw me in the air, call me his beautiful princess, that that was what I wanted from you too? But no, you told him not to be so silly, that he was mussing my hair,

224

showing the neighbours my knickers, that he would "give the girl daft ideas".

I suppose I must have loved you as a small child, although I don't remember it. It's very liberating finally to admit to myself that I don't love you and find that the sky doesn't immediately fall in on my head. I don't hate you either and I never have. What I feel now is pity.

I shall keep coming to see you, every Tuesday, for as long as it takes, bringing you presents and kissing your cheek and telling you that Oliver sends his love because, although your body is there in that nursing home, the woman who hurt me and undermined me for all those years has gone, and I'm not going to waste my time punishing the wrong person.

Your dutiful daughter,
Zoe

The second letter, though much longer, needed only one draft.

She read them both through again then, satisfied, she cleared the fir cones from the grate and burned the letters in the fireplace, as she had once burned requests to Santa Claus, knowing no other address. She burned Jerzi Topolski's file as well, the photographs giving off a foul smell, forcing her to open the windows. She left the grate empty. It would soon be the season for lighting fires and maybe she and Matty would roast chestnuts here together this Christmas.

She would go on believing that, for as long as she could.

She went into her study and looked once more at the photograph of Oliver on her desk. She hesitated for some minutes then pressed a small kiss to the glass face and put it in an unobtrusive place on the bookshelves.

She walked down to the river and turned right along the towpath towards Kew. After a few minutes she came to the pale-green and cream metallic angles of Richmond Lock and she climbed the stairs and walked to the middle. The lock was busy and she waited while a pair of young mothers trailed pushchairs and toddlers across and a fat woman with a dog watched it defecate on the walkway before ambling on, shamelessly leaving the mess behind her.

The tide was high, but turning, ripples surging upstream clashing with ripples trying to get back the other way. She took her wedding ring from her finger and let it fall without ceremony into the water and watched it sink.

She didn't know where it would end up – somewhere far out to sea or on a sandy bank in the estuary. It might lie with the fishes or be salvaged with glee by a man with a metal detector who would get a good price for it. What mattered was that it was no longer hers.

When she got home she ordered a stone for the square patch of earth in the burial ground at Mortlake Crematorium, paying over the odds so that it would be ready for the second anniversary of Oliver's death. It read: Oliver John Barclay Kean, then his dates, then the two simple words,

At Rest.

Missed opportunities

Joanna wielded the bottle of Rioja, topping up her own glass, but Henry placed a hand over his. "Two's my limit when I'm driving."

"I thought you might stay the night."

"I've got an early start. In fact—" he glanced at his watch and got up – "I'd better get off." He put on his old tweed jacket and patted the pockets for his keys the way he always did. "Thanks for the meal, Jo. It was great. I'll pick the boys up after lunch on Saturday, yeah?"

She followed him into the hall. "Henry?" He smiled affectionately at her. "I think we should talk – talk properly – about getting back together again, about giving it another try."

"Ah!" He hung his head, examining the hall floor as if he still found the black and white mosaic pattern fascinating after all these years. "I'm afraid that ship has sailed, love."

"What?"

"The moment when that might have happened has passed."

She couldn't believe what she was hearing. "But, it's barely three months since you last asked me."

"More like seven or eight, I think you'll find. It was before your mother died back in the spring. Anyway, things change. Quite quickly sometimes."

She felt her hand rising to her throat, as if she could push home the lump in it. "Is there someone else?" He didn't immediately reply. "Henry, will you look at me please?"

"Sorry." He raised his head and met her eyes. "I don't know."

"What the hell does that mean?"

"There is someone I . . . but she's not interested. Not really."

"Well, then."

"I live in hope. Anyway, her not wanting me isn't a good enough reason for me to get back with you. We'd make the same mistakes we made the first time round."

"For the boys," she said feebly.

"The boys are fine. Stevie was full of how good his new school is all afternoon, all the friends he's making." He shuffled his feet awkwardly. "Look, it's time we sorted things out. At the moment we're neither fish nor fowl. Two years separation by mutual consent is grounds for divorce."

She felt cold, as if the warm coat she'd always had to protect her against the elements had been stripped away.

She mumbled, "If that's what you want."

"I'll see a solicitor as soon as I can. We agreed the financial things when we parted so it should go through quickly. At least . . . Your mother's house must be worth a fair bit."

"The agent said a hundred and twenty but the market's slowing so I've put it on at a hundred and ten for a quick sale."

"If we – you – could pay off some of the mortgage, it'd make things easier for me financially. I mean, my flat's a bit of a dump and if I'm not coming back here, I'd like to find something better." She didn't answer at once and he said, "Is that so unreasonable?"

"No, of course it isn't. I was just thinking. She left no will, you see, so technically half that money belongs to Valerie if she ever cares to turn up and claim it. I don't feel I can just appropriate it."

"Fair enough. But paying off twenty, thirty thousand would make a big difference."

"Right. OK. Yes." She wiped her hand across her nose and mouth and felt moisture. She had begun to cry, although she wasn't sure when.

"There, there." He hugged her, rubbing briskly – not quite perfunctorily – up and down her back. "There, there. It's all right. It's best to settle things properly, so that we're both free to move on. You'll see." He released her and stepped back. "Goodnight, my dear."

"I still love you, you know."

228

"And I love you, but I'm not in love with you. It was you who wanted us to split up, Jo, remember? I'm not some teddy bear you can take down to play with when you feel like it, then stuff in the back of the cupboard out of sight until the next time."

When she'd heard his car drive away she went back to the sitting room and tipped the rest of the wine into her glass. She raised it in a solitary toast. "Tis better to have loved and lost than not have loved at all . . . I mean, Never to have loved at all!"

She drank it down in one gulp. Then she spent a few minutes giggling at the image of Henry as any sort of teddy bear, of all the inappropriate things. Then she rang her friend Zoe for sympathy and solace.

Autumn

The day becomes more solemn and serene
When noon is past – there is a harmony
In autumn – and a lustre in its sky,
Which through the summer is not heard or seen,
As if it could not be, as if it had not been!

"Hymn to Intellectual Beauty" – Shelley

Reconciled

It was the first week of October and dry thunder was rumbling across the sky. Zoe went to close the French windows. The garden was autumnal. The terracotta pots held gold and purple violas – regal colours – that would bloom into winter. She could hear the Jims doing their duet of "Why do you have to be a heartbreaker?" with Trefor barking counterpoint, as the train to St Margaret's rattled by.

As she watched it began to rain.

It was six weeks since Matty had left for New Zealand and she'd had no word from him. He must now be down in Dorset doing his location shooting. He'd obviously done his thinking and decided that they had no future and that the kindest thing for both of them was to sever all contact.

That was one film she wouldn't be going to see.

She hadn't been idle in his absence, since the incident with the bleach, keeping herself busy working hard on her new novel. There was her work at FILO, visits to the cinema, Sam and Annie, the Jims. Joanna, who had problems of her own.

It was a full life.

She told herself that it wouldn't have worked: that she was so much older: that Matty would spend his working life surrounded by pretty young women in a business that wasn't noted for its carnal restraint; that she'd have tormented herself constantly that he was being unfaithful, even if he wasn't; that the day of his leaving would have inevitably come, the more painful for being later and not sooner.

She wanted him but she couldn't have him and she would survive, because she was strong. She told herself that it was for the best, and only wished she believed it.

233

Sometimes she stood and looked at the empty rails in the dressing room where Oliver's scratchy clothes had hung, the spaces in the drawers where his soft ones had lain precisely folded. She had hoped to fill those gaps again with suits and shirts and springy woollens that smelled of Matty but she saw now that it had been a foolish hope.

Her biggest regret was that her baby would never know its father, because Matthew was much better parent material than she would ever be, but she wasn't going to pull that one on him, the oldest trick in the book. If he came back it would have to be because he wanted her, Zoe, but it seemed that he did not, and so he would never know.

She made an appointment to see her doctor. It was time. The baby – this most precious memento – needed proper pre-natal care. It had already been hurled out of a taxi and bathed in bleach without, admittedly, showing the slightest objection to this cavalier treatment, but from now on it must be her most cherished possession.

Liz Cheney said that she seemed well, that her blood pressure was normal, and that the dangers of a late baby shouldn't be overstated. She hadn't asked about the father.

She went for a scan but it didn't reveal the sex of the foetus.

"Got its back to the camera," the technician remarked. "Shy."

So it didn't take after its father in that respect.

It would be a while before she could have the tests that would reassure everyone else of what she already knew, that the baby was okay, that even though she was over forty it was growing strongly and well.

She hadn't bought anything for it yet. It was tempting: the exquisite wooden crib she'd seen in a shop window, with its lace draperies; the pushchairs and babygros, the prams and bootees. She stood in the smallest bedroom at least once a day and pictured it as a nursery, but she hadn't bought any paint or rung the decorator.

There was plenty of time and she kept reminding herself that her child was not a doll.

This was a complication in her life that she'd never sought,

but it had happened and she was going to do it and she was
going to do it right.

It was almost a week since she'd seen Sam. He hadn't
even been at FILO on Thursday evening to talk over her
counselling session with Mrs Janes in the pub afterwards and
reassure her that she'd said and done nothing wrong either
by commission or omission. He'd left a message with Kate,
perfectly cordial, saying that a childcare crisis had kept him
at home that night.

So why did she get the feeling that he was avoiding her?

She was pleased on answering the door early on Saturday
evening to see him standing there, his hair falling boyishly
over one eye, his hands stuck firmly and habitually into the
strained pockets of his black cords.

"No Annie?" she asked, standing aside to let him in.

"Spending the weekend with her new best friend Lauren.
Her parents have a cottage in the Cotswolds and they've gone
there. She's moving in very plush circles these days. Won't
want to know me soon."

He went on into the sitting room but didn't sit down.

She said, "I haven't seen you for ages. I thought you must
be cross with me for some reason."

"No, Zoe, I'm not cross with you. Why did you lie to me
about your period coming?"

"Oh! So much for doctor/patient confidentiality."

"I don't think that really applies between partners in the
same practice," he said. "It's not as if I don't have access
to your notes at any time. As it happens, Liz said something
about the baby, assuming that I knew, what with you and me
being such close friends." He hesitated. "In fact . . ."

"In fact? In fact, she thought you were the father?"

"It seems it had crossed her mind."

"I trust you disabused her."

"I did . . . But you haven't answered my question about
why you lied to me. Were you in denial?"

"Not exactly."

She explained how she hadn't wanted to see a doctor until
all temptation to have an abortion had passed, about avoiding

the occasion of sin, as the Catholics put it. She laid a hand on her belly where only the faintest curve as yet betrayed her condition. "I've felt the baby inside me, and there's no way I'll ask for a termination now."

"It's too early for the baby to quicken," he said, ever the doctor. "That won't happen for at least another month."

"No, but I know he's there. I can sense him like an intelligence, a personality, a separate identity inside me."

"And the father? This mysterious Matthew, I take it?" She inclined her head. "Did he come back from New Zealand?"

"I assume so."

"I see."

"If you've just come here to lecture me, Sam—"

"Not at all." He stood looking at her for a moment and his eyes were kind. "I've come to ask if you will marry me."

"Is that why you've been avoiding me?" Zoe asked, when she'd recovered from the shock. "While you worked yourself up to that? I think the days when a woman had to be rescued from the terrible ignominy of bearing a bastard are long gone."

"It isn't that. Every baby needs a father and Annie, as it happens, needs a mother, especially over the next few years when she reaches puberty. She's so fond of you, Zo. She'd love to have you for a mother—"

"I'm sure she would."

"Not to mention a baby brother or sister."

"That's hardly the point. I don't love you, Sam, or not in that way."

"We like each other so much, like the same films and plays and books, have the same opinions about so many things. We laugh together. I think it would be a very good arrangement. For everyone. Have we ever had a cross word in all the years we've been friends?"

"It's not enough. You don't even believe in marriage. You and Chris—"

"That was her, not me. I had no problem with the idea of our getting married, but she said it was a bourgeois institution designed to ensure the safe passage of capital and the maintenance of the social hierarchy, not to mention the second-class status of women."

She smiled at his unconscious mimicry of Christine's humourless didacticism, and at the idea that she could ever replace such a woman in his affections. She said, "Which is true, as far as it goes."

"But only as far as it goes. I can't tell you how I regretted it when she died. I wasn't her widower. I wasn't her next of kin. I was nothing."

"I believe in marriage," Zoe said. "Marriage has been good to me."

Sam had always been persistent to the point of pig-headedness. "It's the best basis for a relationship there is at our age. To be with someone who will be kind."

"I might have agreed with you a few months ago. I thought when Ollie died that I could never love again, but Matty showed me that I can, truly and passionately. I may have lost him through my own stupidity, but he's left me hope and I'm not going to bury that hope in a companionate marriage."

"Companionate?" His dark eyes were fiery. "I wasn't suggesting that. You're a very attractive woman, Zoe, and I admit I envisaged us sharing a bed. I'm not . . . I'm not a eunuch."

"I expressed myself badly. I meant to say a marriage without love. I'd rather marry Henry. At least there would be passion on one side."

Sam looked baffled. "Who the hell is Henry?"

"It isn't important. Henry's a friend of mine."

"Dear God, Zoe, I thought I knew you, better than anybody, but you never told me a word about this Matthew, not until he'd gone and left you pregnant and suicidal—"

"Oh, for God's sake! You sound like a Victorian father. It wasn't like that, and you know it."

"And now it seems there's a Henry too. It's as if you've been leading a secret life."

"Sam." She kissed him gently on the mouth. "Dear Sam, I shall always be there for Annie if she needs an older woman to confide in. I shall always be there for you as a friend. I hope we haven't ruined that between us."

"I don't think things can be the same," he said stiffly.

"But we can try?"

"Yes, we can try. I suppose."

"Only I'm going to need all the help I can get because I don't mind telling you that I'm terrified – the pregnancy, the birth, the baby, bringing him up on my own, everything. Absolutely scared shitless."

He melted at once. "I shall be here whenever you need me. Goodnight."

He walked back across Richmond Green like a robot, seeing nothing of its beauty in the autumn evening, hearing nothing of the chatter of the happy couples as they passed him on their Saturday evening revels. Reaching his own silent house at last, he shut the door behind him and leaned back against his drawbridge.

"Idiot," he said aloud. "A good arrangement? Idiot!" What sort of way was that to woo a beautiful woman, with talk of convenience, of what was best for their children?

Why hadn't he spoken to her of love?

Idiot.

Christine hadn't believed in love: she said it was an illusion, made up by man to prettify a purely biological urge. And yet he had loved her. And he had believed then, and still believed now, that she had loved him.

He went into his back sitting room and set up the battle of Waterloo, and fought it for the rest of the weekend.

Zoe wandered back into the kitchen and began to prepare a simple supper. Inviting Sam to stay and join her would have been an anti-climax after all that had passed between them, trying to make small talk across a plate of pasta and salad. She weighed out some rigatoni and was beginning to blanch tomatoes for the sauce when the doorbell rang once more.

Sam come back. Perhaps he could stay to supper after all.

But the shadow on the mottled hall window was not Sam's. It was too tall for one thing and for a moment her heart leaped into her mouth, but she knew immediately that it wasn't Matty either and stifled her hope. The shadow had a bristling quality to it that Matty lacked. Only one man of her acquaintance exuded that restless energy.

She tugged the door open with both hands – it stuck worse in damp weather – and said evenly, "Henry."

He stood there with his hands behind him, his head slightly cocked to one side. "I shall keep coming back," he said. "I'm like dust on the sideboard, however many times you brush me off, I'm there again the next day."

"And just as thick."

"Ha! Sharp as ever, I see."

She stood aside to let him in, saying, "You're just in time for supper," and he walked into the hall, pausing as she pushed the door shut behind him to say, "I'll take a plane to that for you tomorrow, stop it sticking."

Yes, she thought as she followed him towards the kitchen, Henry was that sort of man: useful to have about the house.

"It's been a while," she said to his back.

"I had things to sort out with Jo. And I have."

"Yes, I know. She's very upset."

"She's a survivor and there was really no other way. When a thing is over then it's over."

"You won't take no for an answer, but she must?"

He wasn't going to answer that. He had a bottle of red wine in his hands, a Rioja. He turned in the kitchen, swung it round and up and said, "Corkscrew?"

"I'm on the wagon."

"Yes, you said. Why is that?"

She told him and he listened without manifestation of surprise. When she'd finished, he nodded and said, "OK. I can live with that."

It wouldn't be till the third time, he convinced himself, that he could call it a habit.

She said, "It's Matty's."

"So I should hope. I don't need any other rivals. Nurture counts more than nature, anyway."

"We could argue about that . . ."

"But we won't."

"No."

She'd done arguing with Henry. Charming, infuriating, irreplaceable Henry.

*   *   *

He was working a late day shift the following week, from two till ten, and on Tuesday he insisted on driving her out to Newbury to see her mother, objecting to the needless cost of hiring a car. No one could accuse Henry of being after her money: he wouldn't let her spend any.

She protested all the way. "Mother won't understand who you are."

"So, tell her I'm a friend."

"She's very confused."

"Aren't we all?"

He drove, of course. She could see that Henry would always be the designated driver. She relaxed, snuggled down in the passenger seat, watching the world go by. For a few minutes she even closed her eyes and dozed.

Her mother accepted without comment that this was her old friend Henry Dacres. The two of them got on brilliantly, he friendly and flirtatious, she simpering as she always had in the presence of a presentable male. At they end of an hour they were teasing each other, her tapping him familiarly on the arm as he joked with her.

"Oh, you!" she would exclaim, from time to time. "Oh, you. You're awful!"

Miss Young watched them with a wolfish, voracious but also puzzled look. At one point she caught Zoe's eye and rolled her own heavenwards. Or did Zoe imagine it?

As they were leaving, Zoe's mother held up her pink, powdered cheek for Henry to kiss. He placed a smacker on it and said, "See you soon, Daph."

As Zoe bent to brush the rouge with her cool lips, her mother hissed in an audible whisper, "He's very nice, dear. Don't hang around. You don't want to be left on the shelf."

"No, Mum."

Then her mother playfully tapped her belly and said, "Still think it's just puppy fat?"

So she was reduced again to a gawky girl of nineteen, Oliver magicked from sight, all those years of marriage gone from the alternative universe that was her mother's damaged memory.

At the ends of the earth

At sixty-eight, Ruth Groves was still a handsome woman, wearing her wrinkles proudly, her shock of white hair more unkempt than was considered proper among the matrons of Christchurch. She drove her canary-yellow Mitsubishi with a certain dash on the hour-long journey to the airport to see her son safely on his way back to England.

Ruth had maintained a lively mind into retirement. Arriving back in New Zealand three and a half years ago she'd begun to learn Japanese, accepting that the future of these antipodean islands lay not with their colonial roots – the very name Antipodes placing them geographically in relation to Europe – but with the burgeoning economies of Asia.

She now spoke the language fluently and did guided tours for the small but growing number of Japanese tourists who came to these exotic islands, with their deserted landscapes, so different from the crowded acres of their own shores.

To Matthew's English ears she spoke with a New Zealand accent, although her friends in Christchurch maintained that she sounded like the BBC World Service after thirty years in Surrey.

"You always did go for women with brains and character," Ruth said to her son, "rather than run after pretty faces." He had confided in her on this last private journey.

"If I want to see a pretty face I can look in the mirror." His mother barked with laughter and jabbed him in the ribs before changing gear. "And when a man loves a woman then she is beautiful."

"True. She's older than you, you say?"

"A . . . few years."

"You always did prefer older women. Mary was – what? – five or six years older?"

"Seven. I find girls my own age immature."

"That's being an only child, lots of adult company and conversation from an early age." After a moment, she added, "I didn't say anything at the time because interfering doesn't do any good, but you never seemed happy when you were with Mary. There was a coldness about her I didn't like. I never thought she was right for you."

"Fortunately she reached the same conclusion. Zoe is a widow. Her husband died in a climbing accident two years ago."

Ruth exclaimed, "Poor darling! Was the marriage happy?"

"She doesn't talk about it much but, yes, I'm sure it was."

"Good. That means she has the knack of making it work. Don't understimate that. Has she children?"

"No, she never wanted them."

"Oh." Ruth spoke as evenly as she could, but for a second there was an almost gut-wrenching sense of loss in the revelation that her beloved only son would never make her a grandmother, that her line stopped here. But she knew him well enough to tell that this unknown Zoe, twelve thousand miles away, was the one, the real thing, and she must accept the way things were and be happy for him.

She couldn't resist saying, "That's a pity. You've always loved children, pretty much since you were one."

"It's the thing that's most given me pause, I suppose, but if that's the sacrifice I have to make then so be it. But we're jumping the gun, Momma. It's early days yet. Maybe she won't want me. Maybe she doesn't love me enough."

"I may be biased," his mother said, "but I can't understand why any woman wouldn't love you to distraction."

He laughed. "It won't be plain sailing, that's all I'm saying."

"When was it ever?"

Ruth pulled to a halt outside the airport terminal and looked at him with a mother's true affection over the old-lady glasses she needed for driving. "You'll forgive me if I don't come in with you, darling. Call me old-fashioned but I can't bear to make an exhibition of myself weeping at the departure gate, not knowing when or even if I shall see you again."

"Of course you will, although I don't know when. Anyway, Dad wouldn't even come to the airport."

"Dear Patrick. Always the stiff upper lip and, underneath, a big old softie. Oh, and thanks for letting him beat you at chess last night."

"You don't miss much, do you? He taught me and it'd be no shame to be beaten by me."

"But you let him win anyway." She leaned across, kissed and embraced him. "Thank you for giving us that extra three weeks."

"I wouldn't have been able to if that stupid American girl hadn't sprained her ankle roller blading so the start of filming had to be put back."

"I know, but you could have gone anyway, home to Zoe. I hope she wasn't too upset when you told her you'd been delayed."

"N-n-n-no."

He got out of the car and retrieved his bags from the boot, no better equipped than his mother to bear a lengthy parting. He leaned in at the driver's window and kissed her one last time then walked into the terminal building, not looking back but hearing her car pull away behind him.

Why hadn't he telephoned Zoe when he'd got Jamie's message telling him he didn't have to be in Dorset until the end of October? Had he been trying to punish her for the private detective, to make her feel a little of the anguish he'd suffered that night? If so, he couldn't remember why he would have wanted to do anything so uncharacteristically petty. He'd known before his plane landed in New Zealand that he was going back to her, that it was the only way, however hard it might be.

He felt mean and shabby but he would make it up to her. He'd call her the minute he got to Heathrow and beg her forgiveness.

Erasure

At half past ten Henry drove Zoe to the private clinic in Ham, where she'd elected to have her baby, so that she could attend her pre-natal class. After that she had an appointment with her doctor and he arranged to collect her in two hours time.

It was raining steadily and he shepherded her to the reception area, his umbrella over her, while she told him not to fuss.

"I want to fuss," he said. "I will fuss."

Back in Richmond, he let himself into her house with his key, enjoying the quiet of the place as he stepped into the hall, the smell of well-polished furniture, fresh coffee and books. This morning he was going to make a start on the nursery. He'd insisted. He had been horrified that she should consider paying a professional to do it.

They'd gone round the shops together, chosen a yellow patterned paper with big blue balloons for the walls and navy-blue ceiling paper with the constellations of the northern hemisphere picked out in silver. He had a couple of litres of thick yellow gloss paint, like banana milkshake as it curdled.

He enjoyed decorating, such a useful and manly thing to do.

He was up the ladder when he heard the telephone so he ignored it, letting the machine take it. It couldn't be for him; no one knew yet that he was here. He wasn't here, not full time. Not yet.

Sooner or later one, or both, of them was going to have to find a way of telling Joanna.

Forty minutes later, satisfied with his first coat of paint on the skirting boards and picture rail, with its smooth creaminess, he went down to make himself some celebratory coffee. It had stopped raining and he could make a start on the window soon.

He whistled as he bounded down the stairs, pleased with himself and the world.

While the liquid bubbled in the pot he went into Zoe's study and examined the answering machine with its nebulous red number one. He pressed the play button. The caller was somewhere very noisy and practically had to shout to make himself heard and it was perhaps five seconds before Henry realised who it was.

He sat down heavily on Zoe's swivel chair and bit his lip till the blood frothed, bitter, into his mouth.

"Zoe," the caller said, "it's me. I'm at Heathrow. I got delayed in New Zealand. I should have called you to let you know. Please forgive me, darling. I love you. Can you pick up if you're there? . . . OK, you're not there. I can't say what I need to say over an answering machine, only when I'm holding you in my arms. But I'll try. Can we begin again?"

"No," Henry said quietly, and folded his arms across his chest.

"It's . . . damn, I don't know what time it is. My body clock's all shot to hell. I left Christchurch in spring and come home to a drizzly English autumn . . . Wait, there's a clock on the wall. It's just gone eleven. I'm going to hop in a cab and come straight over and hope you're home by the time I get there. Did I mention that I love you?"

There was an abrupt disconnection. The machine bleeped three times and began to wind the tape first one way then the other in its inexplicable way. When it stopped, Henry sat in silence for perhaps two minutes, then he glanced furtively around. He wasn't sure why, since Zoe was safely at the clinic in Ham, but he wouldn't put it past Fat Jim to be peering in at him through the window, like an eighteen-stone conscience.

There was, of course, no one.

He pressed the erase button. The red one morphed into a big fat zero.

No new messages.

Henry Dacres didn't give up that easily. It was the creed he lived by: if you couldn't win by the rules, then you changed the rules.

Out in the hall the clock began to strike twelve noon. He looked at his watch, which told the same story, doing frantic calculations in his head. There was always a queue for taxis at Heathrow. The journey could take anything from half an hour to an hour depending on the traffic on the M4.

The doorbell rang.

For a moment Henry sat in the chair like a wax dummy. Then, as the bell rang again, he jumped to his feet.

As the newly planed door opened smoothly, Matthew's face changed from eager expectation to frank bewilderment.

"What are you doing here?" he asked coldly of this ghost that haunted him, this man who knew too many of his secrets.

"Taking care of Zoe. Somebody has to."

A black cab waited, blocking the road, its driver mildly interested. So he hadn't sent it away, Henry thought. He wasn't sure. So much the better.

Matthew glanced down at the heavy suitcase at his feet, his hands in the pockets of his raincoat, then raised his head again and looked Henry in the eye. He was exhausted with sleeplessness and jet lag, the bags smudged grey under those cornflower eyes.

They aroused no pity in Henry Dacres.

"Is she in?" Henry slowly shook his head. "Are you sure?" Matthew persisted.

"She's out for the day."

"And what are you? The new cleaner?"

Henry smiled a smile of quiet triumph and said softly, "You're too late, sonny."

Matthew didn't question it, as if it only confirmed his worst fears. He looked at his suitcase again. Slowly, he picked it up, his arm bracing in pain. It had doubled in weight in the last few minutes. He walked down the path, aware of Henry's hostile eyes on him, his trainers leaving ghostly impressions on the wet paving stones before vanishing, as if he had never been.

At the gate he stopped and looked back. "Tell her . . ."

"What?" asked Henry, who had no intention of passing on any messages.

"Nothing. It doesn't matter."

The taxi driver reached out of his window to open the back door and Matthew climbed wearily in.

And was gone.

Epilogue

Zoe opened the door to Fat Jim after lunch two days later. She led the way down the hall into the kitchen, where she busied herself making coffee.

"Himself not home?" Jim asked, knowing the answer, having carefully watched Henry up the road before ringing the bell.

"Henry? He's at work. Or 'on duty', as I suppose one must say. Funny: when I had a proper job I never said I was 'on duty' from nine till five."

"Policemen are different from us mere mortals." Jim lodged a fat buttock on the stool at the breakfast bar, oozing flesh off all four sides. "He's quite sexy, you know – Henry – in a world-weary sort of way."

Zoe laughed. "Yes!"

"Is that why you chose him then, in the end, over little Matthew?"

She felt her face freeze, setting her features, denying the existence of strong emotion to the outer world. She said stiffly, "These things aren't necessarily a matter of choice."

"But you turned him away."

"When?"

"When was it?" Jim pretended to think. "Must have been Monday morning. Drew up in a taxi with his suitcase, rang the bell; then went away again a minute later, with a gob on him like a drizzly Wednesday night in Manchester."

He accepted a mug of coffee, watching her carefully, not deceived by the mask she showed him.

So, he thought, Thin Jim had been right after all.

When he'd seen himself out, Zoe made her way slowly to

the study and sat down at her desk. She couldn't remember
a word Jim had said during the last ten minutes of his visit,
nor what she'd replied, if anything.

It didn't occur to her to be angry with Henry: she'd
learned nothing about him this afternoon that she hadn't
already known.

She stretched out her hand numbly and picked up the
telephone, dialling Matty's number in Hammersmith from
the place where it was safely lodged in her memory. But
after six numbers she paused, her finger hovering over the last
digit, a seven, unable to bear down on it. Half a minute later a
mechanical voice told her that the number she had dialled had
not been recognised and advised her that she should replace
the receiver and try again.

She obediently replaced the receiver in its cradle, but she
didn't try again. She would never call that number. Now that
she was satisfied that Matty hadn't been a conman it was,
paradoxically, easier to let him go.

She had made her decision when Henry last came knocking
at her door. And the moment when she and Matty might have
made a life together had passed away forever that night, into
the realm of dreams.

Somehow, they had missed each other in the dark.